# THE WERELING
# prey

# THE WERELING
# prey

# STEPHEN COLE

**BLOOMSBURY**

LONDON BERLIN NEW YORK

Bloomsbury Publishing, London, Berlin and New York

First published in Great Britain in 2004 by Bloomsbury Publishing Plc
36 Soho Square, London, W1D 3QY

This edition first published in 2009

A CIP catalogue record of this book is available from the British Library

ISBN 978 0 7475 9967 8

The paper this book is printed on is certified independently in accordance
with the rules of the FSC. It is ancient-forest friendly.
The printer holds chain of custody.

**FSC**
Mixed Sources
Product group from well-managed
forests and other controlled sources
Cert no. SGS - COC - 2061
www.fsc.org
© 1996 Forest Stewardship Council

Typeset by Dorchester Typesetting Group Ltd
Printed in Great Britain by Clays Ltd, St Ives plc

10 9 8 7 6 5 4 3 2 1

www.bloomsbury.com/childrens

*To Jill*

# CHAPTER ONE

The full moon shone in on Tom Anderson through the truck window. It felt like a searchlight, hunting him down. He shifted his weight on the rough, pitted leather of the back seat, squirming clear of the blazing light while still pretending to be asleep.

He hated hitching rides, especially at night. The moonlight put him on edge, made him feel shivery and sweaty and caged in. Feigning sleep spared him the ordeal of making conversation with the over-curious truck driver.

Not that he was exactly the focus of attention around here, with Kate up front in the passenger seat. There was no doubt in Tom's mind that it was Kate who had brought the truck screeching to a halt on the highway out of Philadelphia. Tall and slim and dressed all in black, her long dark hair whipped about by the cold November gusts, she was like a secret weapon in the world of thumbing lifts.

Good job. They needed to get to New York fast.

Opening his eyes a fraction, Tom snuck a look out of the window. Beyond the trees that lined the Palisades Interstate Parkway he saw about a billion pinpricks of light stacked in long, tall grids against the night. They were nearing the city – but maybe not fast enough, Tom decided, as the big, bearded driver stole another lingering glance at Kate.

'So, how come a sweet thing like you is hitching, anyway?' The trucker kept smiling to himself, like he was quietly smug at being able to balance his over-sized gut on his knees and make conversation at the same time.

'Well ...' Kate shrugged. 'Hitching's cheap ... and I guess me and Tom just enjoy the freedom.'

*Freedom*, Tom thought bitterly. Sure: freedom to creep and crawl through this horrible new life that had been thrust on him. Freedom to live in fear, constantly looking back over their shoulders. Waking and wondering if today was the day their pursuers would catch up with them at last.

They had to keep moving, to keep one step ahead. But since they didn't have the cash for a bus ticket past Philly, Kate – practical and determined as ever – had dolled herself up and they'd hit the highway. He knew she hated to hitch, loathed the way these long-distance drivers looked her over, like wolves salivating over their next meal.

Nice analogy.

Tom shifted irritably in the seat once more.

'You kids are pretty young to be on the road, now, ain't you? How old are you, sugar?'

'We're both eighteen,' Kate answered. 'Taking a year out before college next fall.'

Life on the run has made you a pretty good liar, Kate, Tom decided. Kate was actually seventeen, and Tom was a year younger. He'd been looking forward to his eighteenth birthday pretty much all his life. He'd always imagined it would be the day he'd walk out the front door and suddenly find himself a man, ready to make his mark in the world.

That was before he'd got tangled up with Kate and her family, and found his future screwed to hell.

Found himself a freakin' werewolf.

'So ...' There was a pause as heavy as the gold chain around the trucker's neck before the next question: 'Is Tom your boyfriend?'

'Not really,' Kate said, turning her head away to look through the window. 'No.'

Tom indulged himself in a bitter half-smile. How could Kate ever begin to think of him as boyfriend material, knowing what he had become? Knowing that if they ever *did* get together ...

He imagined the look on the trucker's face if Kate told him the whole story: that her whole family was lupine – werewolves; creatures believed lost to legend, but in reality part of an active and totally secret sub-culture whose population stretched clear around the world. That, as a pureblood female, Kate's latent lupine nature would be woken if she mated with another 'wolf. And that Tom had been kidnapped by Kate's family and held prisoner in their house while they turned him into future son-in-law material – turned him 'wolf too.

The plan hadn't worked. Kate didn't *want* to embrace her lupine heritage. The thought of it turned her stomach. She was determined to stay human. So she and Tom had escaped. But in doing so, they'd made many enemies in the lupine community – including Kate's crazy mother, Marcie Folan.

The real joke in all this, Tom reflected, was that with all they'd been through trying to stay alive, he had never felt closer to anyone than Kate.

'So you and Sleeping Beauty in the back there ...' The trucker was trying to sound casual. 'You're just good friends, right?'

'Right,' Kate replied, a hard, tired edge creeping into her voice. 'But Tom is pretty special, you know?'

Special.

Uh-huh. More special than anyone could've guessed, Tom thought wryly.

He was what the lupine community termed a silver-blood – someone with exceptional resistance against the 'wolf-change. They'd turned him in the end, but he'd come out of the whole process a wereling. *'Very rare,'* Kate had informed him, quoting some ancient, secret text: *'A wereling is a resister whose humanity and compassion prevails in the 'wolf.'* Which seemed to mean that when the change was on him, Tom could hold on to some struggling, screaming human part of his nature that loathed what he had become.

But each time Tom changed into the lupine state he wondered if this would be the time he would lose control and give in to the intoxicating power and strength of being 'wolf ...

The dark landscape was suddenly neon bright under the orange-pink glare of streetlights. The truck swerved hard and took an exit on to the Henry Hudson Parkway.

'So, this is Manhattan,' Kate observed. Her habitual deadpan voice made it hard to know if she was impressed or just plain bored.

'Sure is,' enthused their driver. 'She's a sight, ain't she? Day or night.'

Tom had to agree. On one side was the wide dark stretch of the Hudson River, and on the other, buildings so high the moon barely peeked over them. As they continued their journey and turned off the Parkway into a crisscross of streets and avenues, Tom felt a sense of genuine awe. It was like he was travelling through a canyon of metal and glass, dwarfed by the gargantuan size of the skyscrapers all around him.

Their driver turned a corner and gave a huge pantomime yawn. 'Say, it's almost two already. Need a place to stay tonight?'

'No thanks.'

'Hey, c'mon. I got a real comfortable place, sweetheart. I even got room for your special friend there, too.'

Kate's voice hardened. 'I said, *no thanks.*'

'Hey, how about a little gratitude, huh?' The trucker's voice got throatier. 'I've brought you all this way. Reckon you owe me something in return.'

Tom clenched his fists. He'd been tense before, but now he could feel his heart beat harder with anger. He was about to speak out when he caught sight of Kate in the rearview, subtly shaking her head at him. 'Not here,' she mouthed.

'Would you let us out, now, please?' she asked the driver.

'Now, why would you want to break up the party?' The big guy pressed a fleshy hand down on Kate's thigh.

'Let go of her,' Tom snarled, grabbing hold of the man's thick arm.

'Yeah?' The trucker took a right turn and broke Tom's grip easily as he did so. 'What you gonna do about it, squirt?'

'He'll turn you into dogmeat,' Kate snapped, 'unless you stop this truck and let us out right now.'

'Him?' The big man tossed an amused glance back at Tom. 'You're breaking my balls, sweetie. In case you hadn't noticed, I'm a *real* man.'

'I might have a surprise for you,' Tom leaned forward and hissed at the driver. 'And you don't want to know how real *I* am.'

Kate was winding down the window. 'And unless you want me to scream down all Manhattan, you'll pull over right now.'

The driver swore under his breath and slowed right down, swinging his rig to the side of the road. 'Who needs this? Go on, get out of here, you teasing little bitch.'

Tom grabbed their stuff and got out. Kate followed him, without a backward glance at the red-faced driver. With an impotent blare on his horn, the man dodged back into the ragged traffic pushing down the avenue.

'Are you OK?' Tom asked her as they crossed to the sidewalk.

'Of course I'm OK,' she said crossly. 'You shouldn't have interfered, I can handle jerks like him.'

'Sorry,' Tom said, a little stung.

Kate sighed. 'It's the full moon,' she reminded him, more gently. 'The more stressed out you get, the more you lose control, the easier it is for the 'wolf to get a hold on you.'

Tom looked down at his scuffed boots, feeling the prickle on the back of his neck from the moonlight. He knew she was right. 'So what do we do now?'

Kate had already taken her guidebook out of her rucksack. 'I guess we start looking for the nearest hostel.'

'Can we afford one?'

'Nope. Not really. But at this hour I'd sooner find somewhere reputable to crash for the night.'

Tom sighed. 'Too bad Blood's not here to lend us an apartment. A bit of luxury would be nice right now.' They'd made one good friend during their crazy time in New Orleans – Adam Blood, a high-class realtor and head of a small network that kept tabs on the dark side of the city. They both owed him their lives. But when he'd taken a stand against Marcie Folan, Blood had gained a formidable enemy. His life had been in great danger, so he'd gone into hiding.

'Wonder where he is now?' Kate murmured a little dreamily.

'Living it up in the sun, somewhere.' Tom forced a smile. 'Lucky bastard.' Shivering a little, he pulled up the collar of his denim jacket and walked to the corner of the street to find a street sign. 'West 107th Street and Manhattan,' he called to Kate.

She nodded and unfolded the gatefold map at the back of the book.

Tom shoved both hands deep in his pockets and pushed out a deep breath. The moon had placed an itch under his skin, like ants were crawling inside him. He paced up and down, avoiding the eyes of people drifting along the street. Any one of them could be a 'wolf, out looking for them. The lupine community was tight-knit despite the distance it spanned, and once the word was out against you, you weren't safe anywhere. 'Do you realise how many people

13

there must be in Manhattan alone, never mind the boroughs?'

Kate knew what he was getting at, and swiftly rolled out her stock answer: 'If Jicaque's here, we'll find him.'

Jicaque. Pronounced, '*Zhi-kar-key*' – or should that be '*Holy Grail*'? He was the fabled medicine man with a tongue-twister name who might – *might* – be able to reverse Tom's lupine condition. From Kate's researches into lycanthropy, Jicaque seemed to be the only chance they had. Unfortunately he was also about as easy to find as smoke in fog.

'Too bad your on-line contact couldn't be a little more precise as to where Jicaque's staying,' Tom remarked.

'He's working on that,' Kate replied.

'Is he? Anyone could've sent that e-mail.' Tom smoothed a clammy hand through his short dark hair, cold sweat spiking it up. 'We've been tricked that way before. The 'wolves could've hacked into his account. Or hacked into *him*, forced him to spill those passwords you agreed …'

'You know, Tom, you're right,' Kate said wearily. This was an old argument. 'We *don't* know we can trust the guy who gave me the info, he's just a name in a chatroom. And say we *do* manage to find Jicaque – we don't know that we can trust *him* either. But since it's the only lead we've got …'

Tom threw up his hands. 'Yeah, yeah. You're right, I know.' His insides felt cramped and jumpy. 'I'm sorry.'

'That's got to be the lamest apology I ever heard.' Kate gave him a faint smile, then nodded toward the moon. 'But I guess it *is* your time of the month, huh?'

Tom shot her a dark look. 'You don't want to make jokes like that when I'm feeling like this.' But Kate was grinning at him, and he found himself smiling back. 'Come on, sick girl. Found any hostels?'

'I have a better idea,' she told him. 'Scratch that: I have a *cheaper* idea.'

'Which is?'

'We're right by Central Park. We could camp out there for the night.'

'Just you, me and fifty muggers. Nice idea.'

Kate shrugged. 'We could bed down in some bushes. It's only a few hours till dawn. Then we can get up and start the search.'

'If we haven't frozen to death first,' grumbled Tom.

'Well, let's hear your great idea.'

Tom sighed, and swallowed hard. 'I ... I guess if we lay close together it might not be so cold.'

Kate's green eyes were cool and enquiring as she looked him over. 'Tom Anderson, is this some kind of sneaky come-on?'

'Get over yourself!' Tom protested, and turned away so she wouldn't see him blushing.

It was weird to see the dark, hunching shadows of so many trees suddenly rise from the centre of the city. The park was quiet and gloomy as they crossed its borders and headed inside.

The wind had dropped, and the landscape held itself as still as the moon. As they pressed on, Tom's senses kicked into overdrive. He drank in the sweet scent of the damp earth and dewy grass. Upwind, a loaded trashcan was brimming over with bad smells.

Further up the path they were taking he heard a

twig snap, and caught a tang of sweat and desperation. Tom could almost picture the figure: some crackhead, turned animal by his need for a fix, shivering in the foliage and psyching himself up to strike should someone pass by.

The moon seemed to shine brighter, and as its light needled Tom with greater strength, he felt a moment's kinship with the crackhead. The animal inside him was desperate for release, to strike out and taste blood, to bring on the change.

'Tom?' Kate was looking at him, concerned.

'Not this way,' he whispered.

They changed direction.

For several minutes they pressed on quietly, searching for somewhere to bed down.

'How about here?' Kate suggested, gesturing to a small huddle of trees and bushes.

But as she started to explore, cracking and rustling through the foliage, Tom hushed her. He could hear footfalls on the wet grass, distant shouts and ragged breaths, getting closer. 'People are coming,' he hissed.

Kate looked around, but it was too dark to make out anything clearly. 'Should we get out of here?' she asked.

Tom peered more deeply into the gloom. Across the open parkland he could see a kid no older than himself, who seemed to be running for his life. A gang of about ten people was tearing along after him, jeering and calling. Tom could smell the fear on the boy, felt his own heart start to pound faster, matching the rhythm of the kid's footfalls.

'Tom?' Kate tugged on his sleeve.

'They're chasing him down. Like it's a hunt or

something.' He turned to her, the hairs on the back of his neck prickling, his breaths coming fast and shallow as though it was him running.

Kate hesitated, then shook her head. 'Leave it, Tom. It's not our fight.'

'I – I can scare them off,' he said, staggering like a drunk, his voice slurring as the change crept closer. 'Just scare them, that's all ...'

'Tom?' Kate grabbed hold of his sweaty face with both hands, tried to make him look into her eyes. 'Tom, no. Don't do this.'

But a familiar heat was coursing through Tom's body. He knew there was no turning back now. He saw the desperation in Kate's eyes turn to resignation. Then she moved forward to yank his jacket off from his back. He fell to his knees, fumbling feverishly with the buttons on his brushed cotton shirt. Too late. His torso was already swelling up, and the heavy fabric splitting at the seams.

He hunched forwards on all fours, a sound raking out of his throat that was half-choking and half-laughter as he went into spasm. Tom's bones were melting under his thickening skin, remoulding themselves into lupine shape. Coarse dark hair pushed out of every pore. He felt a sick tickle in his gums as his teeth sprouted like spikes and his jaw pushed out. His spine twisted and lengthened, pelvis cracking like a gunshot as it clicked into a fresh position, hind legs twitching as new and powerful muscles fixed themselves there.

Tom reached back his head and bit and snapped at the tattered remains of his jeans. They fell away like the last vestiges of his human form. The moon warmed his bare back like a tropical sun. He began to run, luxuriating in the sweet strength of his sleek lupine body. His heavy paws tore up the ground, his blood roaring in his ears. Dimly, somewhere behind him, he caught Kate's scent, heard her running after him weighed down with their stuff.

'They're almost on top of him!' she hissed.

Tom burst out from the cover of the trees just ahead of them all, and roared.

Startled, the boy skidded on the wet grass and fell badly. He swore, his face twisted with pain as he clutched at his ankle. His shadowy pursuers also came slithering to a halt, panting for breath.

Tom leaped over the boy and bared his teeth at them.

The gang stared at the monster before them. But they didn't run screaming. Didn't even flinch. Instead, their breathing grew deeper, hoarser. Their eyes began to shine with a sickly yellow light. One by one, they stretched up their arms and then bent forward on to all fours, as their bodies began to change.

'Jesus,' Tom heard Kate whisper. 'They're 'wolves too.'

# CHAPTER TWO

Kate felt her insides twist. When the change came over Tom he became a powerful, lithe, deep-chested creature, far larger than a real wolf. Tom's lupine form, with its dark, lustrous coat and muscular frame, was almost beautiful in its own sick way.

But there was no beauty or grace in the monsters that were now facing him. Wiry and rangy like the men they had been, their fur was mottled and patchy, their teeth as yellow as their eyes, backs humped and misshapen. Two or three of them howled, a chilling sound like babies screaming. The rest, snapping their jaws, padded back and forth, or in circles, as if easing themselves into their lupine movement.

Tom turned and glanced back at Kate. His eyes were still dark, still his own – the pale glow of the lupine shone there at the start of the change but soon dwindled and died. That set him apart from all other lupines Kate had ever seen, and she thanked God for this, his wereling strength. It helped her remember that Tom was still Tom, whatever form he was forced to take.

Suddenly, Tom turned and threw himself into the pack of awakening 'wolves.

'Tom, no!' Kate screamed.

The noise was dreadful. Barks and bays and growls, full of torment and anger, echoed out into the starry night. But Kate saw Tom was running rings around the creatures; he wasn't attacking them so much as goading them, taking their attention. Distracting them deliberately, she realised, so that she might help the boy and get them both the hell out of there.

She broke cover and ran over to their quarry, who was still down on the ground, slowly edging away from the angry pack. He was kind of pretty for a boy, but his delicate features had been spoiled by a long scar that ran down his left cheek. He was olive-skinned, Spanish maybe, with shaven hair.

When he saw her coming he scrambled up painfully and held out his fists in warning. '*No le quiero hacer daño*,' he said warningly, his voice heavy and scared, 'so get the hell away from me, bitch.'

Kate groped around her ninth-grade Spanish for the translation, holding up her hands open-palmed to reassure him. 'I don't want to hurt you either,' she said at last.

'You ain't gonna get the chance,' he snarled. He turned and tried to run, but his injured ankle gave way under him and he crashed back down to the ground, swearing.

Kate was about to go after him when she caught sight of Tom. He'd broken clear of the pack and was trying to lead them away. Out for blood, the other lupines went bounding and lumbering after him, their sinister shapes soon lost to the night.

Ten against one. They could tear Tom to ribbons.

Worried, Kate grabbed her bag and Tom's stuff and crossed to where the Hispanic kid lay cursing and struggling on the ground.

'What did you do?' she demanded.

'Damn ankle sprained or something.'

'I mean, what did you do to get a pack of were-wolves chasing after you?'

He sneered at her. 'And why are you on my case?'

'Because my friend has just risked his life trying to save you,' Kate responded fiercely. 'You'd better be worth the rescue.'

He snorted. 'Rescue? Sure. I know what kind of rescue you got in mind, wolf-girl.' He mimed slitting his throat.

'I'm as human as you are,' she told him. 'I'm not one of them. But they want me to be. They're chasing after me like they are after you.'

'So why'd you hang out with the howler?'

'Tom's not like that scum chasing after you. Did you see his eyes?'

'I guess,' the boy conceded. 'Didn't look like howler eyes. Looked … normal.'

'Tom is anything but normal. That's why the 'wolves are chasing after us, too.' Kate glanced about. 'Come on. We'd better hide till it's safe.'

She helped him scramble behind some prickly bushes, then they held themselves as still as possible, straining to hear any sound of the 'wolves coming back.

'I'm Kate,' she breathed.

'Name's Ramone,' the boy replied. 'Why're the howlers chasing you?'

'You ever hear of a scuzzball called Takapa?'

Ramone stared at her. 'If you messed with Takapa I don't want nothin' to do with you. He's the one screwing up this place. They say there ain't no howler bigger than him.'

'That big *howler* is actually just a scrawny albino freak with good PR,' Kate told him lightly, but she couldn't repress a shudder. Takapa was making a name for himself among the lupine community as some kind of freedom fighter. He believed that the 'wolves should come crawling out of the shadows to hunt and kill freely in the human world – and was working on ways to make it happen.

Ramone pointed a finger over her shoulder. 'Look who's back.'

Heart lurching, Kate twisted around.

It was Tom, human again, his pale skin laced silver in the moonlight. He'd reclaimed the tatters of his jeans and was leaning heavily against a tree, soaking wet and shivering.

Kate quickly pulled out the last of his fresh clothes from his backpack. 'Are you OK? What happened?'

'There's water back there, a reservoir or something,' Tom said, gesturing behind him. 'I took a swim. They lost my scent and went off the wrong way.' He gratefully pulled on a sweater. 'Lucky for us they're slow and stupid.'

Tom nodded at Ramone, and Kate made some hurried introductions.

'We should get out of here.' Tom eased his arms through the straps on his rucksack. 'Ramone, do you know a safe place we can stay tonight?'

Ramone shook his head. 'No way, 'wolf. You're mixed up with Takapa.'

'This *'wolf* just saved your life,' Kate said tartly. As she spoke, she could hear far-off sirens drawing closer.

Ramone winced like they were going off in his ear. He tried to stand and gasped with pain. 'OK,' he said, scowling. 'You can hide out at my place tonight. But then you're gone.'

'Very generous of you,' Tom observed wryly.

Together they helped Ramone up. His clothes reeked of sweat and cigarette smoke, and Kate nearly gagged. But after a few stumbling steps, they managed to fall into a kind of limping gait that allowed them to move at a pretty fast pace.

'I hope the police don't find those 'wolves – for *their* sake,' Kate muttered.

'They won't.' Ramone shook his head. 'Them 'wolves ain't so stupid as you think, Tom. They stick to the shadows so no one knows the truth.'

Tom shot him a sideways glance. 'And the truth is?'

'That the 'wolves are recruiting,' Ramone said simply. 'Cops don't know they're there ... the nice people of the city don't know they're there ... But in the run-down neighbourhoods, the bad-lit places that my people got to live in, those bastards are getting stronger all the time.'

Ramone's hangout was located in a slum tenement on 110th Street. It was a hell of a walk but somehow they made it. The neighbourhood was run-down and threatening in the cold, mistrustful air of the night.

Tom and Kate helped Ramone up the steps.

He knocked on the pitted, battered old door in a distinctive tattoo. 'You better keep quiet about being a howler,' he warned Tom.

'Sure. Believe it or not,' Tom replied, 'it's not something I like to advertise.'

A minute or so later some bolts were thrown and the door creaked open a little.

A camera pushed its way out. Tom was blinded by its flash.

'Quit that, Polar,' Ramone complained, and shoved open the door.

Polar backed up and shrugged. He was a tall skinny kid with skin the same colour as Ramone's, but beyond that Tom couldn't really say, since Polar kept the camera up at his face. It was a Polaroid self-printing job, which maybe explained his name. He plucked out the developing picture and silently handed it to Kate.

She stared at it, baffled, then slipped it in her purse.

'Life looks better to Polar through his camera,' was all Ramone offered by way of explanation.

They were standing in a filthy, dusty kitchen. Damp mould had crawled up around the black-painted windows, and there seemed to be more plaster on the garbage-strewn floor than on the walls.

The look of disdain was clear on Kate's face.

'Hey, this is just the lobby,' Ramone assured her, and pointed in the direction Polar was disappearing. 'Presidential Suite's through there.'

'Ramone? You back? ¿Tienes algún problema?' A girl's voice, hard and clear in its urgency, carried through to them.

'No es nada,' he called back. At once, he shook off the support of Tom and Kate and stood alone.

Tom understood why when, a second later, a cute girl with a nose stud swept into the scuzzy room. She wore a red cropped top beneath a hooded sweatshirt, and tight black pants. Her thick black hair had been straightened and pulled tight back away from her high forehead. Hands on her hips, her wide, appraising eyes full of attitude, Tom imagined she took some impressing.

'This is Jasmine,' Ramone told Tom with a crooked smile. 'She loves me.'

The girl held up her middle finger to him. 'Bite me,' she said. Her disparaging gaze moved to Tom and then lingered on Kate. 'Who you got here?'

'Kate and Tom. They're OK. Helped me out.'

Jasmine arched one finely plucked eyebrow. 'Why didn't you call me?'

'Lost my cell somewhere in the park,' Ramone replied.

'We heard on the radio some shit was happening in Central Park,' Jasmine went on. 'Tony's gang?'

Ramone nodded. 'Turned hairy on me. No chance of us teaming up with Tony's crew – howlers, all of them.'

Kate was looking at Jasmine in disbelief. 'They broadcast about the 'wolves on the radio?'

'Sure,' said Jasmine, her pretty face twisting into a sneer, 'it went out on Hot 97.'

'We got a police radio out back, 28th Precinct,' Ramone explained. 'We like to know what's going down round here. Who'd they say it was, Jas – kids?'

'Uh-huh.'

'Damn howler could have its teeth round their necks, they'd blame it on kids.' He took an uncertain step towards Jasmine.

'You hurt yourself?'

Tom noticed a flicker of concern on Jasmine's face.

'I broke my ankle, babe.'

'Sure you did, asshole. Twisted it maybe.'

'I'm hurt bad.'

'Whatever.' Jasmine folded her arms, turned and, like Polar before her, disappeared through the door into the next room.

'See?' Ramone grinned at Tom. 'She loves me.'

He limped across the ruined kitchen and, with an exchange of nervous glances, Tom and Kate followed.

The kitchen led into a large room painted blood red, with boarded-up windows. It was lit by a collection of mismatched lamps, lined up in a row along the opposite wall. Cigarette smoke clouded the room, and the bulbs seemed to glow fiercer through the haze, like streetlights in fog.

Six or seven people, all Hispanic, were slumped on cushions or on one of the two battered leather couches ranged in front of an enormous widescreen TV showing highlights from a Giants game. One kid, a little smaller than Tom's kid brother, Joe, was kneeling right in front of it, close enough to count the pixels on the screen. He was shirtless, with grubby-looking bandages wrapped around his shoulder blades. Polar crept up with his camera and photographed the back of the boy's head.

The doorway beside the row of lamps had been knocked through and expanded into a big ragged archway, that showed an unappealing glimpse of the room beyond. Its walls had been smothered in spray paint by someone with all the enthusiasm of a real graffiti artist but none of the technique. Against one vandalised wall was a big table, heavy with beer bottles and spirits, like this was Party Central or something.

But as Tom brought his attention back to the red room, he caught no sense of excitement or even drunkenness in the thick air. This was just everyday life for the occupants of this wreck; late nights and smokes and booze and boredom. And maybe a little fear.

'These are my people,' Ramone told him and Kate, almost like he was challenging the two of them to disapprove.

Various grunts, calls and gestures issued in greeting from the slack bodies in the room as they realised Ramone was back.

But the most enthusiastic reaction came from the little figure with his nose pressed to the TV. 'Ro!' he shouted, and bounded over.

'My brother, Rico,' Ramone announced proudly, knocking knuckles with the kid. 'Hey, could we smoke less in here?' he called to the others. 'You know how it messes with Ric's asthma and shit.'

'Ain't nothing wrong with me, Ro,' protested Rico fiercely.

'Sorry, man,' called a big guy whose bruised face and resigned tone suggested his life was one long losing battle. 'So, how'd it go?'

'Not good, Puff,' Ramone told him. 'They're not interested in banding up. They 'wolf now.'

Puff nodded like he'd known all along, and turned back to the game without another word.

Rico looked up at Kate, his dark eyes glittering in his gaunt face. 'The white girl's pretty,' he observed.

'You think so?' Tom said, mock-frowning.

'Know so.' Rico grinned. His cheekbones were so high and sharp you could cut your finger on them.

'Nice TV,' Tom observed.

'Cicero found it and brought it home,' said Rico, pointing to a stocky, muscular kid with shades and a ponytail, spread-eagled over a large cushion.

'He found it?'

Ramone sniggered. 'Sure he did, Tom. Out back of an ex-rental store on 106th.'

'How'd you hurt yourself, Rico?' Kate asked him, gesturing to his bandages.

Rico looked away, seeming suddenly afraid.

Ramone leaned in close to talk to Kate, as if trying to exclude Tom. 'Howlers done it to him,' he said. 'There was some fighting when the Marqueta gang got turned. One of them nearly took off Rico's shoulder.' He swore. 'Kid's just ten and they done that to him. Jesus, the Marquetas are Puerto Ricans, for Chrissakes. We should be brothers.'

Rico shrugged and drifted off back to the widescreen.

'They *bit* him?' Tom watched Rico sit back down. 'Then ... isn't he 'wolf?'

Ramone glared at him. 'My brother ain't no howler. He got sick for a while but he ain't never turned. Shoulda seen the 'wolf that bit him. Went off screaming, all this froth coming out his mouth ... awesome.'

Rico grinned. 'Guess my blood don't taste good.'

'He's a resister,' Tom noted quietly.

'You got it,' Ramone breathed. 'Shame your own blood ain't that smart, huh, wolf-boy?'

'I didn't turn without a fight,' Tom muttered. 'Now, I think maybe you should tell us what's been happening around here.'

'I need to get this ankle seen to,' Ramone muttered.

'C'mon.' He hobbled into the graffiti room.

Tom and Kate followed him. The view brightened for Tom as Jasmine came back into sight. She was swigging from a carton of milk, leaning against a refrigerator that was so big it half-obscured the doorway next to it. Whatever lay beyond the door was obscured by a long green curtain.

On the worktop beside the refrigerator was a battered police car radio unit, electronic entrails spilling out of its casing. A black power lead had been lashed up to its side, snaking into a socket, and it squawked voices and static quietly to itself like some deranged electronic parrot.

Seeing Kate, Jasmine slunk off to the opposite corner of the room, her snub nose wrinkling like she'd smelled something bad.

Kate pretended not to notice, but Tom noticed a faint blush of colour in her cheeks.

Ramone pulled off his Nikes and rested one bare foot on the table. His ankle was puffy and dark. 'Get me some ice, girl, and make it better, huh?'

Jasmine snorted. 'I look like your mamma?' All the same, she opened the freezer door and started rummaging around inside.

Ramone grinned at Tom and mouthed silently, 'She loves me.'

Kate shot Tom a despairing glance. 'So, Ramone, you were going to tell us—'

'I told you the 'wolves were recruiting,' he announced abruptly. 'Takapa. His people are taking the street-kids, the gangs, the hobos – all the pissed-off poor people in this city – and turning them 'wolf.'

'Turning them against each other,' Jasmine added

quietly, slipping a handful of ice cubes into a bowl. 'Breaking old ties, old loyalties.'

Kate looked at her. 'And these people agree to being … recruited?'

'A lot of them do. Ain't no one else offering them nothing.' Jasmine smiled sarcastically, showing the gap in her front teeth. 'Guess a pretty white girl like you don't know what it's like to be invisible. To spend whole days begging for quarters while people step over you on the sidewalk like you're just trash.'

'You don't know anything about me and my life,' Kate said icily, her green eyes flashing.

'Reckon I know enough just by looking.' Jasmine turned and disappeared through the green curtain. She came back holding a battered square tin, and took out some band-aids, cotton wool and bandages. 'What're you two even doing here, slumming it with us?'

'Lay off,' Ramone told her. 'They running from the howlers like we are.'

'Takapa had captured us both, but we got away,' Tom explained. 'He wants us. Bad.'

Jasmine fell quiet. Her wide brown eyes seemed just a touch wider.

Tom found himself grimly satisfied at a point scored.

'What'd you do to piss off Takapa?' she demanded.

'Oh … stuff …' Kate said levelly. 'Probably safer for you if you don't know.'

Suddenly Tom sensed movement behind him. Cicero pushed past him to grab a beer off the table. He twisted off the cap with his bare hand, then took a long swig and strutted back out, winking at Kate as he did so.

'Looks like it ain't just Takapa who might want you, girl,' Jasmine murmured.

'So these kids that Takapa's agents are approaching,' Kate said, swiftly changing the subject, 'they actually *want* to be 'wolf?'

Ramone shrugged. 'They don't got much choice.'

'You seem to have made *your* choice,' Tom said. 'And screw Takapa.'

'There's nine of us here. Nine kids.' Ramone was looking at Tom like he knew nothing. 'We used to be a gang of almost thirty. This whole building used to be ours, not just one lousy storey.'

Jasmine wrapped the ice in a cloth and passed it over to Ramone. 'Some moved away when Swagger came calling the first time. And some ran out on us to take up with him and the howlers.'

Kate frowned. 'Swagger?'

'He's running things till Takapa moves back for good,' said Ramone, grimacing as he held the ice to his swollen ankle. 'So he says.'

'Swagger couldn't care less about us at first,' Jasmine went on. 'We weren't a threat. Weren't nothing. Then Ramone started stirring. Tried to get some of the gangs together to stand up to Swagger.'

Tom nodded grimly. 'And so suddenly you *became* a threat. And I guess you can't go to the police, get their protection?'

'Nah. Just like *you* can't.' Ramone looked at him pointedly. ''S'why so many are getting turned now. These kids know they'll get it worse from the cops than they will from the 'wolves. They running from home, they running from this and from that ... nowhere to go.'

'And no one to turn to,' Kate murmured. 'So they just give up and take that bite.'

Jasmine shook her head. 'These people, they've felt weak all their lives. If they choose Takapa, they get strong overnight. Then they're not victims no more. They're the hunters.'

Tom shuddered.

Kate was baffled. 'What is Takapa doing?' she questioned. 'Traditionally, the lupine community has always been careful about who it turns; who is chosen to continue family lines. If numbers swell indiscriminately, the community risks drawing attention to itself. But Takapa doesn't seem to care about any of that.'

'Maybe he knows he's not going to get the traditional lupines behind him,' Tom suggested.

'So he's building his own power base here – however he can?' Kate nodded. 'Maybe. But Jasmine, you said he was turning the 'wolves against each other?'

'That's the word out there,' Jasmine replied. 'I've heard that sometimes, they all get together and fight. A fight to the death.'

Tom stared at her. 'But why?'

'Hey!' shouted Rico from the next room. 'The pretty white girl's on TV!'

Tom and Kate stared at each other.

'Come see, come see!' yelled Rico.

They went through to the smoky fug of the TV room. Someone had flicked channels to the news. The mute symbol shone bright and blocky in the top right of the screen, obscuring Kate's picture.

Tom felt the blood drain from his head. He stumbled forward, stepping over people and pillows to get closer to the TV. Now his parents' faces were filling the screen. The camera pulled back to reveal they were seated on a rostrum at what looked like a press conference or something.

Beside them sat Hal and Marcie Folan, Kate's parents.

He heard Kate swear. 'Jesus, what is this?'

'Puff, hit the volume,' Ramone snapped.

'... Anderson, originally believed to have drowned near Seattle in mid-August in a tragic accident, and Seattle resident Kate Folan are both wanted for questioning in connection with a double homicide in New Orleans.'

Two faces were flashed up, a broad-faced Inuit type and a shrivelled old man. Tom felt his world tilt. Both men were in the pay of Takapa. Together, they'd nearly killed Tom. But Kate's mother had arrived on the scene just as Tom had started to fight back. She'd killed both men so she could have Tom herself – and he'd only escaped with his life thanks to Adam Blood joining the fight.

But clearly Marcie was now putting her murders to further use.

The TV cameras came in for a close-up on Marcie and Hal. Flash bulbs popped and glared from the front rows of the conference.

'Whatever you've done, whatever drove you to do it,' Marcie said, her voice studiedly weak with false emotion, 'Tom, Kate, we ask that you give yourselves up now ...'

Hal nodded. The grief on his face looked real enough.

As Marcie looked straight into the camera, Tom felt

like she was staring directly into his own eyes. 'The consequences, should you not, will be so much worse,' she continued. Another flash went off, but Tom knew that wasn't the cause of the unmistakable spark of gold that spun through Marcie's eyes. 'And you have to know your parents need you here.'

A different camera, placed more to the side of the rostrum, zoomed in on Carrie Anderson, Tom's mom. He hadn't seen her for three months but she seemed to have aged about ten years. She looked grey and haggard.

'Tom,' she sobbed. 'I don't know how we can survive this unless you come back to us soon, baby.'

Marcie moved into the shot, placed a comforting hand on Carrie's shoulder.

And with a casual glance at the camera, she licked her lips.

# CHAPTER THREE

The news anchorman rounded things up by announcing the pair were rumoured to be in New York City.

'That was cool!' whooped Rico. 'You're, like, famous!'

Tom turned to Kate. 'Jesus! What the hell do we do now?'

Deathly pale, Kate looked at him. Her eyes were glassy with tears. 'I don't know,' she replied, her voice coming out brittle and high. 'I don't know *what* we do now.'

'Mom and Dad thinking I was dead was bad enough, but – a murderer ...?' Tom paused, too choked up to continue.

Ramone looked at him hard. 'Did you really waste those guys?'

'No!' Tom shouted. 'They were trying to kill me! One was a 'wolf, the other was some maniac trying to cut me open—'

Kate crossed over to him and put her hands on his shoulders, trying to calm him down. 'It's OK, Tom. It's OK. We have to think why she's done this.'

'She's gonna kill my family,' Tom whispered. He felt like he might puke. 'It's a revenge thing, it must be.'

Kate tried to lose the tremor from her voice. 'She

won't kill them. Not yet. She's using them, trying to scare you into coming out in the open.' She wiped her eyes with the back of her hand. 'Mom must've gotten tired of chasing us. Why waste time tracking us down when she can bring us scurrying out?'

'She wants you to go running to the cops?' Jasmine clearly didn't buy it. 'Why? How would she get you then?'

'The cops don't just *know* about the 'wolves,' Kate told her sharply, 'some of them *are* 'wolves. The lupine community can only survive if blind eyes are turned in some pretty high places – so a whole lot of 'wolves make it their duty to climb to the top of the career ladder of all the useful professions. Police, politics, medicine ...'

Jasmine nodded slowly. 'So if you give yourselves up to the cops, what happens?'

'We'll meet with some kind of accident,' Tom assured her. 'Or maybe we'll "escape" and never be found again. Get my drift?'

'Well, whatever,' said Ramone. 'You two are trouble. And we got enough crap going down here without you two bringing your own.'

Kate glared at him. 'This is the thanks we get for saving your life?'

'It's OK, Kate,' Tom said quietly. 'They're just scared. We can't blame them for that.'

'Yo, Ramone,' drawled Cicero, from where he lay stretched out on the floor. 'Seems to me we're missin' a trick. We could buy us some favours – let Takapa have 'em if the howlers want them so bad.'

There was a heavy pause. Tom glanced around the room, steeling himself for fight or flight. All eyes were on him and Kate.

But Ramone shook his head. 'Takapa don't do deals, Ciss. Even if he did, we don't trade with no howlers.' He turned to Jasmine. 'Here's the deal. Rico needs them bandages changin', it's time he got his ass around to Woollard's place. Jasmine, baby, you'll take him in the morning, huh?'

Jasmine nodded. 'Sure.'

Ramone turned back to Tom and Kate. 'Woollard used to be a doctor once,' he explained. 'He helps us out. We help *him* out. And he knows about the 'wolves and shit, even treats some of their victims. Maybe he knows the dude you came here to find. Jasmine, take them with you, baby?'

Jasmine was about to open her mouth as if to argue when several loud thumps at the door rumbled through the room. Jasmine took a couple of nimble steps back in alarm. Rico hit the mute on the TV then jumped for cover behind one of the couches. The others held themselves still as statues except for Polar, who rose automatically – ready to take a snap of their mystery visitors.

Ramone blocked his way. 'Sit down. You think that's the mailman out there or something? It's almost four a.m.'

Kate edged closer to Tom. He felt her icy fingers coil into his own, and squeezed her hand tightly.

There were two more loud knocks, then nothing. The silence continued for what must have been a full minute. People began to breathe again.

Then, with a hideous splintering noise, the front door was smashed in.

The room erupted into movement as people scrabbled up from the floor or their couches, swearing and yelling. Tom and Kate backed away involuntarily, knocking against one of the lamps.

Ramone turned to Jasmine. 'Get the gun,' he told her, but she was already running for the other room. He pulled a switchblade from his jacket pocket just as a giant in biker's leathers burst into their hideout, wielding a sledgehammer. He had a pale, dangerous-looking face. His hair was a greasy crown of thick blond spikes. His heavy-lidded grey eyes sparked with reckless aggression, and his teeth were bared in a wild grin. Scores of tiny zits festered in the chapped, red skin around his mouth.

'Hey, kids!' The man gave a crazed laugh. 'Ain'tcha got no milk and cookies for Swagger?'

Before anyone could react, Swagger brought the hammer's heavy wooden handle up under Ramone's chin. There was a loud crack and the boy reeled back-wards. Puff lumbered towards their uninvited guest, fists raised, but Swagger shoved him aside, sending him sprawling over the couch to land heavily in front of the TV.

Tom tried to help Ramone get back up, but the big man turned, grabbed a fistful of Tom's dark hair and threw him aside.

Tom landed in a heap at Kate's feet, gasping as he banged his head on the sharp plastic corner of a plug socket.

Swagger took two long steps into the room. Two big guys – one black, one white, both dressed in ragged denim over black leather, biker-style – followed him inside, armed with baseball bats.

'Anyone else here want to play the hero?' Swagger enquired.

Jasmine burst out from the other room. Both her hands were clamped hard around a gun. 'Don't make me use this,' she said carefully, no trace of tremor in her voice.

A slow grin spread over Swagger's face. 'Gee, is the little girl gonna pop us?'

Ramone reached up from where he lay and wrangled the gun from Jasmine's stiff grip.

Swagger took a step forward, but Ramone quickly fired over his head. The noise was deafening, and plaster rained down like confetti over Swagger and his sidekicks. The smug expression turned sour on his big ugly face.

Struggling to his feet, Ramone held his gun arm rigid and pointed at Swagger's head. 'Take off.'

Swagger remained still, but gestured with his eyes first at Tom, then at Kate, who shifted uncomfortably under his stare. 'So who you got here? Reinforcements?'

'They're nobody,' said Ramone.

Swagger kept on staring at Kate. 'Figures, if they hang with you, loser.'

Ramone jerked the gun. 'What you come here for, Swagger?'

'I'm giving you one last chance.'

'One last chance to kiss howler butt?' Ramone spat on the floor.

'Uh-huh. And you better pucker up nice and sweet,' Swagger told him quietly. 'Takapa wants you all down at the arena, midnight Friday.'

'Why?'

'To show your allegiance, numbnuts.'

'We don't got no allegiance to shit like you,' said

Ramone. 'Just to each other.'

''S'right,' added Jasmine. 'You think we're stupid? We go down there, we're dead.'

'You got Papa Takapa all wrong, man,' Swagger grinned. 'He wants you to come and *party* on Friday. And he's offering 'wolf *protection*. He wants to look out for you. Who else is gonna do that?'

Ramone got unsteadily up on his feet. 'We got all we need right here.'

'Yeah?' Swagger smiled nastily. 'Not for long.'

As if he'd been signalled, the big black guy hurled his baseball bat at Jasmine, who yelped and fell back. Ramone turned instinctively towards her, and Swagger kicked the gun from his hand. The other intruder brought his own bat down on Ramone's head.

'No!' screamed Rico.

Then everything seemed to happen at once. The gorilla who'd brought down Ramone now waded into the middle of the room and swung his bat into the screen of the TV. Rico yelped as the glass shattered and white sparks spewed out.

Kate crouched down to help Tom up. 'Come on, there must be a back way out of here,' she hissed.

Tom was still dazed. He saw Cicero try to tackle the man with the bat, leaping on his back. But Swagger grabbed Cicero by the neck and threw him against the wall.

Two of Ramone's friends had clearly decided not to stick around. They jumped over Cicero's body and fled the same way Swagger had come in.

'Fleet, China, get back here!' yelled Jasmine. She had picked up the bat that had been thrown at her and was wielding it like she meant business. But the black guy had grabbed Ramone's gun.

He brought it up ready to fire at her.

Kate swore, leaned past Tom and yanked the adaptor plug out of the wall.

The place was plunged into blackness.

All movement stopped. The only sound was a low, male voice, Cicero maybe: '*Por favor, no me lastime.* Don't hurt me,' again and again.

Before Tom's eyes could even begin to adjust to the sudden dark, Kate was dragging him up to his feet. Her lips pressed up to his ear. 'Move,' she said fiercely. 'Refrigerator room. Maybe there's an exit behind that green curtain.'

Tom charged through into the room with the refrigerator but collided with the table. His hip cracked and felt red-hot. The sound of bottles and glasses toppling and crashing filled the air.

'Stop them,' Swagger ordered.

A shot was fired. Tom fell forward again, and he heard Kate yelp – in alarm, he hoped, not pain.

Footsteps were coming towards him. Tom was on all fours, disorientated now, groping for the green curtain. His mind was clouding, he could feel the 'wolf bucking inside his body. He struggled to hold on. If he lost control now, lashed out in the dark, how could he hope to tell friend from foe?

Someone knocked into him as they passed. 'Kate?' The curtain billowed out into his face as someone swept it aside. Tom grabbed a fistful of the fabric, got up and felt his way through into the space beyond.

He found himself in a filthy room lit by the sputtering flames of three stubby candles. Tom stared around trying to get his bearings. A pair of mouldering mattresses had been slung on the floor, rucked-up sleeping bags hunched beside them like great fat slugs. A closet door hung open on a single hinge. Perhaps he could hide there until—

Too late. One of Swagger's heavies came charging inside, the black one with the gun. Tom tripped him up and the guy went crashing to the ground, snuffing out two of the candles as he fell.

Another shape stole into the room. Tom could just about make out that it was female. 'Kate?' he hissed, heart thumping wildly. 'That you?'

'Shut your stupid mouth and follow me,' Jasmine hissed back, crossing to the closet.

Now Tom could see that the wall at the back of it had been knocked through.

'Emergency exit, huh?'

'Gotta be prepared. Cops, 'wolves ... all kinds of assholes want a piece of us.'

'Where does it lead?'

'Next door,' muttered Jasmine. 'Rico came this way. Boy's sick with his asthma. We gotta get after him.'

'You go,' Tom told her. 'I'm going back to find Kate.'

Jasmine was squeezing her body through the hole in the wall. 'She already got chased out the front way with Ramone, I think.'

The fallen thug was rising, a low growl building in his throat. A sudden feral stench filled the room, along with the sound of heavy stitching ripping apart. He was turning 'wolf, Tom realised. The lupine in Tom responded. A shot of excitement tore through him. He shook his head. He *had* to hold on ... He could control this crap – he was a wereling, wasn't he?

Jasmine was now through into the room beyond. 'Get in here!' she hissed at him.

The heavy was no longer human. He was a dark, crouched misshapen figure, panting and snapping his heavy jaws.

Tom darted for the closet door while the creature was still disorientated. He gasped as he landed heavily on the damp debris that littered the floor.

Jasmine helped him up.

'Jas, that you?' Rico sounded lost and small somewhere in the darkness ahead. His hoarse breath had an unsettling rasp to it.

'Stay still, Ric. We're coming.'

'Where's Ramone?' He broke into a coughing fit.

Jasmine shushed at him desperately. 'What happened to your inhaler?' she demanded.

'Don't work,' Rico gasped between awful, whooping coughs. 'Threw it away.'

'Jesus, Ric,' Jasmine began – then an exultant roar sounded behind them.

Tom spun around to find the werewolf that stalked them had pushed its great, bestial head through the hole in the wall. He saw the sick yellow gleam of its eyes, flicking this way and that around the ruined room.

'Out of here!' shouted Jasmine, scooping up Rico in her arms and running for the only chinks of light in the darkness. 'Door's this way!'

But the doorway was boarded up, great wooden planks placed horizontally across the gap. Behind them, Tom heard wet masonry crumble under the onslaught of the 'wolf's massive paws.

Tom gestured at the planks. '*This* is prepared?'

Jasmine turned and dumped Rico on to him. The kid locked his arms around Tom's neck, shaking and wheezing, and the two of them watched as Jasmine knocked two of the planks out with a few savage well-placed kicks.

'They're only tacked over the window,' she muttered. 'What, you want *anyone* getting in?'

'It's us getting *out* I'm worried about,' Tom replied, kicking the last two planks away himself.

A split-second later, Jasmine was leading the way out into the cold dark street. Tom followed close behind, panting with the exertion of carrying Rico.

'We've got to find Kate,' he hissed at her. 'Is there a place you go to regroup after a bust or—'

'Ric's really sick,' Jasmine snapped, crossing over to a beat-up old Lexus over the street. 'We need transport.'

The kid was squirming and coughing in Tom's arms, struggling for breath. 'He's having an asthma attack?'

'It happened before. He nearly died. Little bug won't use his inhaler.' Somehow she'd forced open the driver's door of the Lexus and now she was busy working at the wiring inside.

Tom watched her. 'Wait a second – you're stealing that car?'

'Guess I am,' she said dryly while she worked. 'Hey, d'you think Jesus will still want me for a sunbeam?'

The hunting roar of the 'wolf floated eerily down the dark street, and Tom cast an anxious glance back over his shoulder. 'We might find out sooner than you think.'

The Lexus suddenly growled into life. 'Get over here,' Jasmine insisted. 'We gotta get to Doc Woollard's, fast.'

Tom opened the rear door and placed Rico inside. 'I can't come with you,' he said. 'I have to find Kate.'

Jasmine stared hard at him. 'Get your sorry ass in this car *now*. Look at that kid! He could stop breathing. You want me to give him CPR while I'm driving?'

Tom heard the sound of heavy lupine footfalls tearing down the asphalt, saw a dark, massive blur moving up behind him.

'In!' Jasmine shouted.

With no time to agonise further, Tom ducked inside and Jasmine was speeding away before he'd even pulled the door shut. Rico was struggling for breath, his dark eyes bulging as the coughs kept coming. Through the rear windshield, Tom watched grimly as the hideous creature pelted after them, huge head low to the road like it was scenting the exhaust.

Up ahead was a red light, and a big truck queuing, blocking their way. Jasmine swore as she hit the brakes.

Tom was thrown forwards. Rico gripped tightly on to his hand, wheezing and choking. Tom turned and checked on the lupine. It was almost on top of them.

'It's still coming!' he yelled.

As it readied itself to pounce, the creature opened its great, slavering jaws in triumph.

# CHAPTER FOUR

Kate practically shoved Ramone along ahead of her. 'You've got to keep going,' she urged him, but she knew he couldn't last much longer. His ankle was bad and his head was worse. He had a sticky gash on the back of his skull from Swagger's blow with the bat. Blood had run down and soaked through the collar of his thin cotton shirt.

When he stumbled and nearly fell for about the fourteenth time, she steered him over to rest against the nearest doorway.

While Ramone caught his breath, Kate looked around for any sign of Swagger or his thugs. But the street was silent and empty.

Where was Tom? Kate could've punched the wall with frustration. She'd have been with him now if that hand hadn't curled around her ankle back in the darkened room before she could take off after him. It was Cicero, or Puff, or one of them, sprawled and hurting on the floor – reaching out, confused, scared in the darkness.

Join the freakin' club.

She'd managed to pull away, but then someone small – Rico? – had pushed past her and she'd stumbled and lost her balance.

An oily flame had sprung from Swagger's lighter, inches from her face. Kate flinched from the heat, the big man had grabbed for her, but Ramone had recovered enough to punch him. As Swagger fell backwards, Ramone had grabbed hold of her and together they'd bundled out of the room, through the wreck of the kitchen and the shattered front door, and out into the cold, damp November night.

They'd barely gotten a block away and they'd already reached a standstill.

Ramone's dark eyes were scrunched up in pain and frustration. The scar on his cheek was ugly white against his sweaty olive complexion. 'Why don't you leave me?' he muttered.

'What, and shatter your faith in human kindness?' Kate shook her head. 'No, we'll just rest here for a few seconds and—'

'Don't matter, anyhow,' he interrupted. 'Swagger's won. My people all split, my home's smashed up. It's over.'

'Your brother's out there with Jasmine and Tom,' Kate told him. 'They got away, I'm sure of it. They'll be back.'

'Well, well,' a low, unpleasant voice called out. 'Didn't get very far, did you?'

'Looks like someone else is back first,' muttered Ramone.

Kate felt her stomach sinking into her shoes. She turned to find Swagger standing at the end of the street with one of his 'little helpers'. The streetlight overhead cast a sick sodium glare over his zombie complexion, making him look even nastier than before.

'I ain't going down like this,' hissed Ramone, bunching his fists.

'Very macho,' Kate breathed.

'Come on, little girl,' Swagger called, 'we ain't finished talking to you, yet.'

Kate realised that Ramone, sunk back in the doorway, must be hidden from Swagger's view. 'Stay here, rest, get back to your hideout,' she whispered. 'I'll lead them away.'

She turned and attempted to saunter down the empty street towards Swagger. 'The reason I didn't get very far,' she announced, 'was so that you wouldn't take so long to catch up with me.'

Swagger looked at her, hooded grey eyes beady with suspicion. 'Is that a fact?'

'Yep,' Kate said, forcing herself to look up at him and smile. 'Those losers tried to make me go with them. But I prefer to be on the winners' side.'

Swagger smiled. 'Winners' side is the howlers' side. You like 'wolves?'

'Uh … sure.' She nodded.

A different gleam came into Swagger's eyes. 'Just who are you, sweetheart? You don't look Ramone's type.'

Kate shrugged. 'Don't hardly know him. Me and my friend were just hanging.'

Swagger nodded thoughtfully. 'Hanging at Ramone's, huh? You there to score, maybe?'

It was as good a story as any. 'Maybe.'

'Well if you want to get high, baby,' Swagger grinned, 'you just got to come back with me tonight.'

Kate willed her smile not to shrivel and die. 'But it's almost morning.'

Swagger nodded excitedly. 'And the action kicks off at dawn. My soldiers have been getting psyched all night. Soon they get to play.' He took her by the wrist and led her away. His ape in the denim and leathers moved up close to flank her.

'Where are we going?' she asked, trying to sound casual, up for anything.

'Oh, baby,' said Swagger, 'I am going to give you a high you ain't never gonna forget.'

'Here it comes!' Tom shouted to Jasmine, as the drooling 'wolf leaped through the air, claws outstretched, ready to smash its way through the rear windshield to get them.

'Screw this!' yelled Jasmine. She revved the engine and shot forwards, yanking hard on the wheel to avoid the truck in front.

The 'wolf fell short of them, skidding to a halt, its claws raking up the asphalt. It howled in anger as its prey moved out of reach.

Tom swore as they almost hit a car coming the other way. It swerved aside and crashed into a row of trashcans awaiting an early morning collection.

Jasmine ran the red light, and now swerved hard to the left to avoid a delivery van taking the corner. It blared its horn and Jasmine gave him the bird. But the 'wolf was back up and running for them.

Tom could feel his own change starting to rise up inside him, more insistent than ever. The fear, the panic, the craving for release seemed to have been pumping and pounding through his veins for hours, wearing away his human self. He could taste the sharp tang of blood at the back of his throat. His

49

mouth was flooding with saliva, so fast he could barely swallow it down.

'That thing's not giving up!' he shouted hoarsely, clenching his fists.

'Me neither,' Jasmine replied calmly. Wheels screeched and rubber burned as she steered the car around in a tight arc to turn right on to the next avenue.

Tom saw the delivery truck screech to a halt as the dark shape of the 'wolf bolted out in front of it and caught a glancing blow. At the next block Jasmine took a left and floored the accelerator, and the carnage was hidden from view.

Tom felt the tension that racked his body lose a little of its grip. He realised he'd been holding his breath. He unclenched his fists and saw his palms were scored with nail marks. The taste of blood at the back of his throat soured, turning his stomach. The danger of the change taking hold was fading. For now.

'I think we lost the 'wolf,' he said shakily.

Jasmine nodded, apparently satisfied.

Rico had stopped coughing, and was breathing a little easier now, in shallow wheezes. Tom squeezed his hand. 'It's OK,' he told the kid. 'Everything will be fine soon.' For a second he could almost make believe he was talking to Joe, riding through the night to Seattle in the back of Dad's old Chrysler before this whole nightmare started. He thought back to the press conference on TV. Now his whole family was snared in Marcie Folan's twisted plans ... and where the hell was Kate? He shut his eyes, wished he could think of some clean way through all this.

'You falling asleep back there?' Jasmine enquired.

He sighed. 'I can't imagine ever sleeping again.'

'Good. 'Cause now we gotta go wake up Doc Woollard and get Rico fixed up. Then we can check back with the crew and your uptight little girlfriend. OK?'

Tom just nodded, feeling a strange unease that went beyond the horror they'd just experienced. Jasmine had just seen her home wrecked and her friends beaten up, been shot at and then chased by a hungry 'wolf. And yet here she was, driving along in her stolen car, so calm and so in control. Taking it all in her stride. He couldn't help but shudder. Just what messed-up crap did you have to live through to get that way?

'This is our rink,' said Swagger proudly, leading the way down the central aisle through the tiers of seating. 'Shaun, stay on security.'

'Check.' Shaun the bodyguard stayed by the exit doors, but gestured that Kate should follow Swagger down into the auditorium.

Kate did her best to look impressed as she stared around the ruined expanse, hidden away beneath a cordoned-off derelict warehouse building on East 91st. It was hard to believe this dilapidated, echoing arena had ever been an actual ice rink, a place of brightness and music and fun. Now its surface was damp, grimy concrete, spattered and stained with stubborn pools of dried blood. Dim lights burned high above the endless, empty seating, casting distorted shadows over the arena. If there was any ice left in the place it must be in the air; each breath Kate took chilled her insides, then ghosted out of her mouth in a fine cloud of freezing mist.

Swagger eased himself on to the front row of rotting wooden benches and looked at her expectantly. Clearly her opinion was being sought.

'So,' she managed at last, 'this is all yours, huh?'

'It's Takapa's.' Swagger's chest puffed up with pride. 'But I get to run the events here.'

'Just who is this Takapa?' she asked. She couldn't let Swagger think she knew anything about this.

'Maybe I'll introduce you. I think he'd like you.'

Kate tried to keep the alarm from her voice. 'He's coming here?'

Swagger nodded. 'Tonight.'

'Tonight ... Well. Cool.'

Swagger looked at her strangely. 'You all right, honey?'

*Sure*, she thought. *I can't wait to say hi again to the murdering freak I screwed over. The murdering freak who wants to get with me.* The temperature suddenly seemed a couple of degrees colder, and she knew she had to change the subject. 'You seem to know Ramone's people, were you part of their gang?'

'Had a girl once who was,' said Swagger. 'So I used to hang with them sometimes.'

'When you were just human?' she asked lightly.

He spat on the floor. 'When I was nothing.'

Suddenly the door above them that led to the auditorium was flung open with a reverberating crash. A half-dressed black man greeted Shaun and then came shambling down the steps. As he approached, Kate recognised him as Swagger's other sidekick from Ramone's place.

Swagger didn't seem impressed to see him wearing only a pair of ill-fitting trousers. 'You went 'wolf on them?' he said quietly. 'You lost control?'

The man looked severely pissed off but said nothing.

'Takapa said not to kill them,' Swagger went on. 'You kill them, Eric?'

The big man shook his head. 'Lost them. The little kid, the whitey and that skinny bitch, Jasmine.'

Swagger looked at Kate sharply. 'Seems your boyfriend's got himself some new buddies.'

It was all Kate could do not to collapse with relief. Instead, she just shrugged, kept her face neutral. 'That's cool. So do I.'

He nodded at her approvingly, then turned a more critical eye on the black guy. 'You lost control, Eric. I don't know if I can trust you on my personal staff no more.'

Eric held himself stiffly. 'Sorry, Swag.'

Swagger fixed him with a stare so cold it made Kate shiver. 'Tell you what. Why don't you go get our gladiators down here?'

Eric turned to obey, but as he walked down on to the floor of the rink, Swagger called to him again. 'Oh, and Eric? I want you to fight down there with them. For me, huh?'

Eric froze for a few moments. Then he carried on walking without turning around. The heavy slaps of his bare feet on the concrete sounded around the arena, lingering long after he'd been swallowed up by the shadows.

Swagger patted the bench beside him, indicating Kate should sit down.

Kate forced herself to do so. 'What did you mean, gladiators?' she asked casually.

'I'm an emperor here,' Swagger said proudly. 'We bring people here to fight. Fight for their lives.'

Kate knew he was watching her intently, but couldn't meet his stare. 'For your entertainment?'

'You don't think that's a good enough reason?' Swagger slipped an arm casually around her shoulders. It was all Kate could do not to cringe. 'But, you're right. This ain't about bloodlust. Not just about bloodlust, anyway ... We got plans. Big plans.' He grinned nastily. 'Let me tell you, babe, there's gonna be some changes coming to this city. Everything's gonna be up for grabs, and me and my boys are getting a *big* share.' Then he looked at her meaningfully and added in a softer voice, 'Everything we want's gonna be ours to take.'

Kate pushed a weak smile out of her mouth, but her mind was a whirl. Just what was it that Takapa was planning? Since her mother was here in New York too, chances were she was involved in it somehow. Marcie had been sickeningly impressed with Takapa when they'd met in New Orleans. Whatever, if Swagger wasn't just shooting his mouth off and Takapa really *was* coming here sometime soon – with or without her mom in tow – Kate knew she was in mortal danger.

Like that's anything new, she thought bitterly.

Swagger's sweaty fingers caressed the side of her neck. She wanted to gag, and thanked God when a sudden clatter echoed out across the arena and he pulled away.

Swagger's attention was now exclusively fixed on the old rink itself. He rubbed his hands together with childish glee. 'Here they come.'

Just as Kate was feeling no further tension could be wrung from her body, the sight she saw made every muscle tense up, every nerve jangle. Eric was leading ten people, none of them older than thirty, into the middle of the arena. Their footfalls built from a murmur to a rumble. Some were clutching themselves, either against the cold or with fear. Others walked along vacantly, like this was just some guided tour they were getting.

There were all kinds of people there. Junkie-types, pencil-thin with gaunt faces. Average Joes in jeans and sweaters, staring around glumly in resigned expectation. A couple of muscle-bound types in plaid shirts. And there were two women in the little crowd, looking about edgily: one short-haired and stocky, in denim – and the other a hard-faced blonde with ratted hair, her neck spider-webbed with tattoos.

There was something about the way they looked and moved … Slightly unfocused, jumpy – like they were coming down from taking something.

Eric sorted them roughly into two sides, picking out people and propelling them across the concrete floor to stand together, each group facing the other. The echoes faded as they all stood still as statues, like they were trying to stare each other down in the murky light.

'You expect them to start fighting?' Kate whispered. 'Just like that?'

'Uh-huh. They ain't got a choice.' Swagger sniggered. 'Let combat begin, y'all!' he yelled.

With the words still ringing around the auditorium, Eric lurched into action. First he pushed one of the Average Joes in the first group flat on his ass, then he took a swing at the stocky woman on the opposing side. She cried out and went down. Some of the others eyed each other nervously. One of the junkie-guys just stared down at his feet, clutching his head like this nightmare would all just go away if he only wished hard enough.

No chance. Eric whacked him in the stomach, doubled him over.

Kate looked away, her stomach twisting, but every new shout and cry tugged her reluctant gaze back. She ended up seeing the violence as it unfolded in a series of sickening snapshots. The junkie collapsing to the concrete, clutching his head ... The Average Joe running to kick him while he was down ... The blonde girl raking her nails down a muscle man's face ... The stocky woman grabbing her by the throat.

'C'mon!' yelled Swagger. 'You're not even trying! I know what you need, people. And whoever brings Eric down gets double!'

'*What* do they need?' Kate asked him.

Swagger wasn't listening. He breathed in deep, like he was a soccer coach savouring the early morning air while his team warmed up. 'Work together now! Good job!' He clapped his big hand down hard on Kate's shoulders. 'Don't it make you feel good?'

*You're mad*, thought Kate. *You're truly insane.* But she could only sit there helplessly as the fighting grew wilder and bloodier.

# CHAPTER FIVE

Jasmine banged on Dr Woollard's door so hard that Tom thought she might put her slim little fist right through the wood. He checked his watch: almost five a.m. Rico was leaning on him drowsily. In the car he had kept falling into a fitful sleep, only to wake himself again by coughing.

They had left the stolen car a couple of blocks away and Jasmine had led the way to a shabby-looking brownstone on the fringes of Harlem, overlooking a vacant lot.

'Do you often come calling so early?' Tom asked, as Jasmine knocked even harder.

'He don't exactly keep office hours,' she said. 'And he ain't always strictly sober. But he's plenty smart. Supposed to be a genius or something.' She frowned. 'Least, he was once.'

Tom heard a grumbling voice coming towards the door.

'All right, all right. I'm coming ...' A bolt was thrown, then another; then a third. Finally the door opened to reveal a singularly unimpressive little man, half-dressed in a chunky brown cardigan with nothing beneath it and a pair of striped pyjama bottoms. He stared out at them blearily. His grey hair was mussed up in a dozen different directions, a wild frame for his lined and haggard face. There was a droopy look about him – as if his face and body were giving up to gravity even as you watched. But his eyes were an arresting amber colour. They transfixed you, even though clouded by sleep and drink and God knew what else.

'Hey, Doc,' said Jasmine. 'We need you to take a look at Rico.'

Woollard glanced down at the boy then back to Jasmine. 'OK, I've seen him. Now would you mind leaving me in peace?' His voice was gravelly but he had a refined accent, British maybe. It reminded Tom of Adam Blood's, though *that* posh voice had been a put-on, a front to impress customers. Something told Tom that this man's accent was the real thing.

Jasmine seemed unfazed by Woollard's attitude. 'He's got a howler bite, Doc, remember?'

Woollard knitted his brows together as if trying to recall. 'Rico ... bite ...' He clicked his fingers and swayed drunkenly in the doorway. 'Yes, of course. Rico, our little resister. Very interesting ...'

'He's just had a real bad asthma attack, too, choking and no breath, and all kinds of shit,' Jasmine persisted.

Woollard seemed to lose interest and began mumbling to himself. 'I'm going back to bed,' he announced grumpily.

'Please?' Jasmine opened her beautiful eyes as wide as they'd go. 'I did bring you a real big bottle of JD last time.' She smiled craftily. 'And I might again.'

Woollard's eyes lit up like cigarette-ends. 'Perhaps I *am* being a little ungracious,' he said. 'Come inside.'

With that he turned and shambled from view.

Jasmine ushered Rico inside then turned to Tom. 'As doctors go, he's cheap.'

Tom frowned. 'He looks like he could use a little medical attention himself. You're really going to let him examine Rico while he's in that state?'

'Listen, the sooner we get Rico checked out, the sooner we get you back to your prissy little girlfriend, OK?'

Tom couldn't fault that logic, and followed her into the squalid little apartment. It reeked of whisky and garlic, and there must've been a dozen crucifixes arranged around the walls of the entrance hall. 'He's expecting vampires?' Tom asked quietly.

Jasmine pulled out a cellphone. 'When you've drunk as much as he has, guess you don't know just *what* you're gonna see next.'

Tom nodded to the phone. 'Are you calling Ramone?'

Jasmine shook her head. 'He lost his cellphone in the park, remember? Anyhow, I ain't got no credit left. Incoming calls only.' She hit some keys and waited. Then she sighed. 'No messages.'

Woollard was rooting around in a ramshackle room that was part office, part living room. A bare light bulb dangled down from a flex in the ceiling, so low that Tom nearly banged his head on it. He stepped carefully; the floor was barely visible under piles of clutter and scattered papers. The walls were covered in arcane astrological charts, wax-sealed scrolls and ancient-looking pieces of parchment packed with strange scrawls in stranger languages. Incongruous amid all this mystical bric-a-brac was a dog-eared certificate in a dirty frame; Woollard's doctorate in science from Yale University. The document had been signed almost thirty years ago, and looked as battered and faded now as the man himself.

Tom wondered what had happened to the bright scholar to bring him as low as this dank, drink-stinking apartment. Suddenly, he felt lonely. It was still dark through the open blinds, and he wondered where Kate was right now. Weird. He used to think first of his family when he felt low. Now it was Kate's face that swam into his mind; that look on her face, soft and serious all at the same time …

With a grunt of satisfaction, Woollard finally seemed to find what he was looking for: a dirty glass. He poured himself a generous measure of Jack Daniels, then drained the glass in one gulp. 'I'm sorry that I can't offer you any,' he said, looking at Jasmine and Rico in turn, 'but you're not over twenty-one.' Then he squinted at Tom, as if noticing him for the first time. 'Who is this?' he asked Jasmine.

'A friend,' she answered.

Tom felt vaguely flattered. 'My name's Tom,' he added.

Woollard smiled coldly, then poured himself another drink. 'You've noticed my unusual interior decorations?'

'They're, uh, a little hard to miss,' Tom confirmed.

'And now you think I'm just a pathetic old lush who hangs garlic around his windows and uses black magic to shore up his ruins, hmm?'

'No, sir,' Tom said uneasily.

Woollard fixed him with those burning eyes. It was as if they alone held his vitality, and the rest of his body had quietly withered away around them. 'There are many dark things in this city,' he said. 'Phantoms and fiends and creatures of the night. I've heard them, seen them. I've seen such things …' He glared suddenly at Jasmine. 'Sleep does not come easy to me. These charms and doctrines, fragile though they might seem, lend me a little security.'

This time he sipped from his glass and nodded appreciatively, like he'd suddenly noticed the taste. 'Right, let's get down to business.' He pushed a pile of papers from his desk and on to the floor, and pulled out some cigarette papers and a tin of tobacco from the pocket of his cardigan. 'Rico the resolute,' he said with a wan smile, 'roll me a … herbal cigarette – there's a good fellow?'

Tom shot an alarmed look at Jasmine, but she seemed untroubled.

Rico sat in Woollard's scruffy old office chair and got busy with the papers. It seemed he was adept at rolling joints. Presumably this was another part of Woollard's usual payment.

Tom stared at the shambling doctor, astonished by his behaviour. 'Didn't you hear what Jasmine told you outside? Rico had an asthma attack, a bad one. If you smoke that thing, he could have another.'

Woollard considered Rico. 'Didn't I get you an inhaler for your asthma once before, boy?'

'Didn't work,' said Rico, as he finished making the cigarette. 'Lost it.'

'You have to use it regularly, you little fool,' Woollard snapped. He knocked back the rest of his drink. 'Now, what was it I prescribed …' He pushed the cigarette into his pocket and closed his eyes, trying

to remember. 'Cortico-steroid inhaler, probably ...
Ipatropium? Did we add that to your treatment?'

Rico shrugged.

Woollard sighed. 'Well, Rico. I suppose I should
examine you properly, check what's what. See how
that bite's healing, too ...' he said without much
enthusiasm. 'You know where the examination room
is.'

Rico hopped off the chair and pottered back out
into the hallway. Woollard followed him. 'Excuse me,'
he said.

'And clearly you do,' Tom said to Jasmine once he'd
left the room. 'Excuse him, I mean. Of a hell of a lot.'

She shrugged, and coiled her lithe body into Woollard's old office chair. 'He knows about the 'wolves.
He doesn't ask questions. And he helps us all he can.'

'Because you bribe him with booze.'

'Stolen whisky's cheaper than medical insurance,'
she said, yawning.

Tom shook his head. 'I can't believe you actually
leave Rico alone with him!'

'Rico likes him. Woollard ain't no freak, he don't
mess around touching your privacy,' said Jasmine, her
dark eyes flashing. 'He's just in bad times. We don't all
get lucky in life, Tommy-boy.'

*That's for sure*, thought Tom. Then he heard a
voice, low and furtive-sounding: Woollard. He
strained to hear; he'd learned that if he focused hard
enough, he was able to summon his more sensitive
lupine hearing to his human form.

'I see ...' Woollard was saying quietly. 'What are
your instructions?' A tinny, scratchy voice answered
from the other end of a phone line, but Tom couldn't

quite make out the words. 'Yes, that makes sense. Can you get your hands on some?'

'Jasmine,' Tom hissed. 'Woollard's making a call in there. Come on, let's listen in.'

Though puzzled, she moved quietly as a cat, creeping out after him into the hall.

'Yes, I've got what you've been waiting for.' Woollard's voice was clear enough through the door for Jasmine to hear every word. 'Ready for delivery. Will you pick up or shall I arrange for them to be delivered?'

Tom gripped Jasmine lightly by the arm. 'This is a trap,' he whispered. 'Woollard's selling us out!'

Her face darkened. 'Who to?'

'I don't know, but he's got Rico in there!' Tom pressed his ear to the Examination Room door, but still couldn't decipher the voice on the phone. 'There's only one way to find out.' He gripped the handle, ready to throw open the door.

Kate felt colder than she'd ever felt in her life. A big knot had formed in her throat as she watched Eric grapple with a succession of screaming opponents. She turned to Swagger in shocked disbelief. 'Isn't he supposed to be your friend or something?'

'Sure. But he's got a lesson to learn.' He gave her a crooked smile, then scratched the pustules around his mouth with his dirty fingers. 'It's OK. Eric can look after himself.'

'When it's ten against one?' Kate muttered.

But Swagger seemed to be right. Eric was kicking and punching and knocking heads together like a cut-price Jackie Chan, smashing his way through his opponents, sending them reeling. What he lacked in fancy moves he made up for in raw violence.

'Yup,' Swagger chuckled. 'No need to worry 'bout Eric.'

It seemed the odds were lessening. Kate stared in disbelief at the antics of another Average Joe hovering at the periphery of the fighting. Each time Eric knocked one of Joe's rivals to the ground, Joe would scuttle in and try to finish them off. But the third time he tried it was the last. He'd picked on the stocky woman, who lunged for him, screaming, hands reaching for his throat.

Swagger turned to Kate. 'Think we should let ol' Eric off the hook now, baby?'

Kate stared at him, helplessly. She wanted no part in this, no responsibility for what happened to any of these wretched people.

But Swagger took her silence for tacit approval. 'OK, warm-up's over. Forget Eric,' he commanded, 'and forget any bonus. Stick with your team, now. Bring down your opponents – if you want what's waiting …'

What the hell *was* waiting for these people, Kate wondered. What could be worth all this?

Eric stood back, folded his burly arms and watched as the teams regrouped, panting and gasping, clutching at wounds, wiping blood and sweat from their faces. Then they were bawling and yelling as they bundled together to fight, eyes wild and limbs flailing.

*Make it stop!* Kate wanted to scream at Swagger. *Stop this senseless stupidity now!* But she knew from the maniacal glint in his eyes that nothing she could say would make the slightest difference to him – and it might seal her own fate. She buried her face in her hands as the fighting between the two teams grew even more savage; as the screams got louder and crimson stains bloomed on the cracked concrete floor.

Swagger started to whoop and catcall. Against her better judgement Kate found herself morbidly drawn to see why. Someone was trying to limp away from the struggle, one of the muscle-bound types – he looked the part of a modern-day gladiator but clearly had no stomach to play any longer. The tattooed blonde was sprawled on the ground, roaring at him to come back and fight. Her body was shaking, twitching. With horrified fascination, Kate saw that a thick, pale pelt was bristling out from her darkening skin.

'It's 'wolf time,' cackled Swagger, wiping the mirth from his eyes.

Maybe it was the anger, the fear, the desperation that was palpable in the arena – but the woman wasn't the only one turning 'wolf. Like a yawn being passed on to someone watching, the other fighters began to change too, shucking off their humanity with their bloodied clothes, crouching and yowling. Flesh furred over as lupine cells coursed through their bodies. Bones and ligaments crunched and snapped as they reformed. Lupine eyes shone the same dull, glassy gold as the lights that slow-burned up above.

Only Eric stayed standing on two legs, arms still folded, an impassive, detached observer.

The blonde woman's lupine form was a ragged, scrawny-looking creature. Kate could see welts in the beast's back from the fighting, and one of her legs was damaged, but she could still run at a frightening speed. The muscle man didn't stand a chance. He let out a scream, then went down, his body hidden from view by the 'wolf's bulk. The grunts as she fed on her prey were amplified by the distorting acoustics in the arena.

Kate couldn't keep silent any longer. 'This isn't a contest,' she stormed, 'it's a slaughter. *Murder!*'

'It's survival of the fittest,' said Swagger, looking at her oddly. 'These punks soon learn: they're stronger if they fight as a team. That's what all this is about. That's what we gotta make them see.'

With a chill, Kate saw he was right. The human skirmishes had been scrappy, frantic affairs, but the pack instinct was more dominant in the lupine state. The 'wolves were working together in their factions. Two of the beasts had brought down a third, their great paws pressing down on the creature's neck. Another was methodically herding its wounded opponent towards the slavering jaws of its waiting ally, blocking any attempt to pass, forcing it back.

The fight was clearly coming to an end. Two men and the stocky woman lay twisted and still in their own congealing blood. A 'wolf lay twitching on its side, barely breathing; long gashes scored the length of its body. Three victorious lupines sat hunched over their vanquished opponents, as if waiting for something.

Kate realised they were looking to Swagger.

'The choice is mine,' he whispered, rapt as he drank in the carnage before him. 'All I gotta do is reach out my hand …' He did so, extending his thumb. 'I'm the judge, see? If I raise my thumb, the losers live to fight again. If I lower it – they die.' He looked at Kate and sniggered. 'See that? Got more power in my thumb than most people get to use in a lifetime.'

Kate saw his shadow on the stand before them. In silhouette, the spikes of Swagger's hair could've been a crown of laurel leaves, just like those worn by the emperors of Rome. And here he was gloating over his own private coliseum of gladiators.

'Let them live,' she pleaded.

'Why should I?'

'You made out that there was some purpose behind this fighting.'

'There is,' agreed Swagger, 'but people gotta learn that losing don't count.'

'But they're your own kind. Lupines. Bound by the ties of the 'wolf brotherhood.'

Now Swagger looked at Kate oddly. 'You know about that old-days stuff?'

'Enough to know that 'wolves don't kill 'wolves. It's senseless, there aren't enough—'

'Not enough howlers?' Swagger shook his head. 'You're wrong. Soon, they're gonna be dime-a-dozen.'

'What do you mean?' Kate demanded.

Swagger's smile slipped a little, like he was aware he'd maybe said too much.

Kate swallowed hard, placed her hand on his face and softly caressed his waxy cheek in a desperate effort to distract him. He turned to her, confused for a moment – then smiled. A smug *I-knew-you-wanted-me* smile.

'Please,' she said softly. 'Whatever you're doing this for, let the losers live. Haven't enough people died?'

Swagger looked at her, shook his head a fraction. 'Ain't never enough people died.'

His thumb came down.

Kate closed her eyes and clasped her hands over her ears. But she couldn't hope to shut out the cacophony of baying and howling that filled the auditorium and echoed through the freezing air, as the victors began to feed on their fallen prey.

# CHAPTER SIX

Tom kicked open the door to Dr Woollard's examination room. 'What's going on, Doc?' he demanded. 'Why the private call?'

Woollard looked at him in surprise. He held a stethoscope in one hand, and an ancient cellphone the size of a brick in the other. It seemed he'd just killed the call. Rico was lying placidly on a couch, his filthy old dressings replaced with fresh bandages. He was drumming his fingers on the cracked black leather, staring at a handwritten optician's eye chart and looking bored.

'Who were you speaking to?' Jasmine asked uncertainly.

'Stacy Stein at the hospital centre,' Woollard told her, seemingly bewildered by their behaviour. 'I wanted her opinion on prescribing theophylline for Rico's asthma.'

Tom wasn't convinced. 'Aren't *you* supposed to be a doctor?'

'I'm not a general practitioner,' Woollard replied crossly, resting the phone on a cluttered workbench. 'I used to be a specialist in genetics and haematology.'

Jasmine screwed up her nose. 'Say what?'

'Study of the blood,' Woollard explained. 'I led the

field at Yale. But that was a long time ago,' he added with a sigh. 'The medicine I had in mind for Rico lists heart murmurs as a possible side-effect, and since Dr Stein is more intimately acquainted with his medical history than I, I simply sought her advice.'

'Who is Stacy Stein?' Tom asked suspiciously.

'She sticks needles in you,' chirped Rico, but speaking made him cough again.

'Runs programs, tests, medical trials, that kind of shit,' Jasmine added with a grimace. 'She works with a whole lot of kids on the streets. Always on your case, always judging your ass – you using? You drinking? She don't quit trying to get you straight. 'S'like going to see your mom or something.'

'So you come to Woollard for treatment instead. I guess he's not about to give anyone a hard time about that,' Tom observed. Though he couldn't agree with her preference, at least it made a bit more sense to him now. 'But how come she knows Rico's medical history? She doesn't know about the 'wolves, right?'

Jasmine laughed in his face. 'She knows all right. And she knows Rico's a resister, that's why she's so hot on him.'

Tom nodded thoughtfully. Before this nightmare had begun, he'd have laughed at anyone who said they believed in werewolves. Now he found himself wondering just how many people knew the true situation. He and Kate had been directed here to find Jicaque, but it was feeling more and more like they had been lured into the secret werewolf capital of America.

'Stacy's gonna find a cure for the 'wolves,' piped up Rico. 'Make them just people again.'

'She is?' Tom looked at him, then at Woollard, a jolt

of fresh hope slamming through his heart. Maybe he wouldn't need to find their mystery medicine man; maybe a cure was closer than he could've dared hope. 'Well?'

'That is the ultimate aim of her research, yes,' Woollard confirmed. 'But I fear there's a long way to go.'

Tom felt a dizzying crunch of disappointment in his guts. 'Right,' he said, trying to act casual, aware that Jasmine was looking at him oddly. 'How come you know so much about it?'

Woollard shrugged. 'Obviously the study of were-wolves is not her real work at the hospital. She can only appropriate so much hospital equipment to further her lupine researches.' He puffed up his scrawny chest. 'So she's enlisted my considerable expertise to aid her in her quest ... and uses my private laboratory here, when necessity dictates.'

'Have you heard of a man called Jicaque?' Tom asked him.

'Never in my life,' Woollard shot back quickly. He cleared his throat nervously, setting his chins wobbling. 'Now, are you finished with your questions? Can I get back to Rico here, hmm?'

'Not yet,' Tom replied, bloody-minded at having his hopes dashed again so swiftly. 'You were saying something about arranging for us to be picked up or delivered.'

Woollard gave a bleak chuckle. 'And I thought *I* had a persecution complex. I was referring to *these*.' He reached behind him and pulled back the dull pink curtain that partitioned the room to reveal expensive-looking lab equipment ranged along the back wall, perched precariously on an antique desk. So much for the private laboratory.

He opened something that vaguely resembled a small refrigerator and revealed two miniature milk crates inside, both filled with stoppered test tubes. 'Stacy requests, with some monotony, that I perform specialist treatments on certain lupine blood samples,' he explained with a sigh. 'We're working to perfect a very special serum. She gives me blood samples, I prepare an active solution of serum, she goes and gives it to her lupine patients and I analyse the results.'

'What is this serum?' Tom tried to keep the excitement from his voice. 'A cure for turning 'wolf?'

Woollard shook his head. 'More of a tonic. The serum is intended to pacify lupine aggression.' He smiled thinly. 'I only wish I had one which worked on wilful teenagers.'

'Say you're sorry,' Jasmine hissed at Tom.

Tom felt the heat of her glare and felt himself blush. 'Well, I'm ... I'm sorry for barging in on you like that, Dr Woollard.'

'I'll *make* you sorry if you make me look a fool again,' Jasmine muttered.

Woollard considered. 'There *is* something you could do to make amends.' He lifted the crates from the refrigerator, his shaking hands making the test tubes rattle alarmingly, and placed them in a secure metal chest stowed beneath the examination couch. 'Dr Stein said she needs these treated blood samples urgently – preferably before she finishes her night shift over at Park East Hospital. She'd like to see Rico again, too.'

'I bet she would,' muttered Jasmine.

'I don't taste good to 'wolves,' Rico piped up. 'Stacy likes that.'

'Anyway,' Woollard went on. 'If you'd undertake to deliver them to her right away, I'd be grateful.'

'Sure,' Tom said quickly. 'I'd like to meet her.' Maybe *she* had heard of Jicaque. And if she was working on a cure, maybe Tom's blood could help her out? Then he realised Jasmine was looking at him like he was a freak.

She turned to Woollard. 'Are you sure it can't wait, Doc?' She pleaded, rubbing her eyes. 'It's getting kind of late for me.'

'So I notice,' said Woollard wryly. 'But the trip will be worth your while. Dr Stein has offered to give Rico free drugs for his asthma by way of reward.'

Rico sighed. 'Won't work.'

Jasmine cuffed him lightly around the head. 'They will if you take them regular, Ric! That's all you gotta do.'

'Yeah, yeah,' said Rico sullenly.

Woollard smiled bleakly as if at some private joke. 'You're acting as though the remedy were worse than the disease, boy. That is, if I may misquote Bacon?' He scowled at the blank faces staring back at him. 'Francis Bacon! You've surely heard of him?'

Tom hadn't. But at the mention of bacon, his stomach growled.

Woollard threw up his hands in despair. 'Philistines. Where'd I leave my drink?' He wandered from the room, muttering to himself.

Jasmine turned to Tom. 'Well,' she said scathingly, 'now you've finished making us look totally stupid, why don't you carry that box back to our wheels so we can get the mercy dash done with.'

Tom nodded. But he still wasn't totally convinced by Woollard. 'Isn't it a bit weird that he lives in a dump like this, but he's got all that high-tech equipment lying around?'

'It's his life,' Jasmine replied shortly.

Tom wasn't sure if she meant it was Woollard's choice what he spent his money on, or that high-end science stuff like that was what he lived for. As he hefted up the metal carry-case, he guessed she was right either way.

'Maybe we should go and find Kate,' Tom ventured. 'She could come with us.'

'We get Rico sorted first,' Jasmine said flatly.

'C'mon, Jas,' Rico moaned, 'I wanna get back and check Ramone.'

'We will. Soon as Stacy's checked *you* out,' Jasmine replied. 'Ramone'd want that.'

Rico sighed and nodded, then led the way out. 'Can't you take us there in a real *hot* motor, Jas?'

'You don't wanna know how hot that Lexus is gonna be in a couple of hours when the cops start looking,' she retorted, and then jerked her thumb at Tom. 'And that's another good reason why we can't go cruising about town looking for his girl. But I reckon it'll get us to Park East OK. Then we ditch it for good.'

Tom called a goodbye – Woollard didn't reply – and stepped out after them on to the dismal street. Rico shut the doctor's door, then skipped off after Jasmine. Tom had barely taken another step when he heard the bolts slide stiffly across, one after the other; the old doctor was back in hiding behind his locked doors and empty bottles.

Unable to shake his sense of unease, Tom stared about. There was no one around. The only moving object was a black Porsche, crawling away from him along the kerbside, its engine barely breathing. Soon it rounded the corner and was gone from sight.

Still peering about warily, weighed down with the box of phials, Tom headed after Jasmine and Rico.

Jasmine drove carefully so as not to draw any unwelcome attention, picking a path that took them through the quieter streets. The dirty white of the New York dawn was slowly soaking through the sky. Soon another day would be underway and these wide-open roads would be clogged with the morning's traffic.

Rico was asleep in the back, despite the radio blaring. Jasmine kept switching stations, singing along with songs for a few lines, then tiring of them and hunting down others. The constant chopping and changing was starting to put Tom on edge. He was worried about Kate, and exhausted by the craziness of the night.

Bored with the monotonous low-rise landscape outside the car, he looked at Jasmine instead. Jeez, she was pretty; her dark complexion flawless, the little stud in her snub nose glittering in the dawn light. Tom realised they'd been together for hours and yet he barely knew a thing about her. Maybe he could distract her from the station-hopping with some dazzling conversation.

He nudged down the volume and found his mouth was suddenly dry. 'So, uh ... How long have you been with Ramone?'

She glanced across at him. 'I ain't *with* Ramone, if that's what you mean.'

Tom felt flustered. 'I … Well, I guess from what he said, I assumed …'

Jasmine yawned. 'Truth is, we went together for six months. Longest I've been with anyone. Something special at the time.'

'What happened?' Tom asked.

She shrugged. 'Life, I guess. I don't wanna be tied down at sixteen. He still got it for me, but we're just friends. Good and simple.' She paused. 'That the way with you and Kate?'

'Kind of.'

Jasmine smirked. 'You two seemed pretty tight to me. You been with her, Tommy-boy?'

The question hit straight and hard at some dark place deep inside him. There was no way he could even dream about that kind of relationship with Kate. It was out of the question while he remained 'wolf; it would bring about Kate's worst nightmare – her own lupine change – something she was determined would never happen. And anyway, he doubted she was even remotely interested in him in that way.

He wished he hadn't started this conversation. And he felt a sudden, terrible shame that the creatures who now threatened Jasmine and her friends and the place she called home … they counted him among their number. If Jasmine knew his secret would she scream and shout and kick him out of the car right now?

'I'm taking this silence as a mad big yes, Tommy-boy. You been with her plenty.'

'No,' he said quietly. 'We're just friends.'

'For real?' Jasmine looked at him oddly.

'For real.'

'Well, it ain't no skin off my ass.' Jasmine clicked her tongue. 'But are you sure *she* knows that?'

Tom felt a tingle travel over his skin, but before he could ask Jasmine what the hell she was talking about, a black Porsche came screaming out of a side street, turned and came up fast behind them.

It was the car he'd seen outside Woollard's place. The low, sleek automobile could barely contain the thugs it carried, five of them in all, jostling around inside, laughing and jeering.

The Porsche surged forwards and smashed into the back of the Lexus. Rico was thrown forwards into the back of the driver's seat.

'Seat belt!' Tom yelled at Rico, then turned to Jasmine. 'Who are they? You know them?'

'Swagger's gang,' she replied, trying to accelerate away.

But they couldn't hope to outrun the Porsche. 'Hold on,' Jasmine shouted, as she swung the Lexus around a corner so fast that Tom's head cracked against the window.

'¿A *cuánta velocidad puede ir este coche?*' Rico yelled.

Jasmine gritted her teeth. 'I'm making it go as fast as I can, OK?'

But in seconds, the Porsche was back on their tail. Two of the ugly, brutish passengers were hanging out the rear windows, waving and gesticulating, trying to get them to pull over.

'Bite me,' Jasmine muttered, and floored the Lexus.

The lights ahead were green, but there was a queue of three or four cars ahead of her. Jasmine swung wide out and went careening past them out across the inter-section. Rico whooped in excitement in the centre of the back seat, gripping his seat belt with both hands. Drivers coming the other way jammed on brakes and horns together and swerved drunkenly all around her as she sped through the cars like a sickle cutting a swathe through corn.

But Tom knew that the Porsche, faster and more manoeuvrable, could take the turns better than they could. It was still on their tail, gaining on them, get-ting closer and closer.

'What do they want?' he shouted.

Jasmine tore around another corner. 'I don't think it's to ask us to the prom.' She cursed, eyeing the black motor worriedly in the rearview mirror.

She was so distracted that it was Rico who first saw the garbage truck crawling out from an alley into the street ahead of them. 'Jas!' he screamed.

There was no way they could steer past it, and no way they could miss it at the speed they were travel-ling. Jasmine jerked up hard on the emergency brake – too hard. The rear wheels locked and the Lexus was suddenly spinning right around, out of control. The car mounted the kerb then smacked into a fire hydrant.

Tom felt his heart and stomach swap places as his body seemed to go into freefall. The world outside whizzed past, a blur of brick and metal – then asphalt and sky as the car tumbled over on to its back and scraped across the sidewalk. Woollard's carry-case clunked around in the trunk like a metal beast desper-ate for release, pounding as hard and as loud as the blood in Tom's temples.

Tom felt the ordeal would never stop.

But after long, screeching seconds they crashed into something and finally rocked to a halt. Tom gasped, choking for breath, suspended upside down by his seat belt. 'Jasmine,' he gasped. He could smell smoke, could hear the fizzing of the car's electrics shorting. 'Jasmine?'

She stirred, and groaned. She had a cut on her forehead but she was alive, thank God.

'Rico? You OK?' she asked, her voice slurring a little.

'*Socorro*,' Rico said softly, his eyes tightly shut. '*Socorro*.'

Even Tom knew that meant 'help'. As he fought to unbuckle his seat belt, he could hear anxious voices shouting – the garbage men he guessed. And then he heard other voices, laughing and jeering. Coming towards them. A terrible thought bit at his brain: what had happened to the maniacs in the Porsche?

The anxious voices outside grew suddenly indignant, then angry. Tom heard punches and mocking laughter. Suddenly, he gasped as the bloodied face of one of the garbage men slammed into the passenger window beside him.

A second later, someone else crouched down beside the window and peered in at Tom, smirking triumphantly. A trail of yellow shot through the man's dark eyes.

Looked like he and the other Porsche 'wolves had decided to take out the trash too.

Tom's senses grew sharper, stinging his mind into focus. He felt the now-familiar ache and compulsion; the one that terrified and exhilarated him all at once.

But he couldn't risk the transformation with Jasmine and Rico so close by.

Could he?

The smoke in the car grew thicker, beginning to screen out the leering lupine face at the window. 'Jasmine, Rico! Wake up!' Tom yelled, still fumbling with the clasp on the seat belt. 'We've got to get out of here!'

Jasmine turned her head to face him, her straight black hair hanging down, brushing against the pale roof fabric. 'What's happening?' she murmured.

'Electrics have gone. And I can smell gasoline.' Tom prised his thumbs desperately against the stubborn clasp. 'I think the car's going to explode or something.'

The car rocked again as someone slammed up against it; Tom couldn't see who, the smoke was too thick now.

Jasmine stared about, wide-eyed. 'Is that the cavalry?'

'Cavalry getting their asses kicked,' Tom said. His insides felt on fire. The urge was becoming overwhelming. It would be so easy ... 'No!' he yelled in frustration. 'Come on! Open!' He gasped with effort as he put all his strength into forcing open the stuck clasp. 'Come *on!*'

But his human strength wasn't enough. He was still trapped, powerless to get Jasmine and Rico out of there. His blood burned hot in his body, his mouth stung with the tang of iron. The 'wolves from the Porsche could break in and do *anything* to them while he and Jasmine and Rico just hung there, helpless ...

And then, though his head was swimming, Tom

heard the quiet whoosh of flames igniting. He gave in to the change at last.

As he roared at the delicious pain coursing through his body, the windshield cracked and shattered. Arms reached in eerily through the smoke that belched out from the fusing electrics in the dashboard, fingers urgently groping the air, searching them out.

# CHAPTER SEVEN

'No! Leave us alone!'

To Tom, with his heightened hearing, Jasmine's shriek was almost deafening. Flames were now licking at the window beside him. As his clothes tore open, as his bones warped, and his body refashioned itself into sleek lupine form, Tom fought to retain control, to stop himself from simply tearing into their attackers. He had to focus on getting Jasmine and Rico safely out before the whole car went up. Only that mattered.

But the smoke was being sucked out through the jagged hole in the windshield, and the air was clearing. He was exposed.

Jasmine stared at him, horrified. 'Jesus, you're one of them!' she screamed, tears rolling down her face. She was no longer cool, no longer assured. Her voice was shrill, almost childish; terror and hopelessness shone wetly in her eyes.

The seat belt could no longer support Tom's weight. The fabric snapped and he fell against the roof of the car. One of the groping hands fastened around his throat and he snapped at it, drew tangy blood, began to drool.

Jasmine writhed in her seat, still dangling upside

down, trying to free herself from the belt. 'Keep away from me!' she yelled – at Tom, at the groping hands, at the flames that were now roaring up beside the driver's side window.

A loud clunk from the rear of the car sent a sudden realisation sparking through Tom's clouded thoughts. The hands hadn't been reaching in for them at all. They'd been searching for the switch on the dash that opened the trunk.

The thugs in the Porsche didn't give a damn about Jasmine or Rico or Tom. They wanted the phials of blood from Woollard's apartment, chilled and packed tight in that frosty metal box. Tom didn't know why, and right now he didn't much care. He only wanted to fight back.

With their objective achieved, the hands withdrew. The car began to rock up and down as the heavies attempted to raise up the burning car enough to open the trunk lid and prise out the gory hoard inside.

Tom nuzzled his lupine head into Jasmine's waist. She yelled and pummelled his skull with her fists, but he barely felt the blows. Her musky cologne irritated his sensitive nose, masked the smell of her flesh … His teeth scraped against the skin of her stomach. He drooled over her and she shrieked. If he bit her she would stop. If he bit her he could feed …

*No!* He tore his head away from her, tugging through the fabric of her seat belt as he did so. It snapped, and she fell half on top of him. She recoiled, pushing against him, kicking him, as she struggled to get clear.

'It's OK, Jas!' Rico shouted to her above the din. ''S'OK. It's still Tom!'

Jasmine froze, and stared into Tom's eyes. Her own were streaming from the smoke and the terror, but she didn't blink or break contact. Then slowly, trying not to shake, she nodded.

Rico had wriggled free of his own belt, and was staring at Tom in wonder. Past him, through the rear windshield, Tom saw the Porsche 'wolves dragging Woollard's metal carry-case clear of the car. Rage flared in his belly, his eyes narrowed at the thought of all they had done.

He turned to the front and clawed out the remaining shards of glass protruding like teeth from the frame of the windshield. Then he grabbed the neck of Rico's top with one clumsy paw and backed up and out, hauling the boy clear of the blazing car.

As they emerged, Tom saw the garbage collectors lying beaten and dazed all around their vehicle, where the thugs had cleared them away from their prey. He could hear the slow, whining approach of distant sirens. Laying Rico on the ground, Tom turned to find Jasmine had already crawled out by herself. Clear of the car, she swept up Rico in her arms and held him close.

The thugs were clambering into the Porsche with their prize. Rage growled in Tom's belly. He bounded up on to the exposed undercarriage of the over-toppled car. It rocked under his weight, lending leverage to his leap as he flew at them.

He landed barely a metre from the battered sports car, but it was already reversing. One of the thugs had been left behind. He swung around to face Tom, swiping at him with a metal bar. The bar caught Tom heavily behind the ear, knocking him flat on the asphalt. Everything went hazy.

As the world rolled back into focus, Tom heard the engine of the Porsche receding into the distance. The thug who'd jumped him was pelting away down a side street.

There was a deafening explosion as the Lexus erupted in flames. The force of the blast sent Tom tumbling further out into the road. Then he heard light footsteps, someone running towards him. He tried to move but his limbs were sluggish. He turned his head, bared his dagger-teeth in warning. It was Rico, staring at him with his big, dark eyes.

'Stay away from him, Ric!' Jasmine warned. She was peering around from behind the garbage truck, it must've shielded her and Rico from the blast.

'He's hurt,' Rico shouted back. 'We gotta get him outta here. He got *us* out.'

Tom's 'wolf limbs were cramping up; his whole body was shaking. With the rage literally knocked out of him, he could feel his body preparing to shift back to human form. He would be weak, defenceless, exposed – not to mention stark naked. This place would be swarming with emergency services and crowds of onlookers anytime now. He couldn't be found here.

Rising jerkily to his feet, he limped painfully towards the same side street the thug had taken, then paused and looked back. Jasmine had skirted the burning wreck and stood beside Rico, grabbing hold of his shoulders.

But Rico wriggled clear. 'I think he wants us to go with him.'

'What, so he's Lassie now?' Jasmine retorted. 'Jeez,

Ric, he's a 'wolf. You know what they can do. You more than most.'

'He ain't like them, Jas, I swear it.'

But Tom couldn't listen any longer. He ran stiffly for the side street, felt his teeth ache and his jaw tighten; felt his pelvic bones start to burn and melt as the metamorphosis took hold.

Time and motion blurred, and suddenly he was moving on two legs, not four, and he was freezing cold, slumped naked against a graffiti-strewn wall with his head thumping to the erratic beat of his heart. He gingerly felt for the wound from the iron bar. The speeding of his blood through the metamorphosis had reduced the damage to little more than an egg-shaped bump.

He turned to find Rico and Jasmine standing before him.

Jasmine's eyes had dried, she stood cold and composed. 'Things ain't bad enough already? I got to see you butt-naked now before I even get breakfast?' She held out a bundle of clothes – a fluorescent garbage collector's jacket, grimy trousers, and heavy boots. 'Get these on.'

Rico led them into a nearby vacant lot so that they were off the street, and Tom gratefully slipped on the baggy trousers. 'Nice. I always wanted to dress as a garbage collector.'

'Figured you needed the clothes more than he did,' Jasmine muttered. 'Ambulance is coming for him now.'

Rico smiled. 'Jas can strip a guy faster than any girl I seen.'

'Shut your dirty mouth,' she retorted, and looked

back at Tom warily. 'No wonder you wanted to go see Stacy Stein. You need the cure, don't you?'

'Yeah,' Tom replied quietly.

'So, what – you gonna stay this way now?'

'The urge to change happens when I get real mad,' Tom explained. 'Or scared. Or when the moon's full.'

Jasmine nodded, blew out a long sigh. 'Ric's right. I guess you did help us. I was thinking maybe you were a spy, but now …'

'I'm not a spy. I helped Ramone, too. That's how we met, in Central Park. He didn't want to tell you in case you freaked.' Tom could see the doubt in her deep brown eyes. 'Jasmine, everything Kate and I told you back at Ramone's was true. I'm no ordinary 'wolf. Takapa wants me for study and Marcie Folan – Kate's mom – wants me dead.'

'That bitch on TV,' Jasmine recalled. 'You say she's gonna kill your folks if you don't give yourself up?'

'You a wanted man,' said Rico, his eyes shining like this was just some way cool game. 'So what you gonna do?'

'I figure I've got maybe a day or so before Marcie moves again,' Tom said, as he finished tying his borrowed boots. 'There's supposed to be a man in this city who can cure me, but I don't know how to find him.'

'That *Zhee-khaki* guy you asked Woollard about, right?' Jasmine nodded. 'And you think maybe Stacy Stein knows?'

'If Stacy knows about the 'wolves and is researching for a cure herself …' He shrugged. 'It's the only lead I have.'

Tom tested out the boots. They were at least two

sizes too big, but better than nothing. 'You know, those 'wolves went to a lot of risk and trouble to get those phials of blood before we could take them to Stacy.' He smoothed a hand through his tangled hair. 'Why would that be? Just what is this treatment Woollard's given the stuff?'

Jasmine shrugged. 'Go ask him. Or Stacy.'

'Hold on,' Tom said, thinking. 'Woollard said she needed them urgently. If I can get them back, she'll owe me a favour, right?' He looked at Jasmine and Rico. 'You two go. I'll come find you later.'

'Uh-uh. We're coming with you,' said Jasmine. 'Be good to know what hole in the ground those lowlifes slink back to. Then we can go tell Ramone. Get us some revenge.'

'I just hope he and Kate are OK,' Tom muttered. 'Come on. The guy who slugged me went this way. I think I can pick up his scent, we can follow him.'

Jasmine stared at him uncertainly. 'You can do that shit when you're not howling?'

'Kind of. If I really concentrate.'

'Jeez, Tom, you're freaking me—'

'Quiet, Jas!' Rico slapped her arm. 'Let the man concentrate!'

Trying to hide a wry smile, Tom led the way back on to the street and scented the air. The search was on.

Kate was beginning to wonder if she'd ever find a chance to escape. Swagger was sticking to her like glue, and while he'd mentioned bed a couple of times, she was quite sure sleep was not on his mind.

She shuddered. *Watching 'wolves beating the crap out of each other in a fight to the death may float your boat, freak boy, but it doesn't do much for me.*

So far he seemed to find her reticence somehow cute. She just prayed he didn't tire of it too quickly. She guessed Swagger was used to getting his own way, and probably enjoyed the use of force. Truthfully, she was scared stiff.

While Eric cleaned up the bloody arena, Swagger had announced he would give Kate a guided tour of his headquarters. She had the awful feeling that the tour would conclude in whatever stinking pit he used for a bedroom, and she knew she had to get away before then. But Shaun, his big bruiser bodyguard, was keeping careful pace close behind and every door in the place was locked and bolted. Even if she ran, there was no way out.

Having walked her around the stadium and shown her his cherished video games room – a squalid shrine to all things PlayStation – they'd moved on to the main lobby. Kate was eyeing the boarded-up doors longingly when one of them started to thud and rattle.

Swagger grinned wide, dry skin cracking around his lips. 'My boys are home.' He gestured to Shaun. 'Open up.'

Shaun obeyed in silence, unbolting the doors.

'Your boys?' Kate queried, heart sinking.

'My generals,' said Swagger. 'We rule this city – just that the city don't know it yet. But it will.'

'So,' Kate deduced as Shaun threw the final bolts, 'they've been checking out the other gangs in New York, making sure they'll all be at your big fight come Friday?'

Swagger's eyes were cold, his smile a little less sure on his face. 'Clever kid, ain't you? Yeah, we're about through with the heats. Time now for the main event.'

The doors were opened and four men burst in, in almost drunken good spirits. They were Swagger clones: all acne, black leather and denim. The tallest of them was hefting a metal carry-case. Swagger and Shaun greeted them with whoops and weird tribal salutes.

'You wanna progress report, Swag?' said a barrel-chested man with a whiny voice, whose chest hair curled up to his pointed chin.

'Later, Mikey. When I ain't got company.'

The tall guy looked at Kate and licked his lips. 'See you got yourself breakfast already, Swag.'

Swagger nodded and slapped Kate's butt. 'And damn, am I hungry this morning.' Their sycophantic laughter was sickening.

Kate gritted her teeth.

'So, what's with the new purse, Kes?' Swagger demanded.

'Hope you're thirsty as well as hungry,' said Kes, the tall guy. ''Cause we have brought back a treat.' He opened up the case and pulled out a test tube. A thick, dark syrupy liquid sloshed inside. Blood.

The gang, Swagger included, all stared at the haul like it was solid gold.

Swagger seemed to snap out of the trance first. 'What you even thinkin' about, taking this?'

Mikey shrugged. 'We can handle it, Swag.'

Kes looked suddenly uncomfortable. 'Thought we'd have us a party to celebrate Friday night comin'.'

'You ain't got no orders to!' Swagger advanced threateningly on his so-called generals. 'Where'd you get this? And where's Danno?'

Mikey looked at the others for support. 'We saw some of Ramone's gang taking it from Woollard's place ...'

'And you couldn't help yourselves, huh?' Swagger bore down on him, imitated Mikey's nasal Bronx accent. '*We can handle it, Swag!* Come on, what happened?'

Kate listened in horror as Kes and his buddies told Swagger about how they'd run what had to be Jasmine's car off the road, and how the guy inside had turned 'wolf, and how Danno had slugged him with an iron bar while the rest of them took off. Danno was following on, but the 'wolf wouldn't be going anywhere fast ...

Exhausted, frightened now for Tom as much as for herself, Kate felt tears prickling the backs of her eyes. But she kept them inside. There was no way these animals would ever see her cry.

'You dumb-ass son of a bitch,' Swagger told Kes, suddenly dead serious. 'These tubes were meant for Stacy Stein over at Park East Hospital. She needs 'em, man!'

'*We* need 'em,' said Mikey, and the others agreed.

Kes offered a tube to Swagger. 'Hey, there's two crates of these babies. We can just take some of 'em, and—'

'You're no better than that scum in the locker room!' Swagger snatched the test tube away and smacked Kes in the face with enough force to floor him. 'You don't do shit like this again, none of you, y'hear?' he raged. 'I'm ruling here. *Me.*' He stabbed his grimy finger into Chest Hair Man's shoulder. '*I* say when you can pull this kind of crap, and when I tell

91

you to do something straight, you don't make no circus out of it. Get me?'

Kes got up, wiped blood from his lip and nodded silently. The others signalled their understanding too, the joking around all over, eyes downcast now.

But Kate realised that Shaun had not reacted to a single word or gesture. All his attention was on the phial of blood in Swagger's hand. He was practically drooling, picking at his fingers and shuffling his feet around like he needed the bathroom.

Swagger selected another tube from the crate and handed it to Shaun. 'I guess a little treat from time to time don't hurt.'

Kate grimaced as Shaun pulled out the cork and held it to his mouth, about to drain it, but Swagger shook his head.

'Bad manners, man,' he said. 'First we drink a toast ... to Ms Stacy Stein, the dumbest bitch on the East Coast!'

He raised his tube mockingly at the others, then he and Shaun drank. Kes and the others eyed Shaun balefully now as the sticky red liquid disappeared down his throat. He shuddered and moaned softly as the last of it slipped down. Then he cracked open the glass tube and flicked his tongue over the slivers, determined not to miss a drop.

Kate had never seen any 'wolf get anything like this kick from blood in a tube. It was alien to the whole lupine culture. Their fix was the hunt, the felling of the prey, the opening of veins with scissoring jaws, the tearing of flesh – not just swigging blood from a glass like soda. She jumped as Swagger threw his own empty tube down at Kes's feet.

'Now, you take the rest over to Park East right now,' he commanded. 'And no more dumb stunts, OK?' Then he turned and grabbed hold of Kate's hand so hard it hurt. 'Come on, baby. No more games.' His grey eyes were glassy, and he was squinting like he wasn't quite able to focus. 'It's way past time I saw a little more of you.'

She tried to pull away, but his grip was too strong, he only sniggered.

'What's the matter, sugar? Don't you want us to have some fun?'

Kate wanted to puke in his face. 'Sure I do,' she whispered, trying to keep herself from shaking, 'I just wanna go somewhere more private, y'know?'

Swagger nodded, a slow smile of understanding spreading over his ugly face. 'Chicks,' he said, giving his generals a long-suffering look. 'First time's always gotta be something special. OK, c'mon.'

He dragged her up three flights of crumbling stairs. 'Where are we going?' she demanded.

'My office,' he said, his words slurring a little now. 'You're gonna take some dictation, baby.'

Kate found herself hauled into a fetid, airless dump of a room overlooking the arena. The walls were plastered with tacky posters of bikes and airbrushed bikini-bimbos, and the one table was stacked high with hi-fi separates and computer games. In the corner was a pile of guns, bats and just about anything you could classify as an offensive weapon.

Swagger crouched over a CD player and stabbed at the buttons until a blast of thrash metal spewed out of a huge pair of speakers. 'To get us in the mood,' he said hoarsely, turning to face her.

Kate was beginning to feel nauseous. 'If music be the food of love, party on,' she said, deadpan. Then she tried to curl her lips into what she hoped was a seductive smile. 'Listen, Swag ... D'you have a bathroom? I kind of need to freshen up.'

He took a step closer, his bulk massive and threatening. 'You smell good to me.'

She batted her eyelids. 'Pretty please?'

'Down the hall,' he said, gesturing to the right. 'Don't be long.' He gave her a gruesome smile. 'Or else I'll come find you.'

'I'll be right back, sugar,' she said, all doe-eyed. 'And I don't want to see so many clothes on you when I come back ... stud.'

Swagger guffawed, leaned in and placed a slobbery kiss on her neck.

Kate could smell the blood on his breath. Her flesh crawled and she almost gagged, but she whispered in his ear, 'You won't believe what I'm going to do to you ...'

He grinned and smacked his lips.

He actually believed she wanted him. He'd bought it – and she'd bought herself time. As he turned back to his hi-fi and started fiddling with the graphic equaliser, she discreetly lifted a metal crowbar from his pile of weapons and backed out of the office.

Once alone in the corridor she ran for the bathroom. As she threw open the door, she almost heaved – the air was rank, the floor was wet with puddles of God-knew-what. The toilets were cracked and filthy, most of the doors hanging off their hinges. The bulk of the grimy tiles had long since crumbled away from the damp walls.

And the windows had been boarded up and barred.

Keeping calm, Kate grabbed a slimy wooden mop from the wet floor. Swiftly, she rammed the shaft through the metal 'D' of the door handle and jammed the end of it behind a chipped washbasin. Now the door was jammed shut. It might buy her a little time.

She ran over to the nearest window. Thankfully, the sound of Swagger's music was booming dully down the corridor, and covered the sound of splitting wood as she used the crowbar to lever off a panel and smashed through the dirty glass so she could see outside.

She swore. The bathroom overlooked the street, and safety – but the only way out was a sheer drop down at least three storeys.

'Kate?' there was a loud banging on the door. 'C'mon, who takes five minutes to use the bathroom?'

'I – I'm nearly through!' she shouted.

'Hey, the door's jammed. What you doing in there?'

'I …' She wished she knew. 'I'll be two minutes. It's not like I can get out, right?'

Right.

But Swagger was bored with waiting. And from the way he was beating at the door, he was coming in whether she was ready or not.

# CHAPTER EIGHT

Kate ran for the only cubicle that had a working door and locked it behind her; then she stood on the toilet to reach the small window. She began prising off one of the bars with the crowbar – she'd sooner jump, whatever the risk, than let Swagger get his filthy, sweaty hands on her.

Swagger was still banging at the door. She put all her strength into levering off the bar and finally it fell with a clang on to the floor.

'Hey, what was that? Open up, you bitch!' Swagger started kicking and smashing at the door with greater force.

Kate knew it wouldn't hold him long. She ripped and smashed at the wooden board over the window. It was giving, but slowly. Did she have time to break out before Swagger got inside? Maybe she should hide behind the bathroom door, wait for him to get inside then whack him over the head with the crowbar. No, too risky, he could've brought Shaun upstairs ... the whole lot of them. She imagined them grabbing her, forcing her to this filthy, stinking floor, and then ...

Her fear and anger gave her strength. She swiped harder and harder at the wooden barrier, pulverising it, jarring her hands. At last it split and she ripped it clear before smashing her way through the window.

'Bitch!' With a scream of fury, Swagger finally broke his way inside. 'Trying to split on me, huh? Think I'm stupid?'

Kate said nothing, concentrated on scraping the crowbar around the frame to clear the jagged splinters of glass remaining. But she gasped as the door behind her jumped and rattled under some great impact.

'I'm gonna teach you, girl,' he bellowed, his voice wild and cracked with rage. 'You don't mess with Swagger!'

She pushed herself out of the window, and the ground swam dizzily far below her. The door shuddered as Swagger ran at it again, the bolt nearly snapping clean through. She leaned out through the window to look above her this time – maybe she could climb to the floor above. No, there was nothing, nothing but—

A half-rusted drainpipe ran to the right of the window.

Her heart leaped. It wasn't conveniently placed right beside her like in the movies; she couldn't even touch it with her hand at full stretch. But if she could somehow balance on the narrow ledge and leap for it ...

It was suicide. But so was staying in here.

She heard Swagger pulling off his heavy leathers and throwing them on the ground, breathing hoarsely. Either he was still in the mood or—

Uh-oh. Now she could hear bones clicking and popping, and the first guttural stirrings of the lupine creature inside Swagger.

''Wolf's at your door, baby,' she heard him rasp.

Kate dropped the crowbar and desperately swung herself out through the window feet first. Clinging to the top of the window frame, balancing her butt on the sill, she stretched out her long legs towards the downspout. Edging forward till she teetered on the ledge, she could just grip the rusting drainpipe with both ankles.

With a chilling roar, Swagger smashed down the door at last. She caught a glimpse of matted fur, vivid yellow eyes, sharp teeth snapping for her. Then, her ankles still locked around the downspout, she twisted her body around and pushed away from the window-sill with both hands.

For a sickening second she was sure she would fall. Then, to her amazement, her outstretched palms were slithering over the rusting metal of the downspout.

Swagger's huge head burst through the window, swinging around to face her, snarling and snapping at her. But the window was too small for him to lean out any further. He howled in impotent rage.

Kate knew the alarm would be raised in seconds and began to shinny down. The pipe was cold as she gripped it with both hands, the brackets that held it to the wall rusted and weak. Her lifeline began to creak ominously.

She winced in pain as metal fragments stuck in her palms, and tried to slide down as smoothly as she could, before the pipe gave way all together. Then, without warning, the section of pipe she was clinging to pulled away from the wall. Kate was so horrified she couldn't even cry out. The world whistled about her as she fell, arms and legs flailing, dreading the inevitable crushing impact.

But her fall was broken by a couple of trashcans that – thank God – couldn't have been emptied for weeks. They were filled to overflowing with bags of soft, slimy garbage that worked like smelly airbags. Her landing was only painful and humiliating instead of fatal.

'Would you mind getting out of there? You're making the trash all dirty.'

Kate looked round wildly and saw a dark figure looming over her. It was a garbage collector. Where had he sprung from? Why was he grinning like a—?

'Tom!' she wailed in disbelief.

He helped her up. 'Next time you escape from somewhere, why not try the stairs?' He sounded cool and casual, but the light in his eyes told her how pleased he was to see her. He pointed up at Swagger, still framed in the window. Thick drool was stringing down from the 'wolf's slavering jaws. 'I guess we should get out of here, huh?'

'Right now,' she muttered. She took a few tentative steps – her legs felt bruised and wobbly but at least they weren't broken – then turned and gave Swagger the finger. 'I said you wouldn't believe what I'd do to you,' she shouted, 'you sick, evil bastard.'

The beast stared coldly down at Kate, then abruptly, it vanished from the window.

Tom got up, rubbing his back from where he'd fallen, and took her hand as he hobbled over to the corner of the half-derelict building. Jasmine and Rico were waiting there.

'You was right, Tom,' said Rico, grinning from ear to ear. 'She was in there!'

'Let's move,' said Jasmine, and started to sprint

away down the street. The others set off after her.

Kate noticed Rico was wheezing. 'Is he OK?'

'Not really,' Tom muttered.

'He'll be fine,' Jasmine said hotly, skittering to a stop. 'Ric, get on my back.'

'I can carry him,' Tom protested, as Rico dutifully climbed aboard.

'No,' she said, 'I got him.'

With Rico clinging on around her neck, she moved off again – but at least now at a speed Kate and Tom could better match.

'I thought you were dead,' Kate said.

'So did I,' Tom answered. 'A couple of times.'

'How the hell did you find me at that place?' she panted, gesturing to his outfit. 'Were you emptying their trash or something?'

'Funny. But don't think this uniform entitles me to take any garbage from you!' He gave her a smile. 'We followed the trail of some 'wolf who tried to kill us. Only when it led us to the arena, I could've sworn there was a scent of you about the place.'

She frowned at him. 'You saying I smell?'

'Thought it was my imagination.' He sniffed. 'But now you've taken a bath in the trash ...'

She stuck out her tongue. 'Believe me, there's worse garbage inside that place. You won't believe what those freaks are doing.'

'Tell me later,' Tom puffed. 'But God, Kate, is it ever good to see you.'

'Sure it is,' she said, and put on an extra spurt of speed so he wouldn't see she was smiling.

Jasmine and Rico led them down through a number of narrow, deserted alleyways. Kate was desperate to stop and rest for a few moments, but she was damned if she would show any weakness in front of Little Miss Attitude. By the time they'd turned on to another street, Tom had overtaken her – and just the sight of Tom alive and well and running just ahead of her in his ridiculous get-up was enough for her to keep up the pace. No way was she letting him out of her sight again.

Finally they emerged on to a busier boulevard. Early risers were already trailing up and down the sidewalks, shopkeepers were opening up their stalls and warm, steamy smells wafted out of bakeries.

Jasmine finally called a halt and crouched down so a reluctant Rico could clamber off her back. 'Too many people around here for them to try something,' she said, acting like she'd barely broken a sweat. 'Y'all wait here. I'll fix us some wheels and we can get back to Ramone's.'

Rico nodded approval, but Tom seemed less certain. 'Stealing two cars in one morning? Isn't that pushing your luck?'

'You think we've been lucky so far today, Tommy-boy?' She shook her head, apparently amused, and gave Tom's ass a playful squeeze as she passed by. 'Be ready, people.'

Kate stared in astonishment at Jasmine's retreating figure, then folded her arms and regarded Tom coolly. 'I see you made a new friend.' She doubted his red cheeks were entirely down to running.

'We've been through some stuff, I guess,' Tom said.

'That's the truth,' said Rico brightly.

Kate looked into Tom's dark eyes expectantly, mustering all her usual cool. 'Well, while we wait for her to get back, why don't you tell me all about it,' she suggested, jutting out her chin. 'All the juicy details.' But it felt like there was some screwed-up ball of something sour deep inside her, a spiky feeling she couldn't swallow down. *God strike me dead,* she thought, *all this shit going down and I get jealous for the first time in my whole life.*

'Hey,' said Rico, pointing to a news stand in delight. 'You two are famous outlaws again. Cool! You should get out of sight, fast.'

Kate read the headline screaming off the paper: TERROR TEEN COUPLE SIGHTED IN NEW YORK. 'Cool's one word for it,' she muttered. 'I can think of some other four-letter ones that describe it better.'

Jasmine found them a battered station wagon. 'What did you expect?' she told the disappointed Rico, 'this ain't Park Avenue.'

They all caught up on the car journey back to Ramone's hangout over in El Barrio. Tom could hardly believe Kate's story – his own adventures seemed like nothing next to her ordeal. Maybe she blamed him on some level for running out on her? There was a coldness about her now, a distance – but maybe she just needed some time to lick her wounds.

They spent the last minutes of the journey in silence. Tom shivered as he recognised the slum tenement they'd half-dragged, half-carried Ramone to last night. The door gaped open, hanging on a hinge. People walked by like it was nothing, like they hadn't noticed a thing.

'Ro?' called Rico, first out of the car and scampering up the steps to the ruined kitchen area. 'Ro, you there? *¿Estas bien?*

'Ric!' came Ramone's raw voice from somewhere inside the place.

'Thank God,' murmured Jasmine, and ran after Rico.

Tom turned to Kate. 'You sure you're OK?'

'Sure,' she said. 'Just thinking about Mommy Dearest.'

Tom grimaced. 'With our pictures all over the *New York Times*, how long till we're seen and caught?'

Kate nodded. 'Mom won't be leaving town till she's found us, that's for sure.' She made to go after Jasmine and Rico.

'Wait.' He took hold of her arm. 'Do you think your mom will really kill my folks?'

Kate looked at him. 'I don't know, Tom,' she answered quietly. 'If she does kill them, she'll have no hold over you. But then we know she's crazy ...'

Tom sighed. 'If I could find a cure we'd be free of this nightmare.'

Kate nodded. 'We should get back to looking for Jicaque.'

'Yeah, let's talk to Stacy Stein,' Tom replied. 'Woollard said her own work on a cure has a long way to go, but she might have come across Jicaque through her research.'

'Swagger told his minions to make sure Stacy got those samples back. But then he said she was the dumbest bitch on the East Coast,' Kate said thoughtfully. 'Why would he have said that?'

'No idea – but coming from him that's a recommendation,' Tom growled.

Kate smiled. 'OK, but if we do go see her, what's to

stop her calling the cops the second she sees us?'

'I'm cute as a button?' Tom suggested hopefully.

'Well, some people seem to think so,' Kate said tightly, and she marched inside.

They found Ramone in the wrecked TV room, sprawled on a cushion, clutching his brother tight like a kid with a teddy bear. His olive complexion was waxy, crusty with blood. Polar was standing in the corner, shifting about nervously like he needed the john, his camera raised up over his hooded face. He snapped his flash at Tom and Kate, and another bruised square of paper spewed out from the camera.

Tom found his rucksack discarded under a table and searched it for fresh clothes. No luck; he'd ripped his way through his last pair of jeans.

Jasmine was boiling up some water, and fussing about with the first aid box. 'What are you even doing here, Ramone?' she grumbled. 'You're hurt bad. You need Doc Woollard.'

'Don't need no one,' Ramone snapped back. 'Don't *got* no one.' He looked up at Tom and Kate over Rico's shoulder. 'My people all cleared out. Puff got himself a hospital bed at Mount Sinai. They'll know he's jumped parole, man! Cops gonna be all over his fat ass.'

'Guess he was real scared, huh, Ro?' said Rico.

'And Ciss skipped to New Jersey, bailin' out with Fleet and China and the rest. Only Polar stayed behind.' He lowered his voice, shook his head. 'Just me and the fool. Cosy, ain't it?'

'What's up, Ramone?' Jasmine dabbed several swabs of cotton wool in the hot water. 'We're here. Girls and little kids don't count?'

Ramone glanced over at her. 'Yeah, you do,' he said quietly, 'you really do.' He turned back solemnly to Tom and Kate. 'Ric tells me you looked after him good, wolf-boy. And Kate, you saved my ass from Swagger out there on the street. I owe you both, and I ain't never gonna let you down.'

'So how about you get yourself checked out by this Dr Woollard?' Kate said. 'I'd hate to think we saved your ass just so it could go septic.'

'OK,' Ramone sighed heavily. Rico moved aside as Jasmine came back in and started swabbing at his injuries.

Tom raised his arms in his baggy fluorescent jacket. 'And since I'm fresh out of clean shirts, if you have any spare clothes a little less conspicuous than these ...'

'Got some gear in the sleep room,' offered Ramone through gritted teeth. 'Help yourself to whatever ain't been burnt.'

Tom screwed up his nose as he entered the gloomy room, it reeked of smoke and charred plastic. The fire had done some damage but it hadn't consumed everything in the closet. He pulled out some combats and a black tracksuit top – nice and inconspicuous.

He got back to find Jasmine was cleaning up Ramone's head.

Ramone winced as she daubed antiseptic on to his sticky scalp. 'Jas, you take Ric over to Park East to see Stacy,' he ordered. 'Me and Polar, we'll hit Woollard's.' He looked up at Tom. 'Guess you two'll be shooting off now, huh?'

'Tom says he wants to meet Stacy,' Jasmine broke in.

'We both would,' added Kate quickly.

Jasmine shrugged. 'Guess there's room in the wagon.'

'And, uh ... your cop radio's still working, right?' Tom asked haltingly, and Ramone nodded. 'I was wondering if you'd mind listening in, just in case you hear anything about my parents? The police must be in touch with them.'

'OK, change of plan.' Ramone turned to Polar: 'You wanna stay home and eavesdrop on NY's finest?'

Polar nodded, then slouched past them through to the room with the radio. He dragged out a chair and sat facing the squawking metal box, staring at it through the camera like it was about to scuttle off somewhere.

'So what you waiting for?' growled Ramone to the rest of them. 'Get out of here.'

'Later, Ro,' said Rico, bumping knuckles as the others added their farewells.

''S'right.' Ramone smiled, mussed up Rico's hair with the flat of his palm. 'See y'all later. *Ciudate.*'

Kate glanced back and smiled. 'Keep safe yourself.'

The smile faded from her face as she followed the others out into the cold sunlight, on to the bare, unwelcoming street.

'Keep safe,' Tom echoed softly, and the run-down world around him seemed to laugh in his face.

# CHAPTER NINE

Tom and Kate hung back while Jasmine and Rico marched up to the admissions desk at Park East Virology Unit. They took seats in the waiting room beside a woman slumped in her chair with a brown leather coat draped over her, softly snoring.

'Wish I could grab a few zees myself, now,' muttered Tom, rubbing his eyes. Kate nodded sullenly.

'Rico Carranza to see Dr Stacy Stein,' Jasmine announced to the desk clerk. 'She's expecting him.'

'That's right! I am!' cried the woman beside Tom, scaring him half to death. Jasmine and Rico spun around in surprise as the woman jumped up from the chair like it was electrified and stared at them, her ice-blue eyes wide and bright. 'Good to see you again, Rico. And Jasmine – you thought any more about trying to get yourself on that mentoring programme?'

'Yeah, I thought about it,' Jasmine replied curtly, though the look on her face suggested she hadn't dwelled on it for long.

'Think about it some more. It'd be good for you.' Dr Stein enjoyed a noisy, extravagant stretch, bending her well-proportioned body backwards. 'I've been waiting for you out here since my shift ended – must've fallen asleep. I guessed you'd wandered off somewhere when I collected the package from reception.'

Now it was Tom's turn to jump up. 'The package arrived? Those treated blood samples from Dr Woollard?'

Dr Stein turned to face him. She was probably in her early thirties, her features well-defined and framed by coppery shoulder-length hair. 'You know about those?' she asked, not accusingly, just interested.

Tom lowered his voice. 'And about the 'wolves, Dr Stein,' he confirmed.

She didn't seem particularly surprised. 'Call me Stacy,' she said, but as she held out a hand in greeting, she peered at him closely. 'Your face looks familiar.'

*Please, God, don't let there be a newspaper around here*, Tom thought, returning her strong handshake. 'Just one of those faces, I guess. I'm Tom, I was with Jasmine and—'

'Wait, wait, wait,' said Stacy, shaking her head, her voice falling to a whisper. 'Not with all these people around. Besides, this sounds like a long story and long stories always sound better with hot coffee and bagels.' She held out her hand to Kate. 'Am I right, Miss …?'

'Kate,' she said, shaking the outstretched hand. 'And I think you're the most right person I ever met.'

Stacy led them to a coffee shop deep inside the hospital, and ordered for everyone before bustling over to a hexagonal table. 'Sit down, all,' she said, drumming her fingers on the tabletop until they were seated, 'and let's get the introductions out of the way.'

Tom and Kate told selected highlights from their separate stories over Styrofoam cups of thick, treacly coffee while Rico and Jasmine filled their faces with cream cheese bagels. Tom detailed the chase for the blood samples and the risks Swagger's men took to get them, and Kate confirmed how Swagger himself arranged for what was left to reach Stacy.

Stacy gave a low whistle. 'Weird goings-on, all right.'

'It *was* weird,' Kate said. 'Swagger was furious with the thugs who'd stolen the samples. He said you needed them.'

'I do, they're very valuable to my work.' Stacy seemed strangely moved. 'For a lupine to have said that – he must be counting on me coming through for him and his kind.'

'Er ...' Kate paused awkwardly. 'Actually, he called you the dumbest person on the East Coast.'

Stacy shrugged. 'I'm not in this line of work for the applause,' she said mildly. 'Oh, those poor kids ...'

'Excuse me?' Tom frowned at her. 'Those poor kids are maniacs.'

'Murderers,' Kate added.

Jasmine agreed. 'Did you miss the part where they almost killed *us* to get that stuff?'

'I'm sorry,' said Stacy. 'Of course it's wrong, what they did. But it's not entirely their fault. They're lupine now, desperate for anything that'll help them cope with the new-found needs, with the *conflicts* that being 'wolf entails.'

'So am I,' Tom blurted out, and immediately regretted it. 'Desperate, I mean.'

Stacy stared at him. '*You're* lupine?'

'He's a newblood,' Kate said quietly, 'not long turned.'

'And I hate it,' Tom said. 'When I was first bitten I fought; was able to resist the change – like Rico.'

Jasmine nodded. 'Rico got bitten, but he don't change.'

Tom scowled. 'But unlike Rico, I was bitten, locked up for a month and force-fed turning herbs and potions until my resistance cracked.'

'By my mother,' Kate put in bitterly.

'But Tom ain't like the other howlers,' chirped Rico, chewing on a big bite of bagel. 'He ain't mean and hungry; he don't chase people down. He saved us! And he keeps his own eyes.'

'Tom retains some human control when in the lupine form,' Kate explained. She paused. 'We think he's a wereling.'

'Wereling, huh?' Stacy looked at Tom coolly. 'And maybe a killer too, right?' She turned to Kate. 'With your accomplice, here, natch. I just figured out where I'd seen you before. The TV news on my break last night.'

Tom met her stare. 'It's not what you think, I swear.'

Stacy just raised her eyebrows. 'I don't know. I guess I'm supposed to turn you in.'

'No!' Rico cried, 'you can't!'

Jasmine looked set to chip in too, until Stacy waved them all into silence. 'But I won't. Selfish, I guess – but whatever you've done, I want to run some tests on you, Tom. If your story's true I think you could be a lot of help to me.'

'It *is* true,' he said vehemently, 'and I'll help you in any way I can.'

Stacy smiled and nodded. 'And, you know, maybe I

can help you. Kate, hon, those long black tresses of yours are gorgeous, sure – but just a little distinctive for a girl on the run, don't you think?'

'I never really thought ...' Kate put a hand to her hair. 'What, you think I should chop it all off?'

'And you could give it to Tom to wear, like a wig,' suggested Rico unhelpfully.

Stacy waved a dismissive hand. 'Oh, he's just your average guy. Who'd look at him twice?'

'Gee, I feel much better now,' Tom said.

'Anyway, believe it or not, guys –' Stacy straggled her fingers through her own coppery hair – 'this isn't natural. I've got some henna in my locker, Kate. You'd be welcome to try some.'

Kate shrugged. 'I guess, if you think it will help.'

'It'll help *me* feel happier if I'm caught helping wanted felons,' said Stacy dryly. 'Why officer, this girl *can't* be that killer in the paper, not with that gorgeous red hair ...' She grew more serious. 'Kate, is your whole family lupine?'

'Purebloods. Mom's from the Hargraves family line, Dad's a Folan,' Kate said. 'Two of the oldest families around.'

'So you're a pureblood female, huh?' Stacy nodded to herself, and took a bite of bagel. She chewed it thoughtfully. 'All that lupine potential awaiting activation, wow ... And just doing it with a 'wolf presses the button – that's the way it works, right?'

Kate flinched. 'Your bedside manner sucks.'

'I'm sorry,' said Stacy. 'Really. That's real tough for you.'

Kate sipped her coffee. 'Yeah.'

'And for me too. I won't be able to learn much from

your blood till your lupine cells are in gear …'

Kate looked appalled at the thought. 'Sorry,' she said tightly. 'I'd rather die than let my lupine cells "get in gear". But believe me,' she added, 'my mother's trying to help you out.' She wound a finger distractedly through her hair. 'How about you? How come you're so interested in lupines?'

Stacy shrugged. 'I'm a virologist. I study viruses and the diseases they cause. To me, lycanthropy – the transformation into the lupine state – is just another infectious medical condition.'

'A lot of people wouldn't see it that way,' Tom pointed out. 'These are *werewolves* we're talking about.'

'I don't care for terms like werewolf.' Stacy shook her head decisively, and took a quick swig of coffee. 'People are so conditioned by all that cheap horror movie crap. If they ever found out the truth about lycanthropy – about how many real lupines operate in this city – there'd be widespread panic.'

'Right,' said Jasmine dryly. 'When the poor folk are just hungry, the good people don't give a damn. But when the poor folk grow fangs … that's when the good people take notice.'

Stacy passed her another bagel. 'I know it's tough, but that's the situation we're dealing with. People can't handle the truth. That's why the work I'm doing isn't sanctioned or funded by the hospital authorities, why it has to stay completely unofficial. Just me and a few sympathetic health workers who turn a blind eye when they need to. We're working to do something about the situation before it gets completely out of hand.'

'That's why you have to use people like Woollard,' Tom concluded.

Stacy nodded. 'Funding cutbacks at the hospital last year meant that I lost a lot of the equipment I'd come to depend on in this private little crusade of mine. So, yeah, I turned to Dr Woollard.' Her tone softened. 'Despite the drink, he's still a brilliant man. And he's really helped me out. With this kind of research, you can't outsource sample preparation and testing to any regular lab. I really rely on him.'

'You ever hear of a man called Jicaque?' Tom asked. 'We came here to find him.'

'The big-deal shaman guy – lot of dealings with the 'wolves, right?' Stacy replied. 'Yeah, he got in touch, once. Tried to help, must've heard what I was doing somehow. He sent me some herbs that were meant to boost the body's defences against cellular mutation. But it was so hard to run proper trials that I—'

Tom cut her off. 'You've never seen him, met with him?'

'Never even talked to him,' she admitted. 'Sorry.'

Tom shrugged defeatedly. 'Forget it,' he said. *And so should I.*

'But Stacy, how come *you* got involved with all this?' Kate persisted.

Stacy busied herself spreading cream cheese on another bagel. 'My husband. He was a brilliant man, a top surgeon. Some lupine rich bitch in the Meat Packing District wanted him for a mate, so one night he was turned.' She gave a short, humourless laugh. 'Perhaps that's why lupines don't scare me. The dark mystique of a creature of legend kinda lessens when you have to wash his underpants each week.'

'What happened?' Tom asked quietly.

'He stayed true to his vows ... True to *me* – in spite of all she offered him. He hated what he'd become, but was powerless to fight it.' There was something hard in Stacy's eyes as she looked at Tom. 'Unlike you, unlike Rico, he had no resistance. Oh, he tried, sure ... Tried not to kill ... But in the end the 'wolf grew too strong.'

Tom watched as she gouged big, doughy chunks from the bagel with her fingernails.

'I watched him suffer, day after day. Watched him try to cope. But I couldn't help him.' She flashed a small and watery smile around the table. 'He took his own life. So now I try to help the other victims of this ... condition. As best I can.'

A heavy silence had fallen like a shroud over the table.

'I'm sorry, you did want a side order of sob-story with your breakfast, didn't you?' she joked. 'Come on. Finish off and let's get to work. Rico, I'll write you a 'script for your asthma if you give me some blood, OK?'

He grimaced. 'Some deal.'

'And Tom,' said Stacy, 'I'd like to test some of yours too, see how it compares. Kate, you want to do your hair while you're waiting?'

'I guess,' said Kate doubtfully.

'I'll fetch you that henna. And some surgical gloves.'

Kate looked alarmed. 'Huh?'

'The stuff stains your skin if you're not careful,' explained Stacy, 'so gloves are a must. And plentiful around here.'

'I wondered why you'd dye your hair in the hospital

and not at home,' Tom said.

Stacy smiled tightly. 'That's mainly because this place *is* my home, pretty much. I don't even remember the inside of my own bathroom.' She paused. 'Anyway, don't get me started. Hey, Jasmine, you going to help Kate with her hair?'

Jasmine and Kate looked at each other.

'Mmm, that sounds like fun,' said Jasmine.

Kate scowled. 'I can manage by myself, thanks.'

Oh, brother, Tom thought.

'So what is it you're trying to achieve with your work?' Tom asked, watching the silver needle-point slip under his skin.

Stacy gently eased out the plunger of the syringe, and it filled with his blood. 'I'm working to isolate what I call the "'wolf factor" – the gene in lupine cells responsible for the metamorphosis. Once I've isolated it, I can work on a way of neutralising it.'

'You think that's possible?' Tom asked.

'I'm close, I'm sure of it.' She swabbed at the tiny bead of blood left by the needle in the crook of his arm. 'Thanks to Rico. His blood is special stuff: it contains a highly reactive enzyme that seems toxic to the lupine system.'

Tom settled back on the examination couch. 'What does this enzyme do?'

'It attacks lycanthropic cells, causes fatal mutations in the chromosomes.' She poured the blood into a Petri dish. 'And since the lupine metabolism is far faster than a human's, the cellular degeneration occurs so fast that the immune system is swamped.'

'So, translating,' Tom ventured, 'any 'wolf attempting

to chow down on Rico might as well be swallowing rat poison – except they'll die a lot quicker. Right?'

'Right. So I've been introducing Rico's blood to samples of both lupine and human blood, and comparing the effects on the cells. If I can isolate all the genes affected in the lupine blood ...'

'You'll have found werewolf DNA,' concluded Tom. 'Neat.'

She tapped the Petri dish. 'And your blood could be a great help. Your resister gene should still be present even if it's been mutated by the 'wolf factor. By comparing your sample to Rico's, we can find which genes you share. It should speed up the search.'

'It's been slow work, huh?'

'Damned slow,' Stacy sighed, pushing back her hair absent-mindedly, 'even with a genius like Woollard helping me out.'

Tom frowned. 'I must be slow too. Why would the 'wolves go to all that trouble just to steal some blood samples?'

Stacy shook her head. 'They weren't just blood samples, remember? Woollard treated them – turned them into Stacy Serum.'

'Into what?'

'The interim measure until I find a proper cure: Stacy Serum.' She smiled. 'I believe that the cravings of the 'wolf – bloodlust, aggression, the urge to hunt – are just symptoms of the lupine infection.'

'This is what Woollard was talking about,' Tom realised. 'The stuff in his case.'

Stacy opened the lid of the case they'd taken from Woollard's and produced one of the test tubes filled with crimson liquid. 'You've heard of certain synthetic drugs being used to treat heroin addiction?' she asked him. 'This stuff's kind of similar. It's just blood, but with a special hormone mixed in – a hormone that simulates the kick lupines get from the 'wolf-change and all it leads to.'

'So ... a consequence-free high?' Tom regarded the phial doubtfully. 'They sip that and the 'wolf cravings are satisfied? They lose their bloodlust?'

'I've tried it out on a number of willing subjects,' she said. 'The hospital's linked with a program run for homeless kids. Out on the streets, no place to go, they're easy pickings for the 'wolves. A lot of them were turned against their will and hate what they've become. So I put out the word – Stacy Serum might just help them.'

'And it really works?'

'It *must* be effective. According to my 'wolf informants on the program, the number of turns on the street has gone way down.'

'Down?' Tom frowned. 'But Ramone – Rico's brother – was saying there are more 'wolves on the streets now than ever.'

'Maybe it just seems that way to him,' suggested Stacy. 'I'm talking about the citywide picture. The evidence suggests there are fewer reports of fresh turnings and a greater number of newbloods coming back for more serum.' She grinned at him. 'Don't you get it? The serum fixes the newbloods' cravings without them having to go out and bite someone. And because fewer people are being bitten, the 'wolf population explosion has slowed right down. The results add up.'

'OK,' Tom said guardedly. 'But if you can't make the stuff here, how are you meeting all this demand?'

'This is my starter pack for the latest brand of serum,' Stacy explained. 'It works like a vaccine. Just a few drops added to a beaker of blood plasma "infects" it, turns it into *more* Stacy Serum.'

'And you have access to tons of plasma, 'cause this is a hospital,' Tom reasoned.

Stacy grinned. 'Neat, huh?'

'And are there any side-effects?'

'Nothing much has been reported, but I can't be completely sure. It's still work in progress, not perfected yet,' she said a touch irritably. 'But it's working all right for now. It's all we have, and it's offering the newbloods hope. Hope enough to hang on until I can perfect a cure.'

'But, Stacy – Kate saw Swagger take some of your serum and it didn't exactly calm him down.'

'Its actual effectiveness may vary in degree from case to case,' Stacy said defensively. 'I'm working on that. Perhaps that's why he made sure the rest of the shipment got back to me,' she suggested. 'Perhaps he wants a serum that will work for *him*. He must realise he can't go out hunting the whole time without winding up in trouble eventually.'

'I guess,' Tom said, unconvinced.

She sighed. 'You hate the 'wolves, Tom, I can understand that. But isn't it possible that's colouring your judgement? Making you *over*-suspicious?'

Tom smiled, he didn't want to push the point and risk pissing her off. 'I want to believe you.' He paused. 'And I want to try some of the serum.'

'I haven't checked your blood yet,' said Stacy. 'If there's less lupine in you than in the regular newbloods, the serum may be less effective.'

'Consider me a guinea-pig,' Tom said. 'I feel the blood cravings, doctor, believe me. If there's a way to suppress that, I'll take it.'

Stacy looked uncertain for a moment, then nodded. 'Why don't you try to get some rest first, huh? You look dead on your feet, and it's going to take a while to do these tests on Rico.' She smiled. 'I'll fix you a dose of serum for when you wake up.'

Tom yawned and nodded. 'I guess it has been a long night.'

Kate was catnapping on a hospital trolley that seemed skinnier than she was; she was afraid even to turn over in case she fell out. Her head rustled every time she moved, since her hair was covered by a plastic bag. The henna stank, and she was dreading seeing what she might see in the mirror when she was done.

Whatever, it had to be better than the stuff she was seeing in her restless dreams. Stacy had cordoned off a section in one of the wards so she could get a few hours' rest in private. But each time she dozed she found herself back at the arena, Swagger's big, sweaty body beside her, the violence in the rink being re-enacted again and again.

A cellphone rang close by and she sat up bolt upright. When the tinny melody clicked off she heard Jasmine's voice answer, sleepy and irritable. She must've been getting some rest here too.

'Polar? Jesus, it's a miracle! He has a voice!'

Kate felt her stomach twist. Polar had been monitoring the radio, was he calling with news of Tom's parents?

'A guy? What guy? Say his name again? Zhee-khaki? Hey, I heard of him ...'

Kate was wide-awake now. She jumped off her narrow bunk, tried to follow Jasmine's voice. 'Did he say Jicaque? Keep him on the line.' She yanked aside a curtain and exposed some grouchy old woman getting a shot in the ass from a nervous-looking medic. 'I'm so sorry,' she muttered, pulling it straight back across and moving on. 'Jasmine! Keep him on the line, let me talk to him.'

She found the girl at last, a few cubicles down. As Kate watched, Jasmine killed the call with a precise press of her finger.

'Well, look at the state of you,' smirked Jasmine. 'Bag on your head's a nice touch. No cop's ever gonna recognise you now.'

'Why d'you ring off?' Kate demanded, ignoring her. 'Didn't you hear me?'

'Polar don't like talking to people he don't know,' Jasmine said, putting away the phone. 'Fact is, Polar don't like to talk, period. His daddy beat him every time he opened his mouth, so pretty soon he learned – keep quiet and you keep out of trouble.' She gave Kate a look. 'He's choosy about who he talks to. So I took a message.'

Kate crossed her arms. 'Well?'

'Some old guy came around the hangout. The guy Tom's been looking for. Zhi ...'

'Jicaque. Go on.'

'He wanted to see Tom. Left instructions to meet on Gun Hill bridge out in Baychester. Nine o'clock tonight.'

'That's it? Nothing else?'

Jasmine went sour-faced and shook her head. 'Ain't that enough? What more do you want, faxed confirmation and a map?'

Kate was seething with anger. 'I just would've liked to talk with him about this, OK? You don't have to be such a bitch.'

The girl's eyes widened in outrage. 'Me, the bitch?'

'Look, could you just call him back please?' Kate took a deep breath. 'You're right, Jicaque is the man Tom and I came to New York to see, but the 'wolves know that too. They could be using him to trap us or ...'

Jasmine was shaking her head, looking around like she was bored.

Kate bunched her fists, feeling suddenly helpless. '*What* is your problem?'

'I'll tell you about my problem.' Jasmine stood up and jabbed a finger into Kate's chest. 'I don't want you talking to my friends, OK? We got enough sweat on. Something must've freaked Polar pretty bad to get him talking – and I don't want the people I care about mixed up in your shit the same way Tom is.'

Kate knocked Jasmine's hand away, suddenly furious. 'It wasn't *me* who got Tom involved in all—'

'Save it, honey. Not interested.' Jasmine's dark eyes blazed into Kate's. 'However you dress it up, it seems to me that boy was turned 'wolf because of you. You're trouble. Stuck up, skinny-assed trouble, whatever dumb colour you put in your hair.'

Before Kate could open her mouth to utter another word, a nurse poked his tired head around the curtain. 'You two – take any fights outside, please. You're disturbing the patients.'

'We're done,' said Jasmine. With a last filthy look at Kate, she stalked away, pushing past the nurse.

Kate listened to the click of her neat little footsteps dwindle down the corridor.

Only when the noise had stopped altogether and the nurse gone back about his business did Kate allow the tears to fall.

Tom awoke from a familiar nightmare, sweating and itching inside. He'd been running in his lupine form, chasing after something that was always just out of view; never allowed to quit, his hunger building and building.

Groggily he sat up, his throat thick and filled with the iron tang of blood, like he'd had a nosebleed or something. It was his imagination, he knew, but the taste of it was maddening. On the table beside him was a little paper cup with a viscous red fluid inside. Stacy Serum, he supposed. There was a note scrawled beside it: DRINK ME IF YOU NEED ME.

Tom drained the sticky mixture in one gulp, his head still spinning. It tasted like aniseed but scalded his throat like brandy. 'Half-boy, half-wolf, half-guinea-pig,' he muttered.

'That's three halves,' Kate said, pushing her head around the door.

'Once again, I achieve the impossible.' Tom looked up and did a double take. Kate's hair was now a vibrant red. 'Hey, you look great!'

Kate wrinkled her nose. 'You think?'

'I know,' he grinned.

'I'm not totally convinced.' Kate pulled some strands round to scrutinise. 'I guess I'll get used to it ...'

'Sure you will.' The burn in his throat was fading now, and he felt a lot brighter. 'Anyway, aside from the hair, how's it going?'

'Don't ask,' she said lightly.

Was it his imagination or were Kate's eyes looking a little red too, like she'd been crying?

'As for *where* it's going – that's Baychester, Gun Hill bridge. Get yourself ready.'

Tom listened wide-eyed as Kate related what Jasmine had told her about Polar's call. 'It could be a trap,' he said. 'Scratch that. It's *bound* to be a trap.'

'I wanted to quiz Polar on the finer points,' she said, 'but Jasmine said no. Thinks I'm a bad influence on her friends.'

Tom frowned. 'What?'

'She's *such* a bitch,' Kate said venomously.

He didn't say anything. But from the hurt way Kate looked at him Tom realised he'd been supposed to. *Fell into that one*, he thought, and tried to fumble a reply, much too late.

But Kate spoke over him. '*You* should try and call Polar,' she suggested curtly. 'Jasmine seems to like you a whole lot better.'

'She does not,' Tom protested.

'Oh, please. Just go ask *her* for the number.'

'Well, where is she?'

'Losing your touch? Can't you go sniff her out or something?' Kate held up her hands even before he could register the hurt. 'I'm sorry. Jesus, ignore me, OK? I'm just crabby, no sleep ...' She looked at him hopefully. 'You understand ... right?'

Tom was still mad, and let his face show it.

''Cause Tom, if you don't understand me, I swear to

God I don't know who ever could.'

He looked at her for a few moments. Then he crossed the room and awkwardly held out his arms to her. She rose and held him, and he clutched her back tightly.

A woman cleared her throat softly behind them. They sprang apart.

'Stacy,' Tom said, a little flustered. 'We were just—'

'Hey, no need to explain,' smiled Stacy. 'The new red hair's hot, right? I knew it was a good idea!'

Kate nodded awkwardly. 'Yeah, I like it. Thanks, Stacy.'

Stacy crossed to the table and checked the cup. 'You took the serum then, Tom. How're you feeling?'

'Fine.' He blinked, considered for a moment. 'Actually, I feel great. Better than I have for ages.'

Stacy gave them a mischievous smile. 'Sure that's not young love talking?'

'Eeuw,' shuddered Kate, and they all laughed. 'What's this about taking serum?'

'Later,' Tom told her. 'Stacy, do you know where Jasmine and Rico are?'

'They split,' she said, 'headed back home.'

'Then we can't get hold of Polar and check,' Tom realised. 'I don't have Jasmine's cellphone number.'

Kate smiled sweetly. 'What, you mean she hasn't given it to you already?' she said.

They got directions from Stacy for riding the subway out to Baychester, as well as a twenty-dollar bill for expenses. 'Pay me back in blood samples,' she'd joked. Then they'd headed off.

Kate had never seen Tom in such high spirits, cracking jokes, babbling away about all kinds of nonsense, leapfrogging over trash cans ... She guessed that he was excited at the thought of maybe meeting the man who could save his life – before the worst happened to his family. She waved her new hair in his face to remind him that as far as this whole city was concerned they were wanted criminals; they should keep their profiles low.

'The cops'll never take me alive!' he shouted in some ridiculous gangster voice as he passed through the subway turnstile, drawing a gun from his fingers and pretending to shoot passers-by.

'OK, the infantile jerk thing is wearing a little thin now,' Kate remarked. She was apprehensive; not just about what might be waiting for them in Baychester, but because of this change in Tom's behaviour. What was happening with him? She'd been looking forward to spending a peaceful few hours together, just the two of them, before facing whatever lay ahead. But the new, hyper Tom apparently had no conception of quiet time. It had to be down to that serum stuff; he'd told her about taking it, and she'd scolded him for it: 'There's no saying how it might affect someone like you.'

'There *is* no one like me,' he'd said darkly. 'Remember?'

But Tom calmed down a little once they got on the subway. There were about a million stops on the train. It was only five o'clock, but they'd figured if they got to the bridge early they might get the jump on anyone trying to spring a nasty surprise. Plus, looking at the map Stacy had loaned them, it might take that long to find a bus that would take them even close by.

Tom spent the rest of the journey catnapping, his newfound energy apparently spent. He woke up with a start every time the train lurched or screeched a little too loud, then sank back into a fitful slumber. *Good*, thought Kate. *Sleep it off.*

At last they arrived at their stop, deep in the Bronx. Neither of them said much while they waited for the bus to arrive, but it was a comfortable silence. As it turned out, they didn't have long to wait. The sun was low and dusky pink as a bus took them through a clean, urban landscape of malls and parks and schools; it certainly didn't look like the hotbed of crime and terror she'd heard about from films and TV. But, then, she had learned that few things were ever as they seemed.

Night had well and truly fallen by the time the bus dropped them off. With the time approaching seven-thirty, they crossed a cordoned-off stretch of parkland to reach Gun Hill bridge. It was a dark, ornate structure that hunched long and low over the river below; the water resembled a strip of tarnished silver in the moonlight. An angular mass of scaffolding and tarpaulins clung to one side of the bridge which was closed for repairs. Streetlamps stood flanking it like mute sentries, but they were broken and dark. Only one still shone, rooted in the middle of the bridge.

'Let's make straight for there,' Tom said.

Kate agreed. 'At least we'll be able to see who's coming.'

As they crossed the dark bridge, Kate felt unease tease and itch at the back of her mind. It was too quiet out here. The solitary streetlamp cast strange shadows as its light threaded the intricate ironwork of the balustrade below. Then, Kate felt a shiver run through her. A dark figure was crouched at the foot of the streetlamp.

It rose up as they approached. The light glinted off a square of plastic in front of the figure's hooded face.

'Polar?' Kate shot a surprised glance at Tom. 'What are you doing out here?'

'Where's Ramone?' Tom added. 'Is he with you?'

Slowly, Polar shook his head and lowered his camera. He pulled a photo from the pocket of his grey hooded top and passed it to Kate in silence.

She angled it in the dim light to see what it was. And swore. Bile rose in her chest. Tom snatched the photo away for a closer look. Then let it fall it to the floor.

'Oh, my God,' he said quietly.

It was a picture of Ramone, lying in a pool of blood, his throat slit open.

'Why?' Kate whispered shakily. 'When did this …?' She felt cut up inside. 'Polar, for God's sake, what happened?'

She looked imploringly at the silent hooded figure. And then she caught the yellow gleam in Polar's eyes.

'He's 'wolf, Tom,' she murmured, backing away, panic rising. 'They turned him. *He* did it.'

'No, Kate. *I* did.'

They spun around, though Kate knew who had spoken, knew who had crept up quietly behind them while they stood speechless in shock.

'Mom,' she whispered.

# CHAPTER TEN

'I guessed you would get here early,' said Marcie Folan. Her smile was cold and bleak as the moon above as she looked at Kate. 'Sweetie, what has Mommy told you about dyeing your hair? Am I going to have to punish you?'

Kate said nothing. Tom stared at the scrawny woman facing them; her face pale and gaunt, thin bloodless lips stretched tight over her teeth. The reek of death hung about her. Marcie Folan, the woman who had ripped his life apart, made him half-animal, driven him into the darkness. She had wanted him dead since he'd first crossed her by accidentally killing Wesley, her 'wolf son, in a life-or-death struggle. But Takapa had stayed Tom's execution. He wanted Tom taken apart first. Cell by cell.

So what was Marcie's agenda now?

Tom thought of his parents, thought of Ramone, of all the people this woman had tainted or killed. It was all he could do not to throw himself at her, let the wolf inside him tear into her desiccated hide. But Kate must've seen the way he was tensing because she grabbed hold of his arm, held him back.

'No,' she whispered. 'We have to stay calm. Keep control. She wants to goad us into making mistakes.'

Tom nodded slowly. Kate didn't sound very calm herself, but he knew she was right. 'Where is my family?' he demanded.

Marcie's mocking laughter taunted him. 'Why, here in New York, of course, while the manhunt for their murdering son continues.'

'If you've hurt them—'

'They are safe for now,' Marcie told him, voice smooth as honey. 'How long they remain that way depends on your co-operation, naturally.'

'Co-operate? With you?'

Her eyes gleamed faint yellow. 'It's to be advised, Tom. You've seen what happens to those who don't.'

The photo he'd dropped was caught in a wintry gust and flapped about his feet. He clenched his fists. 'Why Ramone? Why kill him?'

'I wanted him to call his friend, the girl, to summon you here. So much less suspicious than using that monosyllabic little freak.' She tutted. 'But Ramone simply wouldn't betray you, whatever I did to him. Isn't that touching?'

'He swore he wouldn't let us down,' Kate said softly.

'I knew you'd suspect this was a trap,' Marcie went on, as two more dark figures advanced from out of the night behind her. 'But then I realised it really didn't matter. With the carrot of Jicaque dangled in front of your faces, like two dim donkeys you'd follow it anywhere.'

'The carrot of Jicaque,' echoed Tom, playing for time, trying to think through some way of escape. 'That's some voodoo charm thing, right?'

Marcie smiled without humour. 'Yes, your friend

Ramone acted brave, too. Joking till the last. You should've heard the way he laughed when I opened his throat ...'

As she spoke, Tom glanced behind him. Polar was still hovering wraith-like beneath the streetlamp. And from out of the shadows on the far side of the bridge, two more people were advancing on them, hemming them in.

'And to think,' Marcie continued with mock sadness, 'that his skinny hide had just been patched up by that lush over on East 123rd. What a waste of sutures.'

'So you know about Woollard,' Tom said quietly.

'And his work,' she added.

Kate frowned. 'And you tolerate it?'

'Woollard and Stein both have their part to play in our plans,' said Marcie. Her eyes gleamed. 'Like you two. I'm so glad I've found you both again.'

Tom was drawing a blank on any means of escape. He had to keep her talking, buy them some time. 'How did you know we were even in contact with Ramone?'

Marcie assumed an innocent expression. 'I didn't.'

'I told her,' said one of the dark figures, stepping forwards into the better light. But Tom had already recognised the voice and the massive frame, now wielding a baseball bat with a half-dozen nails knocked through the fat end.

Swagger.

Kate took a sharp breath and Tom reached for her hand. She clutched it for a second, then let go. He watched her draw herself up to her full height and stare defiantly across at the towering man.

'You owe me, girl,' Swagger said. 'And I'm gonna collect. Promise.'

'I don't get it, Swagger,' Tom said, trying to distract him. 'You said you wanted Ramone alive.'

Swagger answered, but his gaze still lingered greedily on Kate. 'That was when he still had his gang, and could lead them the way we wanted. Now they've scattered. We don't need him no more.'

'And Polar was the consolation prize?'

'Turned him myself, last night.' Swagger grinned. 'Thought I might need me a spy.'

'Good military thinking,' said Marcie. 'Now I understand why Takapa has appointed you his personal aide.'

'Yeah, until now she couldn't believe that he'd hire such an ugly loser,' Kate added helpfully.

'That's enough. Really, it's so cold out here. So exposed.' Marcie fixed her glacial eyes on Tom, then took a step towards him. Swagger and his heavy kept pace with her. 'Takapa has private lodgings close by. Perhaps you'd care to accompany me there?'

'Nice offer,' Tom said, 'but we've made plans.' He checked behind him and saw the other thugs were advancing closer too. Soon he and Kate would be trapped.

'Ah, *Tom*.' Marcie pronounced his name with an odd relish. 'If only you would give in to your lupine blood, overcome your ancient resister's heritage. What a leader *you* would make.'

'You wanted me dead before.'

'My judgement was perhaps a little coloured ... Takapa has studied the preliminary genetic samples we took from you in New Orleans. It seems there is much we can learn from you.' Another step closer. 'But why should we have to take your body's secrets from you by force? If you were to work with us, *help* us – we would spare your life and your family too.'

'Don't listen to her,' Kate snapped. 'She's trying to trick you.'

Tom's mind was racing. 'And Kate?'

'She must do as she is told,' said Marcie firmly. She took another step closer. 'We *must* continue our bloodline, Tom.'

'She'll give me to Takapa, Tom.' Kate's voice was high and forced. 'She'll have me raped.'

'I prefer the phrase "force-mated",' said Marcie, eyes shining. 'To cement the union of our ideals, the forging of our beautiful lupine future.'

Unable to go forwards or back, Tom and Kate edged towards the side of the bridge, where the top of the scaffolding peeped over the rail, their one teasing hope of escape.

Marcie, Swagger and his heavies began to close in on them. Only Polar hung back, still clutching his camera.

'She's won, Kate,' Tom said bitterly.

Marcie crowed in triumph. 'Broken at last!'

Kate stared at him in disbelief. 'Tom, no!'

Then, suddenly, for a split second the bridge was lit up with a blinding flash – Polar, to Tom's left, had taken another picture.

'You stupid freak!' Swagger shouted, rubbing his eyes, distracted.

And in that moment, Tom and Kate acted.

Kate kicked her mother in the stomach. Marcie screeched and fell back.

At the same time, Tom wrested the club from Swagger's hands. It was a gruesome weapon. But what choice did he have? He hefted its weight, his hands sweaty and arms tingling. A strange tinge of red blurred across his vision. Then he swung the club at Swagger.

Swagger took a hard blow to the head. He shouted out and crumpled to the ground. One of the heavies grabbed Tom around the neck, but Tom shoved the spiked end of the bat up into his attacker's face. The thug cried out in pain, staggered and fell. Tom kicked him to make sure he stayed down. Kate screamed, but he ignored her, swung the bat again and knocked another thug's legs from under him, felt the nails snag on clothing and flesh, and wrenched them free with vicious satisfaction.

'Tom!' Kate was screaming. It sounded like she was a hundred miles away.

The fourth of Swagger's thugs was running away back down the bridge, Polar close behind him, ignoring Marcie's demands that they stand their ground.

Marcie. She must be sprawling somewhere in the reddening shadows. Tom peered about for her, clutching the club tight in his sweating hands. Now he could make her pay, now he would—

'Drop it!' Kate had grabbed him by the shoulders, was shrieking in his face. She was covered in blood. 'Tom, for God's sake, *please*, drop it!'

Suddenly the weapon felt white hot in his hands. He let it clatter to the ground. 'Are you …?' He felt dizzy, sick in his stomach. Her cheek and neck were sticky and dark. 'Are you OK, Kate? You're bleeding …'

'It's not *my* blood, Tom,' she wailed, 'it's *theirs*.' She pointed to Swagger, clutching his head and gasping, and the two thugs who were writhing on the ground in agony.

'I … I wanted to kill them.' Tom stared at them in disbelief. 'More than anything.'

'You were never like this before,' Kate hissed, hugging herself. 'It's that stuff, that damned stuff Stacy gave you, it must be!'

'Jesus, Kate …' Tom started to shake, tears welled up and streaked down his cheeks. 'I couldn't stop myself …'

'Enough,' snarled Marcie. Her eyes were yellow and bright, her features beginning to buckle and shift.

Swagger was pushing himself up on to his hands and knees. His eyes were shut, his forehead gashed open. Tom watched as thick, coarse hair started to sprout from the wound.

'This way, Tom!' Kate shouted as she jumped up on to the wide metal rail that ran along the side of the bridge. 'Tom, come on. Come *on*. The 'wolves can't climb.'

Kate swung herself down on to the top bar of the steelwork scaffolding ranged against the bridge's side and began to clamber down to the planks below.

A low, rumbling noise behind him drew Tom's dazed attention. He looked back over his shoulder.

The dark, nightmarish shape of Marcie in 'wolf form came howling out of the darkness towards him, her foaming, rabid jaws wide open and ready to devour. Swagger ran beside her, a hulking, hideous creature, his sandy coat matted and bloody.

Tom leaped on to the scaffolding after Kate.

But as he swung down to the next level, he landed

badly and started to fall. He grabbed hold of a corner of the thick tarpaulin that shrouded the metal trellis-work. It tore under his weight but slowed his descent – before one of the scaffolding bars stopped it completely as he landed astride it. Pain tore through his body. He struggled to rise, to haul himself up on to one of the planks, but he was tangled in the tarpaulin.

A hot, itching feeling began to surge through his body; his head started to pound. The urge to change. But there was something different. The compulsion, usually nagging and insistent, was all-engulfing. *They want you to give in to your wolf side? OK. Fine. Show them just what that means.* That weird red tint was back in his vision. 'Kate,' he gasped. 'Help me.'

'Hold on, Tom,' she called, somewhere close by.

A terrifying, keening howl echoed out around him.

'No, Tom!' Kate called desperately. 'Please, no, not now! Not like this!'

It suddenly clicked in his head that the howling was his. The change was in full flow. His human flesh and bones were melting away as his 'wolf lunged out from the darkness to dominate. Tom could feel his consciousness slipping away as the lupine will took hold.

'Your eyes,' Kate was shouting, almost hysterical. 'Jesus, Tom, your eyes are yellow! *Yellow! This isn't you, Tom, it isn't you!*'

# CHAPTER ELEVEN

Tom's morphing lupine body tore free of Ramone's clothes. His body looked more bestial, more powerful than Kate had ever seen it. That, together with his eerie yellow eyes, was enough to warn her well away.

This wasn't Tom as she knew him. She could *hear* it, in the way he bellowed his rage up at Marcie and Swagger. The two 'wolves were leaning over the side of the bridge above them, snapping their jaws, their sinister silhouettes blotting out stars.

Kate had seen the rage that had taken Tom up on the bridge, the excessive violence he'd meted out. The glazed, unseeing look in his eyes had reminded her of Swagger and his generals back at the arena – and those unwilling warriors fighting for survival in the rink. Now that rage was back – only, in his 'wolf form, Tom could be unstoppable.

He leaped down from the scaffolding and landed half on land, half in the water. At once, two black shapes detached themselves from the darkness and attacked him. Jesus, there were more 'wolves down there, lying in wait – they'd been surrounded. Clearly Kate's mom was taking no chances.

But just as clearly, Marcie hadn't reckoned with the

change in Tom's personality. Kate saw her standing motionless now, watching the show as Tom fought off the 'wolves with a ruthless determination. His club-like paws swiped through flesh. His teeth tore at fur and muscle and bone.

It was a bloodbath.

Another 'wolf burst out of the blackness to throw itself at Tom, and he went down beneath its bulk. The two monsters rolled over and over till they hit the water with a colossal splash. Kate stared helplessly. There was nothing she could do to help him. She was frightened even to draw attention to herself, for fear of what he might do to her.

While her mom was distracted, she moved down through the planks and poles of the scaffolding as quietly as she could, then jumped down into a clump of long, springy grass. Yet another 'wolf raced by to join the fray, but too quickly to register her presence. She caught a glimpse of its bleeding leg and realised it must be the man Tom had attacked up above, out for revenge – and it sounded like others were on the way. She bit her lip as she tried to decide what to do. She hated the thought of running out on Tom – but what could she possibly do for him now?

She considered heading cross-country in the direction they'd come, but it was wide-open parkland – if she were spotted they'd bring her down in moments. There was woodland the other way. At least it would afford her cover while she waited for Tom – please God – to calm down and come find her.

With a shudder, she crept beneath the bridge. It was almost pitch black, but if she could just pick her way through to the other side …

A low growling ahead told her she'd made a terrible mistake.

Looming out from the shadows came a massive 'wolf. But the shape of it, the smell of it ...

Her heart lurched as she realised she was facing her father.

His glowing eyes bored into her; his salivating jaws creaked open.

Hot tears prickled Kate's eyes. 'Please, Dad,' she pleaded. 'Please let me go.'

The 'wolf that was her father went on staring at her for what felt like for ever.

Then he turned and slunk away.

Kate stood like a statue in the darkness. Maybe some things were stronger than 'wolf bloodlust. 'Thank you, Dad,' she whispered.

She heard the lupine baying and snarling up ahead of her grow fainter. Her father was leading the other 'wolves away.

Suddenly she could hear something else: the droning note of a car engine, and the rattling of a chassis as it bumped and scraped over uneven ground. Kate's heart leaped. But whipped up into such a frenzy, would the 'wolves retreat – or simply attack anyone who dared come near?

She got her answer a few seconds later in the form of an ululating, animal wail close by. It was her mother, crying out in impotent rage. The strange acoustics beneath the bridge took the sound and twisted it, made it echo and re-echo unbearably – but while it half-deafened Kate, the effect it had on the 'wolves was more profound. She saw their shadowy forms shift fleetly past the bridge, answering the keening call, heard heavy footfalls and scuffling all around. They were being summoned away, back into the cold shadows that harboured them.

Kate waited a few seconds more, then emerged from her hiding-place. The dark landscape seemed suspiciously still, the only sound the growling engine of the slowly-approaching vehicle. Then she gasped as something broke the surface of the shallow water.

It was Tom, naked and shivering cold, staring around in confusion.

He saw her, covered his modesty with both hands, and stumbled towards her. 'I'm sorry,' he murmured, his voice slurred like he'd been drinking. 'Kate, I'm so sorry.' He collapsed to his knees on the chill wet grass. 'Kate, what's happening to me?'

He looked at her so helplessly that she ran to him and held him tight. His skin was cold as a corpse, and ridged with deep cuts and scrapes from his struggle. His shivering got more violent; Kate guessed he was in shock. 'You're back,' she whispered soothingly in his ear. 'It's over, now.'

He hugged her closer like he wanted to believe it was true. 'Is it?' he murmured.

The car had stopped, and she heard its door slam shut. 'Tom? Kate?' She could've cheered, or cried or collapsed with relief. Stacy Stein had come looking for them. 'Down here!' Kate called. 'And do you have a blanket in your car?'

Stacy appeared over the rise of the bridge with a torch. Its powerful beam blinded Kate as it picked out her and Tom.

'Oh my God!' Stacy cried. 'Are you guys OK?'

Tom looked up into the beam of light. Kate saw him

force the tiniest of smiles through his chattering teeth.

'Take me to your heater,' he said.

The warm air pumped out on full as Stacy drove them away from Gun Hill bridge in her battered Ford, back to civilisation. Tom was curled up on the back seat, utterly exhausted, sleeping now beneath a tartan blanket.

Kate sat beside Stacy in the front, checking the mirror every few seconds to be sure no one was following. 'Thank you, Stacy,' she murmured for the twentieth time. 'If you hadn't come when you did ...'

Stacy waved away her gratitude. 'Would they have killed you?'

Kate closed her eyes. 'I don't know what they would've done.' She outlined what had happened on the bridge – including Tom's reaction to the serum.

'I can't understand why it should have affected him that way,' Stacy muttered. 'The serum contains agents that excite certain parts of the brain – it gives a lupine all the rush of the hunt and the kill without the need to make it happen for real.'

'Well, this was for real,' Kate said with a shudder.

'After delivering the rush, a downer kicks in, a pacifier,' Stacy continued. She swore softly. 'Why should it have such an effect on Tom? Something to do with his wereling chemistry?'

'I saw Swagger and his generals take some of that serum back at his hang-out.' Kate said. 'Stacy, it didn't pacify *them* either. If anything it seemed to make them more hostile.'

'Maybe I need to perform more tests.'

Kate heard the weariness in Stacy's voice, the reluctance to believe she could've got things so wrong

– and what the ramifications of that could be. 'Maybe,' she agreed. 'Stacy, how did you know the message we got was a fake?'

'I took a call from Jicaque after you left. He wanted to meet up with Tom.'

'What?' Suddenly Tom was wide-awake behind her.

'And *only* Tom. Midnight, some place off of Times Square.' Stacy shrugged. 'I knew one of the messages had to be bogus. The only way to find out which was to come out here and get you.'

'How do we know we can trust this *other* Jicaque?' Kate said bitterly.

'He said something kind of weird about Tom ...' Stacy clicked her tongue as she tried to remember. 'Oh yeah – "This time, put on your pants *before* we meet."' She frowned. 'Make any sense?'

'It's him,' Tom said, struggling forward under his blanket so he could better talk to Stacy. 'We first met in New Orleans ... I'd changed back from the 'wolf and I ducked into some scuzzy old movie theatre to get dressed. He was sitting there – turned out he owned the place – and asked me if I needed any help. I didn't know it was him till way after ... No one else would know that happened.'

Kate nodded. 'And if my mother had got to him, why would she arrange a message to be left while she was tricking us out to Gun Hill?' She looked at him. 'Jesus, Tom. It really could be him. *He's* found *us*.'

'Or Tom, anyway,' said Stacy. 'The message was for Tom to meet him alone at some diner called Vegetarian Kitchen.'

'I guess that's a good sign,' Tom said. 'Sorry you can't come.'

'Maybe he's scared of my mom – wants nothing to do with her daughter ...' Kate said, trailing off as a horrible thought struck her. 'Oh God, I just realised. Someone's got to tell Rico and Jasmine ... about Ramone.'

'Rico's brother?' Stacy asked sharply. 'What about him?'

Kate opened her mouth to tell her, but the words wouldn't come. It didn't seem possible that someone as larger-than-life as Ramone could now be gone. She turned to Tom, her eyes misting over. All she could see was the photo of Ramone's desecrated body.

'It's bad news,' Tom said huskily.

The mood was subdued in the car as they drove the rest of the way into the seething heart of New York. Tom was guiltily glad to have got away, and grateful that it was Kate who would be breaking the news about Ramone.

He felt oddly detached from his surroundings as he wandered down Broadway. Everywhere was bright and well-lit. People surged along the wide-open streets in great waves, spewing out from the theatres and the restaurants in their hundreds. Great skyscrapers ploughed up from out of the busy traffic on every street in sight. And as he finally came to Times Square, there was a sense of something truly giant in the air – not just the massive neon hoardings cranked up high over the city, or the TV screens the size of a condo, or the buildings that outstretched and outshone the night sky. There was a brash, rough-and-ready optimism about the place, the feeling that you could come here and stuff would happen. That *anything* was possible.

Tom tried and tried to give himself up to such

feelings, but he was still struggling to come to terms with his behaviour back on the bridge, and the wild mood swings he'd experienced since taking the serum. He kept getting flashbacks, frozen moments of violence that stung his senses. He hoped against hope that he'd ridden out the side-effects and that now he was normal again – at least, as normal as he could hope to be.

He'd hated the lupine nature within him before, but if he could no longer control the beast and its power ...

At least he felt a little warmer now. Practical as ever, Kate had pointed out that Tom was going to draw some unwelcome attention at his rendezvous if he walked around Times Square naked. Luckily, Stacy remembered a hot tip from one of the street kids in her program: a thrift clothes store on Broadway regularly dumped unwelcome donations outside with its trash. Kate had managed to find him a holey sweater and a threadbare tweed jacket and a pair of tuxedo pants sporting some very suspect stains. They went nicely with the grubby pair of basketball shoes, straight out of the Eighties and a size too small.

But dress sense was the least of his worries, whatever the smirking hordes thronging the sidewalks around him might think. His stomach was fizzing with nerves at the thought of meeting Jicaque, after so many tricks, so many false hopes ...

It was five minutes to midnight. Tom found his step was quickening as he turned on to West 44th Street. Did he dare to think he really could be cured?

The Vegetarian Kitchen was a tiny bistro that had snuck into the street between a 7-Eleven and a tacky video store.

Tom stared at it in disbelief.

It was closed.

He swore. There was no doubt about it: the place was dark, empty, shut up for the night.

'Hey,' a man's voice whispered close by. 'Down here.'

It was coming from an alleyway that ran beside the bistro. His hopes igniting once more, Tom rushed to the mouth of the dark alley to investigate.

Someone grabbed hold of his jacket and dragged him inside. He cried out but a hand clamped over his mouth. *The 'wolves*, he thought, panicking. *How could I have been so stupid?*

Across from the alleyway on the other side of the street, a psychic advertised her services in gaudy, flickering neon. In its pink burn he saw another man, Korean maybe, lurking in the thick shadows.

Tom bit the thick fingers bruising his lips, and with a grunt the man snatched them away. But before Tom could shout for help, the Korean doubled him up with a punch in the stomach, and thrust a knife towards his face.

The other man grabbed Tom again, this time in a neck-lock.

'Give us your money and don't make a sound or we'll make you bleed, kid.'

'Muggers?' Tom gasped. Bizarrely, he felt a rush of sudden relief. 'Thank God.'

He saw the Korean frown. 'Huh?'

'Comedian,' muttered the first man, tightening the neck-lock.

Tom gasped. OK, so they might not be 'wolves – but the city had dangers enough without them, and he had been a fool to forget it. 'I don't have any money ...' he spluttered. 'All I have is the clothes I'm in. Look at me ...' The pressure on his airway was beginning to make Tom feel giddy.

*Change*, he thought. *Change to save yourself ...*

The knife-man frisked him quickly and swore. 'Nothing.' Then he smiled and held the knife to Tom's cheek. 'Maybe we'll take something else from you, huh?'

*Change!*

Tom thought of the hundreds of people coursing through those brightly-lit streets just steps away. After what happened at Gun Hill he knew he couldn't risk their lives to save his own.

And since his last hope had finally failed him, why fight? Maybe it was time just to give in at last.

He shut his eyes as the knifepoint pressed into his cheek.

Then a resounding clang echoed around the alley-way, and the knife fell away. A hand reached past Tom's face and jabbed at the man who held him. With a cry of pain, the man fell back, clutching his eyes.

The muggers, reeling from this sudden assault, retreated quickly down the alleyway and back to the main drag without a backward glance.

In the sputtering light of the neon display Tom stared in disbelief at his rescuer. He was a short man wearing a white coat over checked trousers, an ageing Native American whose silver hair hung down to his shoulders in scruffy braids. His face was lined, his nose like a big, straight arrow through the contours, pointing down to a proud cleft chin. His eyes were amber in the light, twinkling with amusement.

The old man held up a glistening hand. 'Chili oil,' he announced in a voice that held no trace of accent. He gestured to a door in the wall beside him. 'From the kitchens. I think it stung his eyes a little.'

Tom noticed the heavy frying pan in the man's other hand. 'You hit the guy with that?' he asked.

'The use of force is unfortunate,' his rescuer commented, 'but sometimes necessary.' He paused. 'Greetings, Tom Anderson.'

'Jicaque?' asked Tom, shell-shocked.

'Sometimes,' agreed the old man almost regretfully. 'I prefer being Johnny Oldman, lately arrived in Manhattan as deputy head chef of Vegetarian Kitchen.' He brightened. 'You know, my egg rolls are the finest in Midtown.'

Tom just stared at him dumbly.

'But what am I thinking?' the old man went on. 'You've had a terrible ordeal. You need a strong cup of java. I know someplace we can go.'

The old man headed back to the street down the alleyway, still clutching the frying pan.

Tom watched him go, his spirit shaken. This daffy old guy was really Jicaque, fabled medicine man and scourge of 'wolves across the USA? It was a blistering anti-climax.

Heavy-hearted, Tom was about to follow him, when he noticed the door in the wall leading to the kitchens of the restaurant. It was bolted shut and secured with a large padlock. So how the hell did Jicaque get out here?

With a shiver of fear and anticipation, Tom followed the old man as he turned left towards the hustle of the brighter streets.

\* \* \*

Kate dreaded the task ahead of her as Stacy turned the car into the street where Ramone had his hideout. She'd tried rehearsing what she was going to tell Jasmine and Rico, but the words kept coming out all wrong.

Something else was wrong, too.

A sleek, dark stretch limousine was parked outside the slum tenements. It looked incongruous with the housing projects crowding the skyline behind it.

'That's weird,' Stacy observed, slowing down. 'What would a limo be doing here?'

'Look,' Kate said. 'There's someone coming out.' A stooped, bedraggled-looking man was trudging down the steps leading up to the hangout. Something glinted in his hand; metal or glass perhaps, but she couldn't tell what.

'That's Dr Woollard,' Stacy reported. 'I didn't think he ever left his house. Why would he come to Ramone's now?'

She was about to honk on the horn to attract his attention, but Kate grabbed her by the wrist to stop her. 'Oh my God,' she whispered. 'Look.'

A skinny figure had emerged from the limousine to greet Woollard. He was ghoulish-looking, deathly pale, his features bunched up together in the middle of his pockmarked face. His white-blond hair was shaved back to stubble. As he ushered Woollard into the back of the car, he smiled, baring a sharp set of teeth.

'Takapa,' Kate breathed. 'The one who's making all this shit happen.'

Stacy nodded. 'God help us, it looks like Woollard's pitched in with him.'

# CHAPTER TWELVE

Tom glanced around the late-night coffee shop while Jicaque placed their order at the counter. Scattered tables of twenty-somethings huddled together over the yellow Formica, speaking in low, serious voices. Middle-aged men stared out stoically through the menu-cluttered windows, seemingly reluctant to go home to their empty apartments. A couple, he too young and she too old, looked lovelorn at each other over untouched lattes. Tom felt oddly at home here, just one more person in the coffee-shop crowd hiding from the sharp truths of life for a few short hours.

Jicaque returned, placing a cup of coffee down in front of Tom. 'You're disappointed,' he noted, sitting opposite in the grimy booth. 'You were expecting someone more impressive to bear the name of Jicaque, right?'

'No,' Tom protested.

His companion smiled wryly. 'And a bad liar. But you, more than most, should appreciate that outward appearances count for little. Not in the world that *we* inhabit.' He took a packet of cigarettes from his pocket. 'Take these.'

'No thanks, I don't smoke.'

'I mean, take them by way of example. I am an old

man now, and I have survived the attentions of many enemies only through being prepared.' Jicaque's smile grew wilier, and he lowered his voice. 'I don't always carry a frying pan, and I don't smoke, either. But I carry cigarettes powdered with a special compound of magnesium. Should I find myself in trouble, I take out a cigarette and light it. The resultant flare is a useful distraction.'

'Ouch,' Tom said. 'Should I be worried about this coffee?'

'At fifty cents a cup, maybe we both should,' Jicaque replied.

Some oldster music, jazz or something, was piping through little speakers in the corners of the room. Jicaque clearly approved, shaking his head in time to the shifting beat. 'Stan Getz,' he said, with a sigh of contentment. 'Pure genius. You know his work?'

'I think maybe my dad's heard of him,' Tom said.

'Kids.' The old man grimaced, then sipped his coffee. 'Won't you drink?'

Tom felt dazed. He had rehearsed this momentous meeting in his dreams so many times; somehow, he'd never imagined it would take place over a Formica table with corny old records playing in the background. He shrugged, raised the cup to his lips and sipped.

Jicaque watched him intently, expectantly.

'It's good, thanks,' Tom said, remembering his manners. Jicaque went on staring, and Tom shifted uncomfortably. 'Do I have a coffee moustache or something?'

'I thought as much,' the old man said at last. 'The powder I just slipped in your drink would've made you violently ill by now if you weren't what I believe you to be.'

Tom stared at his coffee cup in alarm, then half-rose to his feet. 'There's poison in this?'

'No,' said Jicaque mildly, glancing around to check no one had overheard. 'Merely a combination of dried herbs – an old, old recipe.' His expression hardened. 'I have heard many things, many rumours about you. But I am careful what I choose to believe. If not, I would've been killed years ago.'

Tom sat back down warily and pushed aside his coffee. 'Maybe I should be more careful too. I heard you'd retired from practising medicine.'

Jicaque smiled, his striking amber-coloured eyes twinkling. 'So the 'wolves like to think. You could say I started minding their business a little too closely for their liking. The lupine community does not appreciate human interference in its affairs. They threatened to kill me.'

'They're evil,' Tom said, 'they should be wiped out. Hunted down.'

Jicaque shook his head. 'Like any predator, they have the right to exist.' He sighed. 'Werewolves have been a part of the hidden fabric of human society for countless generations. But they were not always so hidden. Will you listen to an old man's story?'

Tom nodded. 'It has to beat the jazz.'

Jicaque frowned at him, then began his tale. 'No one knows for sure when the first werewolf dragged itself out of the darkness and into the world of men. But according to the ancient texts, a community of Pueblo people in America's southwest suffered particularly from a plague of attacks. As is often the case in nature, they discovered an indigenous remedy nearby. If the bitten victim imbibed a solution of a local herb – in any other situation highly toxic – for the length of one lunar month, then the lupine toxins were unable to take hold. Ancient magics and rites were used to support a body's natural resistance as it utilised the herb to overcome the lupine threat. In modern understanding, antibodies were created. Babies began to be born with natural immunity. Eventually, the community was able to drive out the lupine entirely.'

Jicaque paused to take another sip from his steaming cup. 'They came to be known as the Shipapi; taking their name from the Pueblo word *Shipap*, meaning the womb of the earth, the place from which the first pure human beings entered the world.'

'Go on,' Tom said, fascinated.

'Slowly, the word spread to other tribes that there was a way to fight back against wolfkind. But because the 'wolves hid in human form, the Shipapi's secrets were entrusted only to a very few. They travelled the land, driving out the hidden 'wolves and appointing others in this sacred order.'

'So what went wrong?' Tom reached to take another gulp of his coffee – then changed his mind. 'How'd the 'wolf fight back?'

Jicaque smiled grimly. 'The arrogance of man is often his downfall. The Shipapi grew complacent – even corrupt; the natural protection was diluted through careless mating. The 'wolves became able to infiltrate the ranks of the Shipapi for the first time. Trust dwindled, and so too did the numbers of the Shipapi. So many people died ...' Abruptly, Jicaque stopped, staring into space. A tear trickled down his cheek.

'Are you OK?' Tom whispered.

'Sorry. It's just this sax break here ...' He tapped his skinny chest. 'Gets me every time, you know?'

Tom rolled his eyes. 'Look ... you're telling a great story, but what does it have to do with what's happening now?'

'Be patient,' said Jicaque sharply. 'Though the natural immunity of the Shipapi was seriously compromised, resistance, in various forms and levels, still occurred in subsequent generations and is still evident today in a chosen few.' Now the old man smiled. 'The 'wolves call these *silverbloods*. I believe you've heard of the expression?'

Tom felt the hairs on the back of his neck prickle. *He* had been called a silverblood. 'I'm descended from the Shipapi?' he asked in wonder. 'You mean, like, my great-great-great-great-grandfather was one of these people?'

Jicaque opened his mouth to answer, but hesitated as a departing couple passed by close to their table, trying to squeeze past.

Tom glared at them, holding his breath until they had gone and the old man could talk freely again.

'Indeed, you carry inside you the blood of the ancient guardians,' Jicaque said softly. 'A little diluted, sure – but there, nonetheless.'

Tom grimaced. 'Not strong enough,' he said. 'Marcie Folan still made a newblood out of me.'

'Not entirely; she made you a *wereling*,' Jicaque pointed out. 'As for me, I carry the resistance in a purer form.'

'Like Rico,' Tom guessed. Jicaque looked blank. 'This kid I know,' Tom went on. 'His blood is poison to the 'wolves; he can't be turned.'

'Like Rico, indeed,' Jicaque observed. 'But unlike Rico, and unlike you, I have been aware of my Shipapi inheritance all my life. I was sworn to watch the 'wolves; to help limit their numbers, for the sake of humanity – and their own survival.'

'So how have you gone about it?' Tom asked him.

'Travelled from place to place, guided by others of the ancient order,' Jicaque replied. 'If a lupine community was turning too many newbloods, I would try to cure some of those wretched souls; restore the proper balance.'

Tom finally spoke aloud the question he'd been steeling himself to ask: 'So you *can* cure people who've been turned 'wolf?'

'If a lupine wishes to embrace their humanity once more, then yes,' Jicaque agreed.

'Then can you cure me?'

'I can,' he said simply. 'Though the 'wolves have tired of my meddling and threatened me with death, I will not shirk my responsibilities.' Jicaque sighed deeply. 'I tried to for a while, I confess; turned my back on my ancient calling and went into hiding.' This time, the tears brimming in his tired old eyes were for real. 'In truth, Tom, you're right to be disappointed in me. By turning a blind eye I have allowed the evil of Takapa to fester and grow. The lupine community has traditionally survived by restricting its activities; hunting only when need is at its greatest; scattering its members throughout the population.'

'But Takapa wants to swell the numbers,' Tom said.

'Yes,' the old man said. 'This would-be ruler of the 'wolves seeks to start a fire – a beacon he hopes will lead his kind out from the darkness and into the light. His activities in this city are in preparation for that day. And I fear it is not far away.' Jicaque looked at Tom, his face inscrutable. 'I *can* cure you, Tom. But if I am to fight Takapa, I shall need powerful allies.'

Tom felt uneasy. He sensed what was coming.

'You have great powers,' Jicaque went on. 'Surrender them now and I fear for your safety, and that of Kate, and your family.'

Tom felt like a child cheated of a promised present. 'But Takapa wants me for research. If I was just human again, it would wreck his plans, wouldn't it?'

'Perhaps,' Jicaque agreed. 'But Marcie Folan will still want revenge, Tom. She will come for you. And have you forgotten you are still wanted for murder?'

'You think showing the court I'm a werewolf will count in my defence?' Tom shook his head wearily. 'You're the wise old medicine man; help me out here. Kate's in danger. My whole family's in danger. How can I keep them safe?'

Jicaque smiled gravely. 'If Takapa's plans succeed, who will be safe?' He placed his gnarled old hands over Tom's own. 'I sense the strength in you. The powers you possess.' A flicker of pain, or fear, passed over his tanned, lined face. 'And I sense the balance in you has shifted recently. You must hold on to the good, Tom. Hold on to the good.'

Tom felt a chill pass down his spine. 'I … I took some kind of drug,' he said. 'It was supposed to suppress the lupine in me, to control the bloodlust, but instead …' He shuddered. '*I* lost control. Stacy Stein and Woollard, they must've got the research wrong. They—'

Jicaque pulled his hands away. 'Woollard, you say?'

Tom nodded. 'He's a doctor, over in Harlem, a blood specialist; sometimes helps Stacy out. Do you know him?'

'No. But I've come across the name before,' breathed Jicaque. 'It originated in Saxon England. It means "guardian of wolves". A name given by the Shipapi to humans sympathetic to the ways of the 'wolf.'

'Coincidence,' Tom said uneasily, 'it must be. Stacy's working to develop a *cure* for the lupine toxin.' He glared at Jicaque. 'And *you've* had the knowledge all along. You could've helped her properly, not just sent over a bunch of sappy herbs.'

'It is not for me to say whether a race shall die or live,' Jicaque retorted, 'but to preserve the proper balances of life. Dr Stein seeks to *control* life through her ... *chemicals.*' He spoke the word with a grimace, like it was somehow disgusting.

'She's trying to help the reluctant newbloods control their cravings,' Tom said fiercely. 'While you were burying your head in the sand, Takapa's turned a whole lot of kids 'wolf. *Too* many. It's a bloodbath waiting to happen, and that's what Stacy's been trying to prevent.'

'I know it,' said Jicaque quietly. 'But *suppose* ... suppose her good work has been perverted in some way?'

'But who could've ...' Tom trailed off, his breath catching in his throat. 'Woollard?'

Jicaque met his worried gaze evenly. 'Think of the effect this concoction had on *you.*'

'Then I've got to warn Stacy,' Tom realised, jumping

to his feet. 'Right now.'

'Yes,' Jicaque agreed, rising as well and nodding farewell to the man behind the counter. 'And I must prepare.'

'Prepare?' Tom frowned, following him out of the coffee shop and on to the neon-soaked sidewalk outside. Rain was falling, and people hurried by with their heads down, their coats clutched close. 'What do you mean, prepare?'

'The bloodbath you spoke of,' Jicaque replied grimly. 'It must be prevented. Whatever the cost.'

Tom peered out into the road. 'Do you have money for a cab?' he asked Jicaque, trying to spy any yellow in the traffic. 'I've got to get to Ramone's hangout, quick—'

But when he turned back, he found the medicine man had vanished.

'Jicaque?' He spun around, scanning the sidewalk, picking through the frantic figures fleeing the rain, but there was no sign of him. How could the old guy have moved so fast?

Then Tom realised someone was watching him too. A cop, staring at him hard through the downpour, like he was trying to remember something.

'Hey!' the cop shouted. 'Hey you, hold it!'

Tom swore, then turned and splashed off down the street, muttering under his breath: 'Teenage kid wanted on a charge of Murder One and crimes against fashion ...' The good, the bad and the hairy – everyone wanted a piece of him. And he knew with a sick certainty that any time now his luck was going to run out.

\*    \*    \*

Kate walked gingerly into the hangout to find Jasmine and Rico sitting together in front of the dark screen of the smashed TV. Stacy was close behind her, taking in the squalid conditions, concerned but apparently not shocked. Kate guessed she'd seen worse places than this in her time in the city.

'Are you guys OK?' Stacy asked.

'Jeez,' said Jasmine, jumping in surprise. 'Ric, my man, you are popular tonight.'

'Hey!' Rico looked delighted to see them. 'Kate! Kate, I know where Tom's mom and dad're staying.' He gestured excitedly through the archway that led to the next room, where Kate could hear the police radio squawk and splutter. 'Cops was talking about some other conference or somethin' tomorrow, picking them up next morning from a hotel on Madison. Room 3003.'

'That's great news, Rico, well done!' Kate saw a tiny band-aid on Rico's arm just above the elbow. 'But what did Woollard want here?'

'What all doctors want,' Rico complained. 'Blood, blood, blood, the whole time.'

Stacy smiled in sympathy. 'But why'd he come here, sweetheart?'

'Don'cha know?' Jasmine frowned. 'Lady, they're *your* samples.' When Stacy looked blank, she went on, speaking slowly like the woman was stupid: 'He took those samples for *you*.'

'No, he didn't.' Stacy looked worriedly at Kate. 'Why would he come around here tonight?'

'Maybe because Tom got away?' Kate's mind was racing. 'Mom said Takapa wanted Tom for testing, but maybe he's decided Rico's DNA will do in the meantime?'

Stacy nodded. 'Whatever, Woollard's got some explaining to do. Maybe I should go see him.'

'Takapa's dangerous,' Kate warned. 'If he's there—'

'Hey! Would you mind telling us just what the hell you're talking about?' Jasmine said irritably. 'Any case, where's Ramone and Polar? And Tom?'

Kate felt her stomach ball itself up.

Rico turned his big eyes on her. 'Doc Woollard said they'd gone to meet up with you.'

She looked helplessly at Stacy, who could only stare sadly back at her. 'Uh ... Well ...'

Jasmine looked at her uneasily. 'You got something to say, say it.'

Kate took a deep breath. 'Tom went to meet someone. The *real* Jicaque. The only one who can help us now.'

'What d'you mean, the *real* Jicaque?'

'That message Polar gave you ... was a fake. He sold us out. He's one of them now. Swagger turned him 'wolf last night.' The words ground out of her mouth, mechanically. 'And ... Ramone's dead. He was ... the 'wolves killed him.'

'Dead?' Rico's big black eyes filled with tears. 'This ain't true.' He turned to Jasmine. 'They shittin' us, right? Right?'

Jasmine eyes had zeroed in on Kate's. 'How'd Ramone die?' When Kate didn't respond, she asked again, louder, angrier: '*How'd he die?*'

'Swagger told ...' Kate drew a shuddering breath. 'He told my mom she could get to me and Tom through him. But Ramone wouldn't help, he wouldn't betray us. So ... so ...'

'I knew it,' Jasmine hissed. Her eyes glittered like

ice. 'You got him killed. *You*.'

'That's not fair, Jasmine,' Stacy said gently.

'Oh, right,' the girl sneered, her face contorted with rage. 'You clean-living clever white girls, you gotta stick together, right?'

'That's bullshit and you know it,' Stacy snapped.

'No bullshit,' hissed Jasmine. She rose to her feet and crossed the room, then grabbed Kate by the arms and shook her. '*You* killed him!' she shouted. 'Hear me? *Hear me?*'

Kate didn't react, just stood there and took it, so numb she could barely feel the girl's fingers digging into her flesh.

'Jasmine, stop it.' Stacy tried to come between them. 'This isn't helping, you have to—' But Jasmine knocked her away. The blow sent her reeling across the room towards the archway.

'You killed him!' Jasmine shrieked again in Kate's face. 'If he'd never met you he'd be here right now.'

'Let her alone, Jas!' Rico's voice was high and clear. 'If Ramone never met Kate and Tom, he'd be dead in Central Park. Or maybe dead when Swagger come calling last night. Or maybe alive, sure – shit, who knows? But, he's dead now.' The kid looked up at Kate, wiping his snotty nose, and his voice grew small and quiet. 'He's dead for real ... right?'

Kate nodded, then met Jasmine's pained, crazy stare. 'Right,' she breathed. 'And I'm so, so sorry.'

'Quiet, all of you,' Stacy snapped, rubbing the side of her butt where she'd fallen. 'Listen to this.' The gravity in her voice made even Jasmine relinquish her grip and listen.

A nasal voice was crackling out from the police

radio. '... fits the description of youth wanted in connection with the 'Orleans homicide enquiry. Units in vicinity of West 44th and Tenth, apprehend Caucasian male, black pants, tweed jacket. Proceed with caution ...'

'Oh my God, they're after Tom,' Kate said. 'If the police get hold of him ...' She didn't dare finish the sentence.

'What can we do?' said Stacy.

''S'easy,' Jasmine said shakily, wiping her eyes. 'I'll go get him in the wagon. I know the area.'

Kate looked at her uncertainly. 'You're in no state to drive anywhere.'

'You here in my skin with me? You wanna argue about this so long that the cops get Tom and he winds up dead like Ramone?'

'Then let me come with you,' Kate insisted.

'No way,' Jasmine said fiercely, shoving Kate aside. 'C'mon, Ric.' She grabbed the boy by the hand and dragged him out with her.

Kate went to follow but Stacy stopped her. 'Let her go. Let her cool off and work through some stuff.'

'But she won't be thinking straight,' Kate protested. 'She could—'

'She doesn't need to think right now,' Stacy replied. 'Let's face it, she's got more experience with this kind of thing than we do.'

'So what are *we* supposed to do?' Kate gestured angrily to the radio. 'Hang out, and listen to the running commentary?'

'We go to Woollard's,' said Stacy firmly. 'Waiting around here won't do us any good, and it won't help Tom either.'

'But if there's any news—'

'Jasmine will come find us, with Tom in tow, I'm sure,' Stacy told her. 'We'll leave a note.' She pulled a small notepad and pen from her purse, and gave them to Kate who left a hasty scribble on the paper. 'Now c'mon. I've gone forty-eight hours without sleep. I could use some answers, you know?'

'I know,' Kate said grimly, as she followed Stacy out. 'So could I.'

Tom's lungs burned with the icy air he was rasping down. His sides were splitting with stitches and his legs felt leaden, but he kept on going, kept pushing his body harder and harder. He knew that if he stopped now he would never have the strength to set off again. And if he turned 'wolf ... who knew what could happen.

He'd scaled some tall gates and cut across a school playground, hoping he'd find somewhere to hide – but there seemed to be a cop car waiting around every street corner. Whichever alleyway he ducked down, there was a man in blue racing up it towards him. His ears were ringing with the shriek of sirens.

The city itself seemed to be caging him in; the thundering skyscrapers, stone and glass and metal monoliths, were ranged up around him on every side. The rain poured down through a jigsaw piece of night, the only sky visible beyond the buildings' reach. Tom was soaked through, his feet were cramped and blistered from his ill-fitting thrift store sneakers, but still he kept on running, *running*.

He vaulted a low fence and with the last of his strength, sprinted through a small leafy courtyard and into a parking lot. His footfalls on the wet concrete were too loud, he couldn't hear a single other damned thing. So at last he let himself stop, nauseous with exertion, wheezing for breath. His legs cramped up and he collapsed to his knees, breathing out steam in the freezing rain, his skin chilled, wet and desensitised.

Willing himself to recover, he took a cautious look about him. The lot was quiet and still. If he could just get inside one of these cars, maybe he could hide out till morning and—

'Police! Freeze!'

Tom swore. They'd found him.

He looked behind him, got painfully to his feet.

'You hear me?' The cop was standing at the perimeter of the lot, maybe twenty metres away. He looked young and jumpy, and his gun was trained on Tom's chest. 'I said freeze!'

'I *am* frozen,' Tom muttered.

'Now get your hands up.' The cop gestured with his gun, and started to advance closer.

It's over, thought Tom. It ends here.

He just couldn't accept that.

Before he even realised what he was doing, Tom was running again.

'Hold it!' roared the cop.

But his gun roared louder.

Tom's shoulder burned white hot. For a moment he was flying through the stinging rain. Then he was tumbling over and over on the hard wet concrete and hurting so bad he couldn't even scream. He heard a screech of brakes and came up fast against something that stopped him dead, flat on his melting back, staring up at the distant stars, till the rainwater filled his eyes and he couldn't see a thing anymore.

# CHAPTER THIRTEEN

No one was home at Woollard's place. Kate stood by as Stacy rapped repeatedly on the front door, but no welcoming light appeared at any window, no sound of movement came from inside.

'So now what do we do?' Kate asked dismally, as the rain drummed down around them. She wondered helplessly where Tom was now. She should've gone after Jasmine, got in the wagon and refused to get out. If anyone were to reach Tom and rescue him it should be her, not that girl – and especially not in the state of mind Jasmine must be in now. And whose fault was that, Kate reflected guiltily.

'Gee, this sure is a run-down neighbourhood,' Stacy observed. The tenement overlooked a vacant lot on one side and some boarded-up slums on the other. 'I bet there's a lot of crime.' She walked up to a cracked front window and put her elbow through it. The glass broke noisily.

'Are you crazy?' Kate hissed in disbelief.

'I prefer to think of myself as determined.' Stacy reached carefully through the jagged hole she'd made and unlatched the low window. Then she climbed inside, her lithe figure soon lost to the darkness beyond.

Kate swiftly followed. It was a relief to be out of the

rain, though Woollard's apartment wasn't a good deal warmer than the November night, and it reeked of whisky and garlic.

Stacy flicked on a lamp on the desk, and leafed through a whole stack of papers perched precariously on a chair.

Kate closed Woollard's dusty curtains. Spindly stems bearing withered white flowers had been pinned around the edges. Garlic flowers? 'This is too weird,' she muttered. 'What are you looking for, Stacy?'

'Research notes, papers, tests …' Not finding what she wanted, Stacy impatiently swept the whole pile of papers off the chair. 'OK, then, let's think what the most likely hiding place would be.'

'Takapa drove Woollard to Rico's place in his limo,' Kate suggested. 'So he must've picked him up somewhere.'

'Most likely from here,' said Stacy. 'Woollard lives his whole life in this place. Scared to go out.'

Kate took in the crucifixes on the walls, the cryptic texts in their dusty frames and weird mystical symbols daubed about the place. 'I think I'd be more scared of staying in. But OK, say they met here, to talk stuff over, discuss something?'

Stacy nodded. 'Or demonstrate something. Come on, Woollard keeps his lab in this little examining room back here …'

Kate followed her across the hall and into another room.

Stacy turned on the light and stared around. A low leather couch was strewn with documents, as was a long workbench along the back wall, bowing under the weight of the high-tech equipment that cluttered it.

She grabbed a sheaf of papers and started flicking through.

Kate peered at a padded envelope. 'No doubt about it, Stacy, Woollard's been working for Takapa.' She pointed to the sender's address label on the back. 'It's the address of Takapa's New Orleans hideout. I was held there for a while. He had all sorts of experiments going on.' She pulled out some of the papers inside. 'Cell counts ... chromosome analysis ...'

But Stacy was barely listening, hunched almost double over some lab results scrawled in a spidery script. 'You idiot,' she breathed. 'You blind idiot.'

Kate frowned. 'Who?'

'Me. I've been taking Woollard's comments on the treated blood samples at face value – because they told me what I wanted to hear. The guy's a genius, and I just always assumed he was as committed to the work as I am. And since I don't have the equipment anymore to double-check the results ...' She laughed softly. 'Oh, he's played me for a fool.'

A feeling of unease twisted through Kate's insides. 'What is it?'

'This research seems to run parallel to mine. Takapa must want to study Tom's genetic make-up for the same reasons I do: comparing it to other samples – like Rico's – could help identify and isolate the lupine factor.'

'The werewolf gene,' Kate translated. 'But why would he want that? Takapa's not looking for a cure.'

'No – he's been trying to stop *me* finding it.' She screwed up one of the papers. 'Like with the Stacy Serum ... Woollard's treated my samples as I asked him to – but he's gone further. Altered the direction of my work without my even knowing.'

'Then what does the serum actually do?'

Stacy seemed not to hear her. She looked pale and sick, scanning another sheet of scrawls. '"A chronically addictive psychotropic drug ..."' she read. '"Excitation of the adrenal gland ..."' She looked up at Kate. 'He's knocked out the pacifying effect. The serum doesn't stabilise or soothe the lupine condition – it antagonises it.'

'So Tom's reaction was nothing to do with his particular body chemistry,' Kate said slowly. 'It was just the drug doing its thing.'

'*Woollard* Serum ... all the time.' Stacy threw down the pile of papers in despair. 'But I've been running a register, I've got 'wolves out there on the street reporting back to me. They say the lupine numbers *have* gone down – and a steadily greater number of newbloods have come back for more serum, that's *fact*!' She looked at Kate desperately. 'So the serum *must* be working on the lupine brain in the way it's intended – controlling newblood cravings without them having to go out and bite someone. The math works!'

But Kate was thinking about something else Stacy had read out. The report had said the serum was *chronically addictive*. And Kate remembered Swagger's tempting the gladiators to fight with a promise of *something* ... Something that was worth all that violence and pain. She flicked through the contents of the envelope more carefully. 'Suppose your serum works *too* well? What if taking it's *better* than going out and killing for real?' she suggested slowly.

'What do you mean?'

'I mean, what if someone's been getting newbloods

hooked on Stacy Serum, the ultimate high – so they can control them through it!'

Stacy shook her head. 'I haven't been able to make the stuff in that kind of volume. We weren't ready—'

'Woollard was ready,' Kate said quietly, holding out a small sheaf of papers. 'Top sheet's a fax from Takapa. Ordering Woollard to go ahead with producing the serum in serious volume. It's like he's got some kind of distribution network going—'

'Give me those.' Stacy snatched the papers from her and scanned them. 'Sweet Jesus, it's true.'

'Your 'wolf informants must be in the pay of Takapa,' Kate realised. 'Telling you what you want to hear.'

'So I keep on handing out the drug,' Stacy concluded, tears in her eyes. 'There's me, thinking I'm refining it – but I'm only helping Woollard make it even deadlier.'

Kate nodded. 'Then he just goes and turns a whole load of the stuff over to Takapa to infect *more* street kids.'

Stacy put her head in her hands. 'Shit, Kate, who knows how many 'wolves there could be hiding in this city.'

'All of them more violent and aggressive than any pureblood could imagine,' Kate agreed. 'But being forced to fight each other to the death, just because Takapa wants them to.'

Stacy was practically tearing her red hair out by the roots. 'But we still don't know *why*. Why would he build up 'wolves in such numbers and then decimate them?'

'Swagger told me that some time soon, 'wolves

would be a dime a dozen. It stands to reason that not all of the kids he turns would be fighters, so he's wiping out the weak ones ... forcing them to fight for their lives – literally. He's promising them the drug in return for their service ...'

Stacy looked at her, horrified. 'You think he's breeding, what ... a lupine militia? An unofficial army, ready to fight humanity?'

Suddenly, a bloodcurdling howl sounded somewhere close by outside. Both Kate and Stacy were on their feet in an instant.

A loud crash against the front door nearly knocked it off its hinges. They heard scuffles outside. Someone started banging at the door.

'The 'wolves,' Stacy whispered, fearfully. 'They know we're in here.'

The pounding at the door grew louder and louder.

Tom woke up and wished he hadn't.

It felt like someone had taken a red-hot chisel to his left shoulder and hammered it down into the bone. He was lying curled on his side, his whole body soaked with rain and sweat. And while the ground seemed soft he felt confined, caught in dark and cramped surroundings. He stirred and found something musty and scratchy was covering him from head to toe. An old blanket.

Memories of his ordeal seeped into his mind as he wormed his head clear of the covering. Everything was still black.

'Where am I?' he asked the darkness, afraid of what he might hear in reply.

'Quiet,' hissed a voice he recognised. Jasmine. He

whistled softly in relief but then a hand pressed down over his mouth.

It was Rico, crouched down beside him. Tom guessed he must be back in the stolen station wagon. But while he might be among friends, from the look in Rico's dark eyes, he was nowhere near safe.

Rico pulled the blanket back over him. Tom could hear footsteps passing close by. They faltered, came closer still – then moved away.

'Jeez, that was close,' said Jasmine. She emerged awkwardly from the footwell of the passenger seat where she'd been curled up tight and out of sight, and eased herself back behind the wheel. 'Cops. Still searching the area. Tom, you OK?'

'I'll live,' he muttered. 'Probably. What the hell happened?'

'You got shot,' said Rico, apparently impressed.

'Rookie cop,' Jasmine said by way of explanation, stretching her body in the driver's seat. 'You freaked him out. When he saw you were out cold, he ran to get his buddies. But we got to you first.'

'We heard where to find you on the radio,' Rico added.

'Bullet only nicked you,' Jasmine added. 'Don't think it's too bad.'

'Neither is this dressing,' Tom realised, pressing gingerly at the clean bandages binding his shoulder. 'Thanks.'

Rico shrugged. 'Took 'em from the drugstore. And Jasmine taped you up. Just like she used to tape up Ramone when he'd been fighting.'

Jasmine turned away. 'Shut your mouth, Ric,' she snapped, but Tom heard the tremble in her voice.

'You was always real good to him, Jas …'

Tom saw the pain and the anger in Rico's face, the tears welling in his black eyes. He put a hand on his shoulder. 'I'm so sorry, Ric.'

'Ain't gonna cry,' Rico said fiercely, brushing Tom's hand away, his breath growing hoarse and ragged. 'Gonna get even. Right, Jas?'

'You know it,' she said. 'Now, be good. Take your inhaler.'

'It don't work,' he complained.

'Do it,' Jasmine snapped. 'You gonna keel over before you get even with that mad bitch who did Ramone?'

His young, clear face still screwed up with emotion, Rico took two wheezy puffs on his inhaler.

'Thanks for coming after me,' Tom said. 'Thank you both.'

'Forget it,' Jasmine said distantly. 'With the guys gone, Polar turned 'wolf and Ramone … Well. Guess we got to look after the friends we got left.' She started the wagon's engine. 'And that means getting you to a doctor. I patched you up the best I could, but Woollard should take a look. He's got some good pills, they'll help with the pain.'

'But he lied to us about Stacy wanting my blood,' said Rico, rubbing his forearm.

'I'm not sure we can trust him,' Tom agreed, 'and neither is the man I met tonight.'

Jasmine cut the engine, looked at him gravely. 'The real Jicaque, right?'

'Right.' He winced as he tried to straighten his shoulder.

Jasmine sighed heavily. 'Well then, I guess we get

Stacy Stein to take a look.'

'And hook up with Kate at the same time,' Tom added automatically.

'Don't worry, Tommy boy.' She put the car in gear and pulled out into the dark, silent street. 'I ain't forgotten your sweetheart.'

Kate turned to Stacy as the banging on the front door grew louder. 'There must be a back way out of here?'

Stacy nodded. 'Let's find it.'

But as they reached the hall, they heard a frantic voice at the door rise above the banging: 'Stacy! I know you're in there – I can see your car outside. Let me in! He'll get me! I can't find my keys, let me in!'

'That's Woollard,' Stacy breathed, heading for the front door. 'He sounds terrified.'

Kate hung back in the hallway as Stacy fumbled with the door latch and finally got the door open.

Woollard shambled in on his knees, clutching his stomach, and pitched forwards. 'Dr Stein,' he gasped. 'How'd you get in here? Close the door, for God's sake.'

Stacy tried, but Woollard's legs were blocking the way. 'Help me, Kate!' she said.

Kate took the doctor by his clammy hands and dragged him forwards. To her horror she found he was leaving a thick trail of blood in his wake, a crimson stripe across the floorboards.

While Stacy locked the door and slammed the bolts home, Kate turned Woollard over as gently as she could. A large wound had been gouged in his flabby stomach.

'Knife.' He stared up at her with clouded eyes.

'Hurts. Get me a drink.'

She looked down at him and shook her head. 'We know what you've been doing. We know you've been working for Takapa!'

He nodded, and clutched at Kate's wrist with sticky red fingers. 'Takapa,' he rasped. 'Got all he can from me. I've made his dreams come true.'

'What are you talking about?' Stacy said angrily, coming to join them.

'Mass production.' Woollard smiled bleakly. 'Add just a single drop of Stacy Serum to a phial of ordinary blood plasma ... In under an hour, the blood is pure serum. Ready to go to work on another poor 'wolf junkie ...'

Kate pulled her wrist away in disgust, and Woollard winced.

'The serum is now as addictive as it can be,' he croaked. 'So Takapa thinks it's high time I was turned 'wolf too.' Woollard gave a weak mirthless laugh that turned into a cough. Blood appeared on his lips. 'It was the threat of that hanging over me that made me work for him in the first place.'

Kate looked down at him helplessly. 'Takapa did this to you?'

Woollard feebly shook his head. 'Still out there,' he murmured, wide-eyed. 'Tried to run, but—'

Suddenly there was a glassy crash from the living room. Before Kate or Stacy could react, the main light snapped on and a large shadow fell over them as a hulking figure appeared in the doorway.

'Oh, Jesus.' Kate shut her eyes; felt a terrible cold take her body. 'Please, no.'

Swagger stood towering over them in his long,

black leather coat. He must've ignored the bolted door and simply come in through the window as they had. His beady eyes were bloodshot and wild, his wide, crusty mouth hung open in a lascivious grin. A vivid gash ran across his forehead, clumsily stitched; the sutures looked like black flies feeding on the wound.

'Well, well,' he said, glancing between her and Stacy. 'Look who we got here.'

'Don't hurt me anymore,' Woollard begged feebly. 'Please.'

'You could've been something, Doc,' Swagger told him. 'Could've stood beside Takapa and me and welcomed in the new world. All you needed was guts, old man.' He giggled. 'Guess they fell out through that hole in your belly, right?'

Kate stared across at Stacy in dismay. Swagger was looking spaced out, euphoric, like Tom had looked on the bridge. 'He's taken the serum,' she hissed.

''S'right,' Swagger agreed, 'and I'm in the mood to party.'

Kate winced as he hauled her up by her hair. 'Liked you better with black locks, sweetheart,' he hissed. 'But it was sweet of you to make the effort for ol' Swag.' She tried to struggle free, but when he held the switchblade to her throat, still wet with Woollard's blood, she stayed very, very still.

'Now get into the examination room, Stein,' he snarled. 'Or this little prick-tease here's gonna be gargling blood.'

Kate held her breath. She could feel the muscles in his arm clenching, smell the rank odour of his sweat saturating his clothes. He kept shifting his weight between his legs like he couldn't hold still. The blade pressed harder against her neck as he marched her inside the examination room after Stacy.

'I got to get every piece of paper out of this hole,' Swagger told her. 'Takapa wants all his science research shit back. You got brains, pick it all out for me.'

Stacy nodded, cowed and pale, and started to collect together the scattered papers. Outside, Woollard was moaning softly in the hallway.

'Shame you had to find out about this, Stein,' Swagger snarled. 'Takapa likes you. You been good to us.'

'You tricked me,' she said quietly.

'We coulda gone on trickin' you, too. Used you a whole lot more and then given you the bite like your poor little hubby. But Takapa saw you watching when he was outside Ramone's with the doc tonight. Guess he could hear the penny dropping right the way across the street.' He giggled again. 'He said you'd come here. Said you'd work it out.'

Stacy finished collecting the papers and held them out to him.

He put the knife away so that he could take them. Kate let out a shuddering sigh of relief.

'Now, let her go,' said Stacy, trying to sound brave. And failing.

'Nuh-uh,' said Swagger. 'But you won't care, nohow. 'Cause now you gotta die.'

Stacy stared at him, speechless for a second, before his big fist crashed into her chin and sent her reeling back over the couch, where she lay still.

'No!' shouted Kate, but he tightened his grip around her throat, choking her off.

'Sure is cold out, tonight, ain't it?' laughed Swagger.

'Still, a little fire will warm us all up.'

Struggling and writhing in his grip, Kate was dragged out of the room. She saw Woollard feebly rocking on his back like an upturned tortoise.

'You ain't going nowhere, gutless,' Swagger shouted, pulling Kate into the living room. 'So, babe. Just you and me now, huh? Where's your freak boyfriend?' He clumsily folded the papers and put them in his coat pocket. 'I aim to have me some fun with him.'

'He's … he's left,' she croaked. 'Gone.'

'Like I believe you,' he said, pulling a cigarette lighter from his pocket. 'But if that little bastard *has* skipped town, I hope he said bye to his folks first. 'Cause Marcie's gonna make sure he won't get the chance again.'

'Where is she?' Kate asked fearfully.

'Yakking with Takapa now he's back in town.' Swagger held the oily flame up close to her cheek, and she flinched. 'But later, when it's nice and quiet, she's gonna creep up to Tom's mommy and daddy and …'

Kate gasped as he held the lighter flame to the thick curtains. The heavy fabric smouldered for a few seconds then caught alight. He crossed about the room, starting more little fires here and there, until the room was filled with dark smoke and eager, orange flames.

'Once a fire takes a hold of one of these old places …' Swagger whistled. 'They're gonna be using dental records to tell Woollard and Stein apart.'

'No!' Kate cried. She'd never felt more helpless as Swagger kicked the last glinting glass teeth from the window frame and carried her out through it. The cold night air fanned the flames, and soon smoke was billowing out through the broken window.

'You can't do this,' Kate sobbed, praying someone would pass by and see the flames, go for help. But the street was quiet and still; only the dreadfully familiar form of Polar stood close by, a silent spectre as ever, leaning back against a black car and viewing the spectacle through his camera. 'Swagger,' she tried again. 'For God's sake, let them go.'

'Nuh-uh.' He shoved her towards the car, and Polar turned and opened the rear door for her. 'But don't worry, baby.' Swagger leaned forward and hissed wetly in her ear. 'You'll be begging me to let you burn when you find out what I got lined up for you.'

# CHAPTER FOURTEEN

Tom saw the smoke the second they rounded the corner into Woollard's street. 'That's Woollard's place! Come on!'

'Firefighters are gonna be out in force here soon,' Jasmine warned him. 'The cops, everyone.'

'Then we'd better be fast!' Tom yelled at her. 'We don't know who's trapped in there!'

Cursing under her breath, Jasmine stamped on the gas and they accelerated down the street.

Tom berated himself for not agreeing to come straight here. He'd thought it safest if they all confronted Woollard together, and assumed that Stacy and Kate would be waiting at Ramone's. But they'd already taken off. Kate had left a brief note that confirmed the worst:

*Tom – if you're not OK I'll kill you. ;-) Gone to see Woollard*
  *K*

Just like her: she'd leave him a scribbled emoticon, but never so much as an x.

Jasmine found him some painkillers, and then they'd all headed over to Woollard's.

And found an inferno.

Jasmine hit the brakes and the wagon skidded to a halt on the wet tarmac.

Tom jumped out, looked at her expectantly.

'I'll stay here,' she announced, 'and you'd better be quick. When the cops come calling we're out of here.' Her pretty face softened. 'Don't take any risks you don't have to,' she added quietly. ''K?'

'OK,' Tom told her solemnly. 'Rico, you'd better stay here too.'

Rico said something noisy and probably very offensive in Spanish, and leaped from the wagon to join him.

A few night-owl neighbours across the street were staring in wonder from windows, but Tom didn't care who saw him now. 'Kate!' he yelled. 'Kate, are you in there!'

'Back way,' said Rico, racing toward the vacant lot adjacent to the house. 'Fire might not have reached there yet.'

Tom chased after him.

Rico was right. The flames hadn't yet reached this part of the building. The wood of the back door was slimy with mould. Tom thought of all Woollard's locks and bolts and mystical protections to keep the dark things out – and yet the shell of his apartment was so old and worn that it wouldn't keep out a determined field mouse.

With a couple of well-placed kicks, Tom booted open the door. Stinking black smoke choked out in his face. He recoiled, coughing and spluttering.

'Better leave this to me, Tom,' said Rico confidently. 'If you turn howler in there, you gonna burn your fur.'

And with that, Rico rushed inside.

'Come back!' Tom yelled, his eyes streaming. 'Rico!'

There was no reply. Tom dashed in after him, and found himself in Woollard's kitchen. He yanked down the yellow curtains from the windows and soaked them in the sink. Then, crouching down low where the smoke was less dense, he draped the wet curtains over his head and pressed on through to the passageway.

Woollard's body lay prone outside the living room. Tom felt his neck for a pulse.

So much for answers. He was dead.

Tom peered into the lounge. The fire was fiercest here. The arcane texts that papered the walls, the charms, the feeble garlic flowers, all were blackening to a charred mass. Glass cracked as a heavy frame tumbled from the wall to land at Tom's feet. He saw it held Woollard's doctorate, hard-won in a brighter time.

'Tom!'

His heart leaped; that was Stacy's voice, from across the passageway. Tom crawled from the room, the damp fabric heavy about his head and injured shoulder. He placed the doctorate beside Woollard's corpse as he passed by.

He squinted into the smoky room. Suddenly Stacy came into view, coughing, eyes streaming. Rico appeared just behind her.

'I woke her up!' he wheezed in triumph.

'Where's Kate?' Tom asked Stacy, handing her the other soaked curtain.

She took it and wrapped it around herself and Rico. 'Swagger took her.'

Tom stared at Stacy blankly, the flames and smoke suddenly nothing to him.

'We have to get out!' she shouted, grabbing Tom's arm.

Tom gasped at the wrench on his injured shoulder. The pain was enough to snap him out of his despair, sparking and strengthening his resolve. He swiftly led the way back outside, where they all three gulped down icy sharp breaths of the damp night air.

'Got your inhaler, Rico?' Tom asked.

The boy coughed thickly. 'Don't work,' he muttered.

'Take the damn inhaler,' Stacy barked. 'You think we want more trouble than we've got already?'

A distant wailing carried to them over the gloating roar of the flames as they consumed more and more of the apartment. Sirens.

'We may not want it, but here it comes,' said Tom huskily. 'Let's get out of here.' He led the charge back around to the front of the building to where Jasmine waited.

The streets in the neighbourhood were crawling by now with fire trucks, cop cars and ambulances, blue lights blinding the night, sirens screaming past.

'Close,' Jasmine remarked when they'd stopped at the next lights. She was half-smiling at Tom, her dark eyes suggesting approval.

'Too close,' he agreed. 'But we were too late to help Kate.' He felt sick inside, and utterly helpless.

'You shoulda seen it in there, Jas,' Rico chirped from the back seat.

'Rico was fantastic,' Stacy said with feeling.

'Dragged me off the couch and on to the floor where there was less smoke. Helped bring me round.'

Rico shrugged. 'Wasn't nothing.'

'OK, heroes!' Jasmine called. 'Where the hell am I driving?'

'To the ice arena, I guess,' Tom said grimly. 'That's where Swagger and company will be. And Kate.'

'I'd better tell you what happened at Woollard's,' said Stacy.

There was silence in the wagon as Stacy told her chilling story.

Tom's heart sank like a rock as he heard how Kate had been dragged away, kicking and screaming. 'So Takapa's back in New York, and Marcie's come to join him. Whatever his plans are, they must be close to coming together.'

'Midnight, Friday,' Jasmine recalled. 'Swagger said he wanted us all to check his dumb skating rink at midnight on Friday to swear allegiance or whatever.'

'Something must be going down,' Stacy agreed, checking her watch. 'And we're four hours into Friday already.'

'Screw Takapa.' Rico pouted. 'What about Kate?'

'My thoughts exactly,' muttered Tom.

'Reckon Swagger's ...?' Jasmine sounded kind of awkward for once. 'Well – d'you think he'll have killed her?'

'I don't think so,' said Tom, praying he was right. 'Otherwise, why not kill her at Woollard's? And both Marcie and Takapa want her pretty bad.'

'This Takapa's a son of a bitch,' Stacy said. 'From what Kate has seen, it looks like he's breeding his own militia.'

'Nice thought.' Tom shook his head. 'Just imagine. Kids off the street, all the flotsam and jetsam of a city ... trained like soldiers to fight and to kill, but with the strength, the speed and the senses of a werewolf.'

'I don't want to imagine that,' muttered Jasmine with a shiver.

'Better still, they're all hooked on a drug so addictive they'll follow any command to get it,' sighed Stacy. 'All thanks to me: dumbest bitch on the East Coast.'

'I met dumber,' Rico piped up matter-of-factly.

'Oh, God.' Stacy clapped both hands to her face. 'I just remembered. I was so out of it, I can't be sure, but ...'

Tom frowned. 'What?'

'Swagger. I heard him say, Tom, after he'd hit me, while I was whacked out on the couch ...' She looked at him, and bit her lip. 'I'm sure I heard him say Marcie Folan was going after your parents – later tonight.'

Tom felt his world fall away. He tried to speak but the words withered up at the back of his throat. 'That evil bitch,' he managed to croak. 'She's taken so much ...'

'Well, I've taken a whole bellyful of *her*,' said Jasmine fiercely, taking a corner. 'She ain't hurting nobody else.'

'We know where his mom and dad are,' chirped Rico. 'It was on the cop radio. First Western Hotel, over on Madison, room 3003. We could go get them. Pick them up.'

'And do what?' Tom said bitterly. 'Tell them their son's a werewolf? And that the woman they think is another poor grieving parent is actually planning to tear them apart?' His voice was rising higher. 'You think they'll buy all that? Sure! "Oh, sorry, son, we thought you were just a murderer, not the freakin' 'wolfman!"'

Jasmine placed her hand on his arm. 'OK. Enough, Tom. Come on, cool it.'

Tom massaged his temples. He felt exhausted, and his shoulder was still throbbing, setting his whole spine on edge. 'I'm sorry,' he muttered.

''S'all right, Tom,' Rico told him. 'I know you ain't mad at me.'

'We need a proper plan,' said Stacy. 'We need to think about this.' She shut her eyes, and started muttering to herself.

Rico watched her, intrigued.

'That brainy stuff might work, sure,' said Jasmine quietly, seriously, as she pulled up at the next set of lights. 'But, seems to me you gotta fight fire with fire.' She shot Tom a dark look. 'Know what I'm saying?' She held open her jacket. Protruding from her jeans pocket, glistening black, was the handle of Ramone's gun. She must've grabbed it from the hangout.

Tom stared at it, framed against the creamy brown skin of Jasmine's midriff.

'I've got an idea,' Stacy announced.

Jasmine let her jacket hang back down, hiding both the gun and her bare flesh from sight. 'So do I,' she muttered, her eyes wide and maybe just a little scared, holding Tom's.

The ice arena looked no more appealing by starlight than in the cold, grey light of yesterday's dawn. To Kate, its squat, rounded shape gave it the silhouette of some giant black beetle hunched over the land.

Swagger was half-dragging, half-carrying her through the rubble-strewn parking lot, away from the main entrance. 'We're taking the back way,' he informed Polar, who followed on mutely behind. 'Hell, will you dump that camera, man? You look like a friggin' retard.'

Polar reluctantly lowered the camera.

'You could pick up some tips from Polar, Swag. You'd look a whole lot cuter if we couldn't see your face,' Kate goaded him. 'And just why are we skulking into your sleaze palace the back way?'

'I don't want no one seeing you come in,' he told her. ''Cause ain't no one seeing you come out again.' He passed Polar a key to open the heavy padlock on a set of mouldering fire doors. Then Swagger yanked them open and forced Kate inside.

They were in the arena's cavernous locker rooms. The stench was worse than the last time she was here; sweat and urine and stuff she'd rather not dwell on. She soon learned the reason why.

The place had been converted into a kind of holding area. All around, people were gathered in groups, slumped on the floor or against cracked tile walls. Their eyes were glazed, their bodies stiff and lifeless. They were being held in crude pens fashioned from welded fenders, girders, bits of scrap iron – presumably anything Swagger's thugs could lay their hands on. A bucket made do for a toilet. The damp concrete floor was their table, littered with assorted fast food debris: empty buckets of chicken, burger wrappers, soda cans.

It was like a detention camp for all the poor souls Swagger and his kind had snatched from the streets.

Polar stood beside Kate, looking down at his scruffy sneakers as if trying to blank out the rest of his surroundings.

'Why are you keeping these people here like this, Swagger?' she demanded.

'They won't be here long. Arrived last night. Winners of the national heats, shipped in from all over the country.' He tightened his vice-like grip on the back of her neck. 'My gladiators. Ready for the big rumble. Midnight tonight.'

Kate shivered. 'That's when you wanted Ramone's gang to come here.'

'That was the plan.' He sniggered, and clapped Polar on the back. 'I like my troops to be well-fed before battle.'

'So anyone who won't take the bite becomes the pre-match snack, is that it?' She glared at Polar beside her. 'And I guess *you* decided you'd rather chow down yourself than be part of the meal.' Then she paused, as the full significance of Swagger's words sank in. 'Troops? Gladiators?'

Swagger leaned in close, nuzzled his big greasy nose in her ear. 'They're here to prove themselves, see? Only the strongest, the fiercest, have a place in Takapa's private army. He's been recruiting in a dozen states, and the big face-off is right here – with me presiding. This is where we build the real crack force, right here, in New York ...'

'Crack force?' Kate snorted. 'Crackheads more like.'

Swagger was oblivious to her scorn. He spun her around to face him. 'They'll fight for me, *die* for me.'

'Not for you,' Kate argued. 'For the drug you've tricked Stacy into creating. Once they're hooked on that filth they'll do anything for a fix.'

'That's right. And only the strongest will live.' His eyes shone as he stared into the distance, and Kate was glad she couldn't see what he was seeing. 'We gotta make fighters out of this scum, gotta make them the best. So we gotta *keep* them fighting, see? Make them faster, sharper, meaner. Strip out the weak till we got us an unbeatable army, ready and waiting ...'

Without warning he snatched the camera from Polar's hands. The carry strap snapped and Polar gave a weird, high-pitched squeal, like he'd lost a piece of himself. Swagger opened a locker, tossed the camera inside and turned the little key in the lock. Then he threw the key into one of the pens.

'You're watching *her*, now,' Swagger told him. 'With your own eyes, not through a lens. Retard.'

Polar slumped his shoulders, and slowly nodded.

Some of the people in this makeshift prison were roused by the clang of the locker door slamming.

'You bringing us the stuff?' a man called, and one by one the others began to rise and take up the call. Some even got to their feet, hanging from the rusty bars of their cells, first angry and threatening, but soon pleading and pathetic. All clamouring wildly and violently for their fix.

'They can shout all they want.' Swagger shoved Kate out of the locker room into a grimy reception area. 'But they'll just have to wait. When they wait, the kick's even better ... and the fighting's so much sweeter.'

Kate massaged the back of her neck, turned to face

him. 'You're sick.'

Swagger dropped his voice to a stage whisper. 'You might want to keep real quiet, now.' He turned to Polar. 'Watch her.' Then he disappeared around a corner.

Kate heard him knock on a door.

'Well?' came an imperious voice, a hint of something European in the accent. Kate recognised it at once, and it chilled her. Takapa.

She heard Swagger open the door and go inside. This was it then. Takapa would come out of his office now and find her. She glanced at Polar. He was looking back towards the locker room, thinking about his camera, no doubt. If she could catch him off guard ...

She took a slow step towards him but he caught the movement, whirled back around, and slowly shook his head.

'Stein and Woollard are dead, sir,' she heard Swagger announce. 'I burned 'em, along with any remaining evidence.'

Now Kate heard the rustling of papers.

'Ah, my documents,' purred Takapa. 'Invaluable research. The fruits of which shall quite transform this feckless human society.' He paused. 'With Stein dead, you can liberate the remaining serum from her offices at the hospital. Our fighters must be well-fed.'

'Already arranged, sir,' Swagger reported. 'Kes is dealing with that now. Serum supplies to be dished up at eighteen hundred hours.'

Takapa sounded amused. 'Meagre rations, I trust. Then we'll leave them to simmer for six hours. Their aggression levels will remain high and their cravings will be at their most extreme. Excellent, General Swagger.' His voice suddenly hardened. 'Now, have you found the wereling and the Folan girl?'

Kate shut her eyes, held her breath.

'Not yet,' said Swagger. 'But I got people working on it. I'm expecting news soon.'

A reprieve? Why was Swagger risking his own life with a lie that size? Kate bit her lip, more scared now than ever. There could only be one reason.

Swagger had his own plans for her.

'Marcie Folan is resting now in my private suite,' Takapa said. 'If the wereling is not found, she intends to inflict damages on his parents at dawn to draw him back out into the open.'

'I know that. She told me herself, coming back from Gun Hill.'

'It would be ... good public relations if we could spare her the risk and the bother and find him first.'

Kate looked imploringly at Polar, his face a dark shadow beneath his hood. 'Let me go,' she mouthed. 'Let me warn them!'

He didn't move, stood still as a statue.

'Make no mistake, we still want that wereling, Swagger. He has much to contribute to our plans.' Takapa paused. 'And *I* want the girl. Her own contribution shall be sweet indeed.'

'Understood, sir. If she's still in the city, we'll find her.'

Kate heard the sharp tap of Swagger's heels clicking together, then his heavy footsteps before the door closed behind him.

A second later he was back, his gargoyle grin large on his heavy face. 'Why, there you are now!' he whispered. 'Ain't that a surprise.'

Kate took a shuddering breath. 'What are you going to do with me?'

He just smiled, and took another step closer.

# CHAPTER FIFTEEN

'Coast's clear,' whispered Jasmine.

Tom followed her stealthily across the hotel lobby. It was five-thirty a.m. The night receptionist was on the phone, her long hair hanging down over her face. She didn't notice them tip-toe into the large elevator. Tom held his breath until the heavy brass doors closed, and their upward journey was underway. His palms were slick with sweat but his mouth was dry.

Jasmine was staring into space, cool, placid and serene. Like she planned this kind of thing every day.

Stacy had come up with a good plan, brilliant, even. But no matter how clever, it was another stop-gap measure; more time spent hiding in the dark till the bogeyman went away. And Marcie Folan wasn't going away anytime soon – unless they made her.

As the elevator crawled up to the thirtieth floor, Tom had never felt so alone. No one but Rico even knew they were here. Good old Ric. Together with Stacy, he'd saved Tom's parents' lives, at least for now.

Tom sorted through the night's feverish memories.

'Here's what we do,' Stacy had announced in the back of the wagon. 'I'm a virologist. So, if we get Tom's parents to the hospital, I can fake an outbreak of something nasty and highly contagious, and have them placed in isolation. That way, *no one* can get to them.'

'But your colleagues, other medical staff,' Tom argued, 'they'd question your diagnosis the second they looked at them.'

'Careful management, Tom. Blind eyes and sympathetic ears,' Stacy said. 'If I call on the right people, we can have your mom and dad transferred to another hospital out of state, no questions asked.'

'You gonna tell his momma and papa about the howlers?' Rico was wide-eyed. 'They be locking *you* up for being crazy.'

'All they need to know for now is that Tom's OK, that he's not a murderer, but that their own lives are in danger.' She looked at Tom. 'I'll leave you to explain to them what else you feel you can.'

'I can't see them.' Tom shook his head. 'Can't face them. Not until this is over. Not until ...' He broke off, swallowing back the threatening tears. 'Damn it, where's Jicaque vanished off to? He's supposed to be helping us ... and what's happening to Kate?'

'One thing at a time, Tom.' Stacy put a comforting hand on his shoulder. 'And if Jicaque's all you say he is, he'll come through for you.'

*We'll see,* Tom thought.

He had written a note to his parents on the back of a postcard, telling them to go to Park East Hospital and ask for Stacy, and not to tell Marcie or Hal Folan where they'd gone. Never to speak to them again. Asking them to trust him.

Once Jasmine had dropped Stacy at the hospital to make the necessary arrangements, they'd driven over to the First Western. First, they'd sent in Rico on a commando-style mission to slide the postcard under the Andersons' door.

Then they'd waited.

Tom's heart had lurched in his chest when he saw his mom and dad emerge from the hotel ten minutes later. They jumped in the back of a yellow cab and drove away. 'We did it,' he breathed. 'Marcie can't get them.'

'For now,' Jasmine added. 'I don't have no mom or dad, Tom. But I want you to hang on to yours.' She tapped her hip where the gun was hidden. 'Let's go. Ric, wait in the car.'

'Aw, Jas,' Rico complained. But she gave him a stern look. He made a face and nodded reluctantly.

Quickly, quietly, Tom and Jasmine walked towards the hotel's reception ...

*Ping.*

The elevator's electronic chime jarred Tom from his memories. They had reached the thirtieth floor.

'Let's finish this,' muttered Jasmine.

The corridor was quiet. Jasmine soon picked the lock on room 3003, and Tom followed her inside.

The moment he breathed in the still-lingering smell of his dad's deodorant, a wave of almost unbearable homesickness overcame him. His mom's clothes lay strewn on a chair. The same suitcases they'd taken to Seattle, where the whole nightmare had begun, were stowed beside the TV in the corner of the room.

Tom felt hot and flushed, and opened the window a fraction. Then he sat heavily on the king-sized bed.

Jas joined him, saying nothing. She took the gun from her pocket and turned it around in her hands.

'You ever use that on someone?' he asked.

'You kidding me?' She shot him a dark look. 'How's that shoulder of yours?'

'Hurts like hell.'

'Just a scratch, Tommy-boy. Just a scratch. You ever seen someone shot dead?' Jasmine's voice trembled a fraction. 'I did once. This guy I knew? He was shot in the guts ... He was kind of crazy, but he had this great smile, you know ...' She sighed softly. 'So much blood when he got shot. Everywhere. We couldn't stop it. We watched him die for hours and hours, too scared to do jack shit, too scared to go to the cops ...'

'Who shot him?' Tom murmured.

'The guy's best friend,' said Jasmine, weighing the gun in her hand. 'They'd ripped off some gas station, got really high. Tried to split the cash between them fair and square, but they couldn't count straight ... started fighting over a ten-dollar bill or something.' Her voice was drained of all emotion. 'And this guy I knew with the cute smile ... he lost the fight. His whole life just bled out of him over this dumbass ten bucks. 'Cause his dumbass friend had a gun like this one, loaded and ready to go.' She looked at him. 'Kind of a waste, don't you think?'

Tom just nodded dumbly.

Jasmine kept talking, her voice dull like the sheen on the black metal of the gun barrel. 'Looks kind of cool, don't it? In the movies and stuff, I mean. And these punks, they think all they got to do is pick up a gun and suddenly they're a real man. Puff got a hold of this one. Got it from some guy over in Queens ...' She passed it to Tom. 'Don't look like so much, does it? But one shot from this and ...'

He looked at her. 'Murder?'

She shook her head, and when she spoke again she sounded fiercer than he'd ever heard her. 'Not if you use it against this Marcie bitch,' she said. 'That bitch that killed Ramone. That bitch who thinks she's gonna kill your parents here tonight.' She passed him the gun. 'This ain't a murder. It's an execution.'

'An execution,' he echoed. 'I guess, I guess I should do it.' He still felt the tingling traces of Stacy's serum in his veins. Was that why he was going along with this? A few months ago, just holding a gun would've freaked him out. Now he found himself lifting the gun, aiming it at the door, curling his finger around the trigger, picturing Marcie coming into range ...

Jasmine had picked up a picture from the bedside table. Mom's side, he guessed.

'Look at you,' she murmured. 'And who's the cute kid?'

'My brother, Joe.'

'He ain't staying here?'

'Guess he's at Aunt Rachel's or something.' Tom wiped wetness from his eyes.

Jasmine put the photo back on the table, shifted a fraction closer to him. 'You must miss your folks real bad.'

'I do.'

'Never had much family myself. Hanging with Ramone, Puff, Ciss, Ric ... that was my family.'

Tom nodded. 'And the 'wolves ruined everything.'

'For the both of us.' She slapped her hand down on his, jokily. 'But hey, we're still standing, ain't we? Or sitting, anyway.'

She wasn't moving her hand away. It was cool and reassuring on top of his own.

'I guess you just have to get through stuff in life,' Tom ventured. 'You have to adapt, you know?'

'Oh, yeah. I know all about adapting.' She looked at him with an intensity that made his skin tingle. 'First time I met you, I thought you was a real pussy. Then I thought you was the big, bad 'wolf, some scary howler spy or somethin'. But I've been watching you, Tommy-boy. Stuff you've done. The way you handle yourself.' Her fingertips were caressing the rough skin on his knuckles. 'And I want you to know, I'm impressed.'

He shrugged. 'I've been lucky, that's all.'

She laughed softly. 'Boy, you don't know what lucky is.' She leaned in closer, angled her face towards him. 'Do you wanna know?'

Jasmine pressed her mouth against his.

Tom felt a light flick of her tongue, found himself responding. Suddenly they were caught up in a hot, wet kiss. Tom's thoughts were scattered and lost. All he could feel was the heat of the kiss buzzing through him, the sweet smell of Jasmine's sweat, the taste of her tongue snaking around inside his mouth. He went to slide his arms around her – and felt the gun, cold and heavy in his right hand.

He jumped away like a shock had bolted through him.

Jasmine stared at him, scared and vulnerable. 'What? What'd I do?'

'I can't do this,' he muttered.

In a blink, the old, hard look was back, set on her face like a mask. 'What, you suddenly got religion or something?'

'This isn't who I want to be,' he said. The gun

195

weighed heavy in his hand. 'The guy you think I am, the stuff you like about me … that's the stuff I hate.'

'Sure,' she said coldly. 'I guess that's why you hang with Kate. Nice, clean, smart shoulder to cry on, huh?'

'No, it's not that,' he protested. 'I … I'm sorry.' He turned away, placed the gun on the dresser.

'You having second thoughts about that too?'

He closed his eyes. 'I know it's the only way to be free of her and Takapa. To protect the people I love.'

'Like Kate?' Jasmine said quietly.

Tom didn't answer her.

He heard Jasmine rise up from the bed and walk to the door. 'I'll be waiting outside with Ric,' she announced, her tone as cold as the night air gusting in through the window. 'When she comes in … just don't miss.'

The door clicked shut behind her.

Tom sat on the bed, one hand on a little pile of his parents' clothes, one on the gun. He registered that the sky was starting to lighten, but his attention was fixed wholly on the closed door. The minutes stretched by. His shoulder ached. A part of him ached for Jasmine to come back. To feel someone beside him, to help him do this thing he knew he—

There was a scratching, scraping sound at the lock.

Tom jumped up from the bed.

The doorknob was turning, very slightly, very slowly.

He held the gun in both hands and aimed it at the door.

The door jumped a fraction as the catch released.

Tom held his breath. Gritted his teeth. Checked his grip on the gun. Felt his world start to tilt as the door swung open, slowly, so slowly …

The dim light of the breaking dawn was enough to cast only the faintest of shadows. But Tom still caught the movement behind him.

He whirled around. Someone big and ugly was standing behind him, his fat fist swinging towards Tom's face.

Then the world jarred into blackness.

For Kate, the hours were passing slowly and uncomfortably in claustrophobic darkness. Swagger had forced her inside a cramped locker. There was no room to move, and her long legs were buzzing with pins and needles. It was hard to breathe; she had to sit with her mouth pressed up against the grille in the narrow door, snatching gasps of the foul smelling air. Her muscles ached with inaction, and she had to fight the rising panic that kept threatening to overwhelm her. What was he planning for her?

'Better keep quiet,' Swagger had hissed as he'd squeezed her inside. 'If you start screaming, remember your mom's right across the hall.'

It was impossible to tell how much time had passed. She'd been stuffed inside the locker around seven in the morning, and left for what felt like for ever. Swagger, or one of his men, had allowed her out twice for a few minutes' 'exercise'. What a joke. By the time she'd finished flailing about on the damp floor trying to ease the cramps in her arms and legs, they were ready to bundle her back inside. Her back throbbed with pain, her head was splitting; this was torture, pure and simple, but she was damned if she would let Swagger see how much she hurt.

What was he going to do to her? Was this just some sadistic payback before he handed her over to Takapa? Or was he planning to have her himself? The cold thoughts rolled around till her whole head felt bruised.

Six o'clock in the evening had rolled around at last; she knew because Kes and the rest of Swagger's mangy generals had come to distribute little phials of serum – liberated from Stacy's labs? Or had Takapa brought his own supplies with him?

In her darkest moments, Kate wished she'd been left behind in the blaze at Woollard's place; anything would be better than being trapped here in the dark waiting for the end to come. But as she heard the so-called gladiators moaning and screaming and fighting for their meagre fix of the drug, she found herself counting her lucky stars that she wasn't amongst them.

That relief had soon passed, of course. As the hours edged on towards midnight, she felt she was going out of her mind, trapped like this, unable to sleep or stretch or—

Suddenly, she saw Polar come creeping cautiously into her narrow field of vision. 'Please,' she whispered. 'Let me out, Polar. Just for a minute. *Please!*'

He hadn't come to see her. He was pulling at the lockers lining the adjacent wall. Of course, looking for his camera. But Swagger had thrown away the key …

'Hey! Kid!' Kate squinted through the rusting grille. A skinny woman was beckoning to Polar from one of the makeshift pens. Her bleached hair was greasy and matted, her eyes bruised and blue, and she was forcing a crooked smile. 'I think I got what you need.'

Polar turned to face the woman. She was tapping a tiny key against the bars of her cage. Polar immediately rushed over to get it.

But the woman snatched her hand away. 'What you gonna give me in return, sugar?' She smiled like she was trying to flirt, but it came out like a grimace. 'You got some more stuff? We need some … Just a little. You know you got it …'

Kate saw the woman's companions in the cage feign careful disinterest in what was happening. Saw them pass looks and shift subtly into crouching positions. 'It's a trick, Polar!' she yelled. If she could get some favour with him maybe—

But her warning came too late. He had reached in to the pen to take the key, and one of the men had grabbed his arm. Polar was yanked forwards and his head crashed against one of the cell bars. While he was held up against the door of the pen, helpless, the other men searched his pockets.

'He doesn't have any!' shouted a man in ragged clothes. He turned on the bleached-blonde woman. 'You dumb bitch, you said he'd have some.'

'How was I supposed to know?' she yelled back at him. 'He's one of them, ain't he?'

'We can hold him here,' said an Asian guy, 'threaten to kill him if we don't get more!'

Someone else in another cell started up. 'If you're getting some stuff, *we* should get some!'

Soon the call was taken up by countless others. The noise boomed through the cavernous room, making Kate's locker vibrate and rattle. She shut her eyes, clasping her hands over her ears.

'All right, simmer down!' Swagger looked like he'd come looking for trouble. 'What is this?'

'We want more stuff!' snarled the Asian guy.

'We'll kill your buddy here!' added the guy in the ragged clothes.

Swagger sneered around at his pet prisoners. 'You ain't getting nothin' more till you earned it.'

The blonde woman yanked Polar back against the bars. His head struck the metal with a low, melodious chime. 'We mean it!' she said, shaking, almost frothing at the mouth.

Kate watched the big man make a great show of thinking about it. Then finally he spoke.

'Go ahead. Kill him. Retard's next to useless anyhow.'

He turned and strutted over to Kate's locker, ignoring the cries and the clamour that greeted his words.

She shrunk back from the grille but there was nowhere to go.

He winked at her. 'Enjoy the show.'

As he moved aside she caught a glimpse of Polar, still pulled up helplessly against the bars, while the blonde and the rest of her cellmates beat his body like a punchbag, egged on by the other prisoners, screaming out their frustration and rage.

She waited for Polar to transform, to let loose his 'wolf. But maybe they'd hit him too hard, too quick. He only broke his silence with a long, loud scream of despair that twisted her guts.

Kate turned away, shaking uncontrollably. How long now before she was thrown to these animals herself?

# CHAPTER SIXTEEN

When Tom became aware of the world again, he was tied to a chair in a dingy office. Fatigue viciously defined every muscle in his body. His head pounded like a deranged child was banging a drum in his ear, and he felt weak as a kitten.

Behind the desk in front of him was a pink-eyed, skinny man in a dark suit that emphasised his ghostly complexion. A silver helix earring snaked down from his only ear. His skin was cratered with acne scars, his white hair speckled out of his flaking scalp. He bared his sharp yellow teeth in a knowing grin.

'Takapa?' Tom croaked.

The man nodded. 'Here we are, face to face at last. You've been a tiresome strain on my resources, Tom Anderson. Thank you for allowing yourself to be captured so easily.'

'How did that guy get in through a window thirty storeys up?' Tom muttered.

'The platform used by the hotel window cleaners was fortuitously placed,' said Takapa smugly. 'Perhaps that's why Marcie booked that particular room on the Andersons' behalf.'

Tom felt disgusted with himself. 'I can't believe I didn't check the window,' he muttered.

'He and Marcie took you out of there in the same way so as not to arouse suspicion. But, come now.' Takapa rose from his chair. His suit hung baggily from his skeletal frame. 'I suspect you're relieved in a way, no? I don't think that you're a killer, Tom.' He smiled down at his captive, his watery eyes gleaming. 'I believe that if Marcie or myself had walked through that door, you could not have brought yourself to shoot.'

Tom flashed a big, fake smile back up at him. 'If you're that curious, how about we stage a reconstruction?'

'Then you'll be needing me.' The door swung open and Marcie Folan walked in. Like Takapa, she smiled down at him gloatingly, her skin taut over her cheekbones.

Tom felt a jolt of pure fear. Maybe he should try to bring on the change, try to escape. But he knew he was faced now by real adepts. They could change quicker than he could, and against the two of them he knew he wouldn't stand a chance.

'Forgive my intrusion,' Marcie went on. 'Say, Tom, how about we take the reconstruction back a step further – where are your parents?'

Tom looked away. 'Where you'll never find them.'

'Are you sure? You know how persistent I can be.' She took hold of his bruised chin in her bony fingers and forced him to look at her. 'And where is my dear daughter?'

He frowned, a spark of hope stirring somewhere inside. 'I thought *you'd* got her.'

'Did you indeed,' Marcie remarked icily, her dark eyes boring into him like she was trying to read his thoughts. 'Takapa, I do believe he's telling the truth.'

'We'll find her.' With his pink eyes, his short white hair and long narrow face, there was the look of a lab rat about Takapa. 'In the meantime, after the fun tonight, we'll ship him over to my Chicago headquarters, prepare him for experimentation.'

Tom yawned noisily. 'Didn't your stooges find out enough the last time you had me tied up?'

'*This,*' Takapa hissed, 'will be the last time. I can assure you of that.'

'I know what you want,' Tom informed him, trying to sound confident, hoping to catch them off balance. 'You're after the same thing as Stacy – lupine DNA. Once you've got that isolated, you can *really* refine her serum—'

'And make my army the strongest, the most vicious it can be. Bravo,' said Takapa dryly. 'But it's more than that. With the 'wolf factor fully synthesised and in my control, I can create a lupine toxin that will overcome the defences of even the strongest resister.' He tittered, adopted a scandalised expression. 'Everyone we bite will turn, no exceptions.'

Marcie nodded. 'Think how many humans Takapa's army will be able to bite in a single night.'

Tom didn't like to. 'And then what? You make sure they all take your super-addictive serum and get full control of them?'

'It's all in the marketing,' purred Takapa. 'Those who embrace the 'wolf will be told it makes them faster, makes their senses keener. Those who attempt to reject the 'wolf, well – we'll just sell it to them as a cure.'

Marcie smiled. 'There will be other poor dupes like

Stacy Stein, desperate to help these poor victims.'

'So the state gets flooded with random 'wolves …
and then the next state? And the next?' Tom looked at
Marcie for confirmation, and she nodded. 'Doesn't
that go against all the old-fashioned stuff about quali-
ty and purity that 'wolves like you believe in?'

'These street-trash 'wolves will be an inferior race.
Servants to the true breed – and through the drug,
dependent on us for everything.' She smiled. 'They
will do anything for their pureblood masters.'

'So that's what makes it acceptable to polite werewolf society, huh? A whole new race of soldiers and
servants.' He repressed a shudder. 'And you really
think the rest of the world will just sit back and watch
you create a Werewolf nation?'

'We are not fools,' said Takapa coldly. 'We are real-
ists. We shall start small. I am furnishing the next generations of 'wolves with the tools and knowledge they
will need if they are to flourish. I am going to unite
the 'wolves as never before.' He punched his fist into
his palm. 'It shall truly be *das Zeitalter des Werwolfs*.'

'Wolf time,' Tom translated. 'With the support of a
dried-up pureblood bitch and the stolen biology of
resisters like me and Rico.'

Marcie slapped him hard around the face.

Takapa leaned in close. His breath stank of raw
meat. 'Once I overcome the child's resistance, there
will be no human defence that can stand against me.'

'Oh yeah? Not even Jicaque?'

Takapa reacted angrily. 'That old crank is a spent
force. He is nothing.'

'So why do you flare up even at the sound of his
name?' asked Tom mildly before turning to Marcie.

'And why did you frighten him out of New Orleans with death threats? Just for laughs?'

'You are a rare creature, Wereling,' Takapa said smoothly. 'Your dual nature is near perfectly balanced; you draw on the best of your humanity and the best of the 'wolf. Once I have cracked the genetic code that allows you to do this, I shall use it to enhance the natures of the most loyal soldiers. They shall mate with pureblood females and sire a new breed, more powerful, deadly and more numerous than ever.'

Tom looked away. 'Spare me the global domination bullshit. You're crazy.'

'No he's not,' said Marcie coldly. 'And Kate will help us in that task. Yes, I feel she will be a most fertile 'wolf mother over the coming years. However loudly she howls about it.'

'You'll have to find her first,' Tom taunted.

'I will,' Marcie calmly assured him. 'Now, come, Takapa. My husband has been out searching for Kate, but he will be joining us shortly. We should prepare ourselves for tonight's celebrations. It's almost time.'

Tom noticed a clock on the wall. It was eleven o'clock.

In an hour, the slaughter would begin.

Despite the fear, despite the tension, Kate found herself catnapping in her tiny prison. She felt totally exhausted, feverish almost. When Swagger opened up her locker and dragged her out on to the floor, she barely reacted.

'Time to get you ready for your big night,' Swagger said quietly. 'Let's go.'

Two familiar henchmen, Shaun and Eric, hauled her

up without comment and half-carried, half-dragged her out of the locker room.

'You know, your daddy's come to watch the show, too,' Swagger informed her. 'Quite a reunion. Shame you'll miss out on it.'

Kate felt doubly dismayed. To know her father was condoning this horror ... Her mother had been psychotic most of her life; Kate expected nothing better of her — but her dad had always been cautious and careful. He hunted only sparingly, and had always tried to keep Marcie's bloodlust under control.

Often he'd failed. Perhaps now he had given up entirely.

'I thought about picking up where we left off,' Swagger told her lightly as they moved through the dingy corridors, 'but then I thought why should I give you pleasure when I could give you pain?' He flashed that macabre smile at her. 'Anyway, I know you got off on watching the fight before. So how'd you like a real ringside seat?'

Kate closed her eyes as fear crept back into her disinterested body. She didn't bother to ask his meaning. She knew she'd find out soon enough.

Swagger kicked open the double doors that led to the rink itself; this must be the same route she'd seen Eric lead the fighters down when she was here before. A dark, brooding atmosphere hovered over the quiet arena, a cold air of anticipation.

Between two of the many supporting pillars that ringed the periphery of the arena, a great length of chicken wire had been strung like a hammock several metres above the arena.

'What's this?' she asked.

'Your hiding place, sweetheart,' said Swagger. 'See, that wire net there's gonna hold the victory feast. Three hundred pounds of raw, tender meat fresh from the slaughter – spiked with serum, of course – and little old you packed in alongside.' He giggled like a kid. 'When Takapa calls the winners, my boys are gonna slash those supporting ropes and – WHOOSH! – down comes the food.'

Kate shuddered. 'And me with it.'

'You got the idea.' Swagger nodded.

'But Takapa needs me!' she argued desperately.

'You really shoulda been nice to me, sweetheart. I don't know what your mommy and the boss had planned for your pretty little ass, but they ain't never gonna get it now. 'Cause when you come tumbling out of that net, you're gonna be eaten up alive.' He laughed in her face. 'And what a beautiful sight it will be!'

'They'll know you did this,' she whispered. 'They'll kill you.'

'No they won't. They'll just think you were hiding out here, trying to find a way to rescue your little boyfriend Tom, when you got disturbed, ran for cover, got caught up in all this and – oh, dear …'

Kate tried to rise but her legs were too cramped. 'Tom's here?'

'I heard he really misses you.' Swagger wiped a make-believe tear from one of his piggy eyes. 'He's all cut up over it. Well – he's gonna be. Cut up in little pieces by the time Takapa's through.'

Swagger guffawed with laughter and looked at Shaun and Eric. They managed a couple of sycophantic sniggers, but turned at the sound of a whining electric engine getting closer. Some kind of forklift truck was coming slowly across the stained concrete, piled high with boxes.

'Meat wagon,' Swagger announced, with evident pleasure. 'We're ready to roll. Tie her up, gag her, then let's get her up there.'

Kate recoiled from Eric and Shaun as they advanced on her, but she knew she had nowhere to run.

Tom struggled against the ropes that bound him until his wrists were raw, and he was still no closer to escape. The situation seemed hopeless as the hands on the clock edged closer and closer towards midnight. He pictured Takapa and Marcie and Hal, her husband, talking and sipping cocktails upstairs together like VIPs, looking forward to their midnight arrival as guests of honour for the big fight.

A sound from outside startled him – a loud thump against the wall, then a dragging, sliding sort of noise.

The door handle turned. Someone was coming to get him. Tom braced himself.

Polar stood in the doorway, the hood of his black sweat top covering his face as ever, hands thrust in his pockets. Slowly he advanced.

Tom strained against his bonds but it was useless.

Then Polar crouched down in front of him. 'I told you not to miss, what the hell happened back there?' he said.

Only it wasn't Polar's voice.

The hood was shrugged off to reveal Jasmine crouched down in front of him. 'Well, dumbass?'

Tom slumped back in his chair with relief. 'A thug came in through the window.'

'Typical,' muttered Jasmine, roughly untying his knots.

He flinched as the ropes chafed against his raw skin. 'So, you and Polar swapped outfits or something?'

'Looks like Polar won't be wearing anything 'cept a bodybag,' she said brusquely. Now Tom looked more closely he could see dark stains stiffening the sweat top's material. 'We broke in through the locker room. Place was empty, he was just lying there, beaten up bad. Stacy said she don't care much for his chances.'

'Stacy's here?'

'Shit, we're all here, Tommy-boy.'

'Kate too?'

'Ain't seen her. But your Indian pal with the dumb name's here.'

He blinked in disbelief. 'Jicaque?'

'Uh-huh. Regular cavalry.' She regarded him sternly. 'D'you think I'd walk out on you, just 'cause you're a dumb jerk with no taste?'

He smiled to himself. 'Not for a second.'

'Good. Else you'd be a dumb jerk with no nuts, too.'

The ropes came free, and Tom gratefully massaged his tender wrists. 'Jicaque's here to stop the fight?'

Jasmine shrugged. 'Sure hope he's got somethin' planned. Him and the others are waiting in the lobby, out of sight. I came here alone – those asshole generals didn't take no notice of me dressed like this.' They crossed to the door and she indicated the unconscious thug who'd been guarding his door. 'Not till it was too late, anyway. Come on.'

As they sprinted down the corridor, Tom heard a plaintive *beep-beep* sound from Jasmine's wristwatch.

'Midnight,' she breathed.

Kate was almost glad of the thick tape over her mouth

– the consequences should she hurl right now was about the only thing keeping her turning stomach in check.

She was half-buried beneath a pile of raw meat. It was hard to breathe, but maybe that was a blessing since the stench was so disgusting. The feel of the cold, dead flesh on her skin was almost unbearable. Her clothes were saturated with rancid blood, and the weight of it all was crushing her against the chicken wire hammock, the cold metal biting into her back.

And now the gladiators were entering this cut-price coliseum, herded in by a handful of Swagger's goons armed with automatic weapons. The prisoners shambled in, two hundred or more, ranging from kids no older than Rico to bag lady types in their fifties.

Kate stared on in horror as the people split off into groups and took up position around the rink, some directly beneath her, facing each other in groups of twenty or so. They were silent, their sallow faces blank, their sunken eyes dark and burning. The armed guards ranged themselves around the rink. A spiteful charge was building in the air.

'Listen up, everyone.' Swagger's voice reverberated around the arena. 'Before we begin tonight's spectacle ... a few choice words from our glorious leader: Papa Takapa.'

There was no applause, no real reaction at all. A few of the fighters turned to gaze upon the man they were fighting for, the scrawny albino who stood in the front row of the bleachers beside Swagger. A few rows back, Kate saw her parents. She squirmed, tried to rock the hammock, to get herself noticed; she would do anything to delay the proceedings. But she could barely move beneath the mass of raw meat. No one was going to see a thing unless the people directly below looked up and saw her.

And if they did ... what would happen then?

'Greetings, my warriors,' Takapa said vaingloriously. 'You stand before me now because you have survived a number of trials by combat. Those who fight and triumph tonight shall rank as officers in my private army. You shall enjoy power and privilege. A place in the new order I am bringing to the lupine community.' He paused, impressively. 'In ancient Rome there were many kinds of gladiator. The Samnite, a helmeted warrior with sword and armour ... The Thracian, with his curved dagger and shield of bronze ... Retarius, the net fighter, a bloodied trident clamped in his hand ...'

Kate surveyed the motley crowd shifting impatiently about below her, muttering and whispering. They seemed unimpressed with Takapa's lecture. Perhaps he guessed this, because he cut it short:

'But you! You are a fresh breed of gladiator, a new invention. You have no weapons save your cunning and your savagery. No armour save the toughened hide of the magnificent creatures you can become. Fight well for me in your factions, and you shall no longer be caged, treated no better than animals. I will bestow honour on you, give you purpose. You shall be allowed to serve me and all our kind.'

Again, he paused, and this time the people in the arena stayed silent.

'I promise you blood!' he shouted, exultant. 'I promise you carnage. I promise you the future. Now – *fight*!'

No one moved. One or two of the guards raised their weapons threateningly.

Then Swagger rose to his feet. 'You want your next fix? Get going! Now!'

Had the Emperor Nero ever had this kind of trouble? Kate thought darkly.

But Swagger's practical threats clearly won out over Takapa's rhetoric. A few half-hearted scuffles were breaking out amid the different factions. Soon the skirmishes were escalating to full-on fistfights – and suddenly, just like in some bad Western movie, everyone was getting caught up in the fighting. Throughout the arena men and women were shouting, threatening, throttling, tearing into each other; just like she'd witnessed before, but on a much grander scale.

Then suddenly the wire mesh hammock supporting her lurched. She felt herself drop a fraction. One of the ropes lashed around the concrete pillars, securing the vast net in place, was giving way under the sheer weight of the doctored meat. It slipped again. The net tilted a little to the left, then a little more, threatening to ditch its haul.

If the hammock gave way completely she would plunge ten metres down into the heart of the bloody battle below.

# CHAPTER SEVENTEEN

Tom followed Jasmine down into the arena's dirty lobby. Stacy and Rico came out from behind a crumbling concrete pillar as they arrived. 'Are my parents safe?' he asked Stacy.

She nodded. 'And looking pretty perky considering the number of scary viruses they're carrying.' She fanned her face with her hand. 'It was looking kind of hairy for a while, but the plan worked.'

'When you didn't come outta the hotel, we knew the 'wolves had snatched you, so we went back to Park East,' Rico said, chewing noisily on some gum. 'There were all these weird guys there in, like, radiation suits or something.'

'Hazard squad,' Stacy explained. 'Your parents are isolated. No one can get to them.'

'Shame we can't say the same about us,' said Jasmine, looking around nervously.

'And while I was busy organising everything for them,' Stacy went on, 'some thugs ransacked my laboratory. Took all the serum samples I had.'

'I heard Takapa discuss it with Swagger,' Tom interrupted her. 'He and Marcie will be in the arena now. The fighting must've started. I *wish* I knew where Kate was.'

Stacy looked surprised. 'I thought she'd be locked up with you?'

'Takapa and Marcie said they were still looking for her. So either she escaped from Swagger or else ...' Tom sighed. 'Where's Jicaque? How'd you hook up with him?'

Stacy frowned as she stared about into the shadows that pooled thickly in each corner of the hall. 'He was waiting in my lab at the hospital – had to hide when the thugs came searching for the serum. He came and found me, said he was here to gather us together; that we would be allies for one final battle. But now I don't know—'

'I am here.'

Tom whirled around to find Jicaque standing right behind him, wearing a long dark overcoat over a shabby linen suit. His deep brown eyes seemed troubled. 'Tell me, Tom, have those poor souls caged in the locker room been given their fix of Stacy's serum?'

'I guess so,' Tom reported. 'They were due a dose at six.'

Jicaque nodded gravely. 'There will be terrible bloodshed tonight.'

'So what do we do?' Jasmine wondered aloud. 'I guess getting the hell out of here ain't an option?'

'Not without Kate,' Tom shot at her.

Jicaque nodded. 'We must get inside the arena. Stop this madness once and for all.'

'Nice thought,' said Stacy. 'Any practical ideas how we do that?'

But Jicaque had already turned on his heel and was striding away, his long silver hair trailing behind him like a comet's tail, his dark overcoat flapping about his ankles.

He led them along the dank corridor and up a flight of crumbling stairs. 'This leads to the upper tiers of the seating,' Jicaque informed them. 'The lower entrances are blocked to prevent any escape attempts by those forced to fight.'

The stairway ended in a set of peeling double doors. Beyond them, rising in volume and pitch, the unmistakable sounds of violent battle carried: shouts and crashes and shrieks of agony.

Jicaque tried the doors, but they wouldn't budge. Tom lent his weight, pulling on the handles with all his strength, but it was a hopeless task. The doors were locked firm.

'They don't want no one getting in, neither,' Rico observed, wheezing a little after taking so many stairs.

'You taken your inhaler?' Jasmine prompted him.

Rico pulled the puffer moodily from his pocket. 'I keep saying, it don't work.'

'Let me see it,' Jicaque snapped.

Rico produced the inhaler and Jicaque extracted the little pressurised canister from the plastic housing. 'Yes,' he muttered, 'that might just do.' He delved in his pocket and pulled out a few crumbs and lumps of some silvery-white powder.

Stacy watched him suspiciously. 'What's that?'

'Jicaque?' Tom looked at him uncertainly. 'Is that more of your magnesium?'

'Hair elastic,' Jicaque snapped, holding out his other hand.

Jasmine obliged him with a puzzled glance at Tom. 'Magnesium?'

215

Tom nodded. 'He powders the ends of cigarettes with the stuff. If he's in trouble he lights up and the magnesium blinds whoever's close by.'

'Cool,' said Rico happily.

Jicaque secured the white lumps to the canister with the hair elastic. 'Now, Rico, that gum you're chewing.'

Rico duly handed over the gum, and Jicaque used it to fix the little canister to the lock on the doors. But as he produced a disposable lighter from his pocket, Stacy snatched it away.

'You can't set light to that stuff!' Stacy said, appalled. 'That's a pressurised container.'

Jicaque shrugged, untied a string from one of his scruffy silver braids of hair. 'And these are locked doors. Any other suggestions?'

The grunts, the yells, the echoing thuds and crashes from the arena were getting louder and louder. Jicaque used a small gob of the gum to secure the short string to the magnesium.

'They're killing each other in there,' Tom muttered.

He nodded. 'We must act now.' Suddenly the lighter was out of Stacy's hand and back in Jicaque's. He struck the flints and a flame jumped from its end. 'Tell me Tom, have you heard of Chet Baker? Great jazz musician.'

Tom shook his head wearily. 'Is this the time for a history lesson?'

Jicaque shook his head disapprovingly. 'You haven't heard a trumpet till you hear Chet speak through it.' He paused, apparently transfixed by the smoky flame. 'You know, jazz is a lot like life. All a matter of timing.' He set the flame to the string, his makeshift fuse. 'Back down the stairs, everyone.'

Tom covered his eyes as the magnesium compound flared with blinding intensity. Jicaque shooed him away down to the turn in the stairwell to join the others.

With a deafening blast, the pressurised canister exploded. The echoes of the explosion slammed around the concrete walls, ringing in Tom's ears.

'So much for Rico's inhaler,' sighed Stacy.

'Guess it *does* work,' Rico said, a slow grin spreading over his face.

Tom peered around the corner. The doors were blackened; the lock had been punched right out.

'Now the danger truly begins,' Jicaque murmured. 'Who will stand with me?'

'I will.' Tom glanced around at Jasmine, Stacy and Rico. 'But maybe you guys should hang back here and—'

'Forget it,' said Jasmine.

'People might get hurt,' said Stacy. 'I can help.'

And Rico nodded too. ''S'time to get even.'

'Then let's go,' the old man said, moving off into the wreaths of smoke coiling from the charred hole in the doors.

Kate had finally managed to work her mouth free of the tape that gagged her. She bit and chewed at the knotted ropes that bound her wrists, trying desperately to free herself. All around the arena the fighting was escalating, far more slick and savage than the scrappy bouts she'd witnessed here before. Swagger was right; these people had been trained, conditioned to fight for their survival. The fighters worked with their team-mates, pitilessly targeting their victims. There was something feral about these men and women as they tore through the opposition, drugged-up and blank-eyed, that chilled Kate to the bone.

Across the arena, in the safety of the bleachers, she saw her mother watching rapt beside Takapa, palms pressed together as if praying the carnage would never end. Her father looked on at the spectacle impassively. If she could only signal to him …

She gasped as the mesh net lurched and dropped a little lower. Joints of meat went tumbling as the net tilted, and fell around the maniacs fighting below.

A woman looked up, wildly, as if suspecting an attack from above. It was the bleached-blonde girl who'd tricked Polar back in the locker room. Her eyes were gleaming yellow. Saliva flooded from her leering jaws as her body began to warp into lupine form.

Kate knew what a tempting target she must make, trapped here helpless, surrounded by a half-ton of bloody flesh; and she knew with horrid certainty the woman meant to kill her. Sure enough, with a frenzied roar the blonde leaped for the net, her broken nails extending into talons mid-jump.

The creature scraped against the chicken wire close to Kate's head, then fell back down. Kate realised she must still be out of reach. But for how much longer?

A man rushed to tackle the blonde before her metamorphosis was complete, pounding his fists down on her distorted face. But others had noticed the net was disgorging its bloody haul. And more and more of the fighters were starting to turn.

Kate bit at the knots in the rope with a new desperation. The net shook again and she saw another 'wolf had jumped up and was hanging from the thick chicken wire with its claws. But the metal soon gave way and the animal fell to the concrete with a thud, soon set upon by two more slavering, brutish lupines.

Then suddenly Kate heard a sharp, percussive crack. Before the echoes had died away, the entire arena seemed to shake with a single bellowed cry.

'*Enough.*'

The sound lashed around the arena like a steely whip.

The 'wolves slowed in their struggles then stopped altogether, panting hard, backing off from their private fights and scenting the air for this noisy interloper.

Swagger's guards patrolling the perimeter raised their weapons, hunting out the intruder through rifle sights.

Then Kate saw Tom standing at the top of the steps that led down through the bleachers, Jasmine, Rico and Stacy standing alongside him.

In front of Tom was a slight, silver-maned Native American man. All eyes, human and beast, were on him now.

'Please,' Kate muttered, shutting her eyes and praying to any god that might listen. 'Please, Jicaque, make this good.'

Tom stared in disbelief as the 'wolves in the arena overcame their urge to attack and paused in a sudden, uneasy truce, as if on some deeper instinct.

He felt sick with fear. There were so many of the creatures in here, trampling human corpses beneath their hefty paws as they milled impatiently around the blood-soaked rink. At any moment the violence might ignite again – and all that was stopping the 'wolves taking the fight out of the arena and into the bleachers were a few of Swagger's generals with guns. Guns that were aimed now at him and Jicaque, guns that would tear them apart in a single burst of fire.

Hal and Marcie Folan rose from their seats. Hal looked at Tom without emotion, but Marcie's lip kept twitching as she watched him, like she was about to bare her teeth. She kept glancing at Takapa impatiently; this was his territory, Tom supposed, and she was giving him a chance to handle the situation. How long before her patience was spent?

Takapa too had risen, his face contorting into odd expressions as he struggled to find an appropriate way to express his rage. He turned to Swagger. 'Get down there,' he said in a low voice, gesturing to the rink. 'Make sure that scum don't get out of hand. This won't take long.'

Swagger hesitated, glaring at Tom hungrily. Then reluctantly, he turned and strutted down the steps as ordered.

Takapa's pink eyes blazed furiously at Jicaque. 'You dare to interfere, old man?' he said hoarsely at last. '*Now?*'

'I have let your activities go unchecked for too long,' Jicaque said calmly. 'That was my mistake.'

'No. Coming here tonight was your mistake,' hissed Takapa. He looked past Jicaque to face Stacy. 'The rumours of your death are exaggerated, I see.'

'Don't look at me, I didn't start them,' said Stacy.

Takapa smiled, then gestured to the bloody rink, to the beasts that prowled there. 'But you started all this.'

'And maybe I'll help finish it,' she said fiercely.

As the exchange went on, Tom felt someone tug on his arm. Rico. He was pointing across the vast arena. Tom swore. Unseen by Takapa, Marcie and the rest, someone was balanced up on a mountain of meat hanging above the rink, waving furiously. 'Kate,' he breathed.

'I'll sneak down, try to help her out,' Rico whispered.

'Stay out of it, Ric,' Tom warned him. 'You're only a kid, you can't—'

'Watch me.' With that, Rico slipped into the bleachers to Tom's right.

Tom held his breath, but miraculously, it seemed no one had seen him go.

'You've played me for a fool, Takapa,' Stacy was saying.

'And it was so deliciously easy,' the albino murmured.

Tom kept a subtle eye on Rico's progress. He could see he was making his way down through the bleachers in a purposeful zigzag, heading for the rink.

'I suppose,' said Jicaque thoughtfully, 'that Dr Stein could be said to be the founder of the feast here.' His voice hardened. 'Such a shame for you that the feast is poisoned.'

Takapa narrowed his pink eyes. 'What nonsense is this?'

'The drug you have been synthesising, the means of controlling your rabid army here ...' Jicaque waved an angry hand at the teeming monsters in the rink. 'Your minions stole the doctored samples from Stacy's laboratory, and I guessed you would be using them tonight. So you see, before the supplies were taken, I did some herbal doctoring of my own to those samples.'

'Well, whatever you did, you wasted your time,' snarled Takapa. 'The contents of those phials were added to my own stocks of the drug.'

Tom held his breath as Jicaque went on.

'Excellent. Then I have contaminated your entire supply.' The old man smiled. 'I have neutralised the effects you sought to engender in these unfortunates you would have fight for you.'

Takapa was shaking his shaven head now in angry disbelief. 'No. You're lying,' he snapped. 'Are you blind? They *are* fighting for me!'

'As humans, sure.' Jicaque clicked his fingers. 'But now they have transformed to the lupine state, my remedial herbs are taking effect.'

Tom gripped Jicaque's arm. 'The cure? It's working on them now?'

'The first step of many – the restoration of human will. But I can only cure those who wish to be cured,' Jicaque reminded him. 'There are many here who relish the strength and power their 'wolf lends them.'

'It's a trick!' Takapa spat, with the fury of a cheated child. 'A filthy trick!'

'For your sake, Takapa,' hissed Marcie, 'it had better be.'

The albino raised his arms and fell forwards into a crouching position. His form seemed to blur and run like watercolours in the rain.

Tom flinched to see a lean, sinewy 'wolf suddenly facing them, eyes narrowed and burning with malice.

'A further mistake,' Jicaque announced calmly. 'In

that form, you cannot issue orders to your men.' The old man raised his voice, cupped his hands to his mouth. 'Hear me! This degenerate before me has sought to use you, to make you fight for his own callous ends. But now you are freed from the hold he has over you!'

With a roar of hatred the rangy white 'wolf arched its back and then pounced forward, jaws snapping for the old man's throat.

# CHAPTER EIGHTEEN

Tom shoved Jicaque out of the way. The old man staggered and fell between two benches.

Jasmine shrieked as Takapa landed at her feet. She kicked him hard in the head with her pointed boots. The werewolf growled, swiped at her with one massive paw, but Jasmine leaped for cover among the rotting wooden benches. Enraged, the creature moved to follow.

'Rise up!' Jicaque shouted at the 'wolves pacing the arena. 'Fight for yourselves, now, against the people who would use you!'

'All right, enough!' Marcie bawled. 'Swagger, kill him!'

Swagger didn't need telling twice. He opened fire, spraying the gangway with bullets. One by one his generals joined in the attack. Stacy dived for cover back through the double doors, and Jicaque huddled down behind the benches in front.

Takapa broke off his attack on Jasmine, staring around in confusion. Bullets whistled noisily through the cold air. But then the white 'wolf saw Jicaque in his hiding place, and readied himself to pounce once again.

'No!' Tom shouted and threw himself at the

creature, locking his arm around its sinewy throat. Takapa bucked and writhed, snapping at him, but Tom was just out of range of the monster's dagger-like teeth, and holding on for dear life. Finally Takapa threw himself into a full body roll. Tom couldn't hold on, and his bad shoulder smashed against the concrete of the gangway. He cried out in pain – then he heard a howl of anger. Dazed, he opened his eyes.

Jicaque was nowhere to be seen.

But the low growl, the bestial eyes narrowed in his direction, told Tom that Takapa had found a new target. He tried to pull himself away, but the 'wolf was preparing to spring.

'Get out of here, you fool!'

Takapa reacted to the voice as if stung.

Marcie was shouting at him. 'Come on! We can't fight them all!'

Takapa turned in confusion.

'My God,' breathed Tom.

A whole pack of werewolves had broken free of the confines of the rink. Swagger was no longer firing at Tom and his friends, but into the slavering mass of the enraged werewolves. The creatures were thinking for themselves now, acting on their own unfettered instincts.

And, clearly, they wanted revenge.

Marcie and Hal were running for an emergency exit to their left, pursued by eight or nine of the lupine monsters. With almost balletic grace, husband and wife dropped down to the ground and brought on the change as they fled.

Takapa roared in defiance at Tom one final time, then chased after them, hurdling the benches in the bleachers, a white blur disappearing into the shadows.

Tom nodded grimly as Hal and Marcie smashed through the emergency exit and vanished from view, Takapa close on their heels. But the cold rattle of more gunfire riveted Tom's attention back to events in the arena. The men were firing wildly; some of the beasts bayed in pain as the bullets tore into them. But there was no way Swagger and his generals could take them all. The 'wolves had been trained well, and now were using their skills as a team to slash their persecutors to ribbons.

Tom swallowed hard as he looked at Kate, still perched high on her mountain of carcasses. She waved with both arms, trying to be sure he'd seen her, and Tom waved back. But his stomach was churning. How could he get to her, caught between bullets and claws – and where was Rico?

Turning, he staggered over to Jasmine, who was shakily getting to her feet. 'You OK?'

'Sure,' she said quietly. 'I'm good.'

Stacy burst back in through the shattered doors. 'What happened to Jicaque, is he …?' Her hand flew to her mouth. 'Jesus. How long was I out?'

It was true, Tom reflected. In seconds, everything had turned around. Now, with Takapa and his honoured guests gone, scores of 'wolves were roaming the bleachers, howling and roaring their anger and frustration. Many more were feeding on the tough corpses of their fallen opponents – and the remains of the men with guns who had sought to control them. Swagger himself had either been killed or ducked out of the fighting, he was nowhere to be seen – but two of his surviving generals were standing back to back beside one of the supporting pillars, terror in their eyes, shooting at any lupine who came too near.

*I can only cure those who wish to be cured*, Jicaque had said, and clearly some of the 'wolves weren't ready to stop now. They craved more violence, more blood; a few ringleaders were snapping at their fellows, trying to pick up the fight like nothing had happened.

'Some of the 'wolves are changing back,' Stacy realised. 'They'll become targets for the others, just like we are.' She set off through the tiers of seating, heading for a young girl who stood naked and shivering, gazing around the arena in shock. 'We have to help them, get them out of here before the 'wolves notice them.'

'Maybe round them up into a group,' Tom called, and Stacy nodded distractedly. He guessed the thought had occurred to her.

And then Tom saw it.

The net supporting Kate had started to give way; it was sagging seriously at one end. Huge hunks of meat were tumbling into the arena, exciting the waiting 'wolves that paced below. But seeing their hungry eyes, Tom knew they craved soft, tender, wholly-human flesh.

Jasmine looked around, suddenly panicked. 'Where's Rico?'

'Trying to reach Kate,' Tom said worriedly, 'I couldn't stop him.'

Jasmine looked appalled. 'He'll get himself killed!'

'Work your way around the stands,' Tom told her, signalling the direction Rico took. 'I'll take the direct route.' He ran down the gangway, mercifully free of wandering 'wolves, picking up speed as he hurtled down the steps. He had to reach her, save her somehow before—

'Hey, freak,' shouted Swagger, jumping up from his hiding place near the front of the bleachers. He wielded his gun like a club and brought it around in a savage arc.

Tom couldn't stop in time. The weapon caught him under the chin and he fell reeling back with a yell of pain.

Swagger advanced on him, gun raised. 'Guess who?'

'The tooth fairy?' Tom spat out a thick gobbet of blood. 'Say, Swagger, are you out of bullets, or did you just forget how your gun works?'

'Don't need bullets for scum like you.'

Tom heard a whistling rattle as the wire netting holding Kate was attacked by another 'wolf. He knew he couldn't waste any time. 'It's over, Swagger,' he hissed. 'Now, get out of my way.'

'You and your dumb friends ruined everything!' Swagger bellowed, his scarred face livid red, the piggy eyes screwed up in rage. 'I was gonna *be* somebody. I was gonna count!'

'I don't have time for this!' Tom hurled himself at Swagger, hoping to overbalance him, but there was true madness in the thug's eyes now. His big hand closed around Tom's throat, and threw him flat on his back on the concrete.

'What's wrong with you? You fought good last night. You really hurt me, man.'

Tom heard Kate yell in alarm. He tried to get back up but Swagger pushed him back down to the ground.

'Now you're gonna hurt, too.' Swagger's crazed

eyes shone with malice. He adopted a child's sing-song voice: 'And so's your little girlfriend.'

'No!' Tom heard the guttural edge to his own voice, heard Kate scream again for help, felt the anger flooding through him. Swagger was laughing at him, his eyes burning yellow, his features beginning to bulge and twist into bestial forms.

'You took away everything I had that was good,' the big man said hoarsely. 'Now, ain't nothing left but the bad.' He crouched down in front of Tom. 'Wanna see?'

The big man was starting to shake. Thick, coarse blond hair was curling from his hands and face. His jaw extended outwards, his teeth began to curl out sharply from his red gums.

But the change was on Tom, too. As his fear, his anger, all those dark emotions pounded through his body and urged on the metamorphosis, he knew that this fight wouldn't be over until one of them was dead.

Now that she'd untied herself, ready for escape, Kate found she had precisely nowhere to go. She was clinging on to the remnants of the chicken wire hammock for dear life; it was hanging down almost vertically from the pillar. Many of the 'wolves, their anger spent and Takapa's hold on them broken, had ceased fighting; they were roaming about the stands, transforming back one by one into their human forms. Stacy was going to them each in turn, trying to give help and comfort.

The firing had all stopped now; the last of Swagger's henchmen had been split open by razor claws the second he ran out of ammo. But there was still danger in the arena.

229

Like the two lupines prowling around below her.

One was grey and wasted, the other bloated and black. The creatures were surprisingly single-minded amid the chaos in the rink; the stretch of wire just beyond her toes had been ripped clear away by their teeth and claws, and she doubted they were about to give up now.

Her fingers were red, the mesh biting into them so keenly she'd lost all sensation. She sensed the beasts beneath her willing her to give up, to slip and fall right into their drooling jaws.

Kate looked away, trying to blank them out, and saw Tom running towards her. She cried out in dismay as Swagger burst out and ambushed him.

Swagger. The good soldier left to carry the can while his commanding officer fled with his tail between his legs. But then, she didn't have Swagger figured as the type to give up gracefully; he was always going to take a piece of the world with him when he went.

Now Swagger was turning 'wolf, and so was Tom. Clothes split and fell away, bones bent and cracked as the metamorphosis ran its course. Finally, she was watching two animals warily circle each other on all fours; Tom sleek and well-proportioned, Swagger the biggest, mangiest 'wolf in the arena.

Tom's eyes had remained brown; he was his old self, the savagery of Stacy's drug out of his system. But the knowledge sent a spasm of fear through Kate. She knew now that if it came to a fight, Tom didn't stand a chance.

She swore as the grey 'wolf leaped up at her again. This time its jaws snagged one of her sneakers, wrenched it from her left foot. 'Get away from me!' she yelled.

Right. Like it would listen.

But someone had heard her.

'Hey, Kate!'

The hoarse whisper barely carried over the snarling of the two 'wolves, but Kate recognised the voice at once. 'Rico? Where are you?'

A small olive-skinned face emerged over the rink's crash barrier. 'Listen up. I'll lead those two away, you drop down and run like hell. Is it a deal?'

'Rico, get out of here!' she hissed. 'Get help!'

She saw Tom had tried to dodge past Swagger to reach the rink. But Swagger had moved with incredible speed, swiping Tom's hind legs from under him. He somersaulted through the air and splashed down hard in a puddle of blood.

'No!' she yelled. And her fingers were slipping. Below her, the 'wolves were licking their bloody chops in anticipation.

'Hey, boys,' a supercilious voice called. 'Either of you two got a light?'

Kate turned her head to find Jasmine leaning casually against the crash barrier, with three cigarettes clamped in her mouth. Rico was peeping out from behind her legs.

The grey 'wolf emitted a low roar at the sight of these new prospective morsels, and its partner's drool hung from its jaws in great sticky strings. They approached Jasmine cautiously, as if suspecting a trap.

But the girl was just standing there.

The beasts drew closer, *closer*.

And Rico passed her a lighter. 'Sorry, boys,' she said

coldly, 'I found one already.' She closed her eyes and placed the flame to the tips of the cigarettes – which flared like blowtorches.

The grey, skinny wolf gave a shrill, ululating howl and skittered away. But the dark one was enraged. It lunged forwards, jaws opened wide to take off her head.

Jasmine dodged, and stubbed the flaming cigarettes out on the creature's snout. It roared in terrible pain and bounded away, gnashing its teeth. 'I'm not running anymore!' she screamed after it. 'You hear me?'

Kate dropped down to the filthy concrete, half-blinded, her stinging fingers red-hot and numb. She tried desperately to blink away the bright blobs on her vision left by the light show. 'What the hell brand are those?' she gasped.

'Jicaque's self-rolled,' she heard Jasmine mutter.

'You stole 'em!' said Rico accusingly.

'Sure. I got light fingers, he got big pockets. Figured I could find a use for them smokes.'

But Kate was no longer listening. As her vision started to clear she saw that Swagger had batted Tom back to the ground. He looked a gory mess, his coat matted black with blood – how much was his and how much he'd rolled in she couldn't tell. Before he could get to his feet, the Swagger-wolf was on top of him, stamping down on his barrel-like rib cage. His sharp teeth raked a neat crimson line along Tom's throat.

Rico broke free of Jasmine's grip and raced across the rink to where the two 'wolves struggled.

'No!' Jasmine yelled. '¡Para, Rico! There's nothing you can do!'

Then everything seemed to be happening in slow motion.

Rico was sprinting across the bloody arena, his breath coming in short puffs, steaming into the icy air.

Kate and Jasmine were running after him.

Too slow.

As Swagger opened his massive jaws ready to scissor straight through Tom's neck, Rico shoulder-charged him. Swagger growled and snapped instinctively at Rico's arm, his teeth sinking easily into the boy's flesh. The sharp yellow teeth were soon bright red with blood.

Rico screamed with pain – but Swagger was howling louder. He spat the boy out, who fell lifelessly against Tom's flank.

The huge blond 'wolf twisted and writhed, his deep, bellowing roars modulating to high-pitched screams as he switched back to his human form in a series of sick spasms. It was like he'd swallowed acid and now it was burning its way through his entire body.

Finally he laid still, eyes dull and glazed, a thick white froth seeping from his cracked mouth.

As she ran to reach Tom, it dawned on Kate what she had just witnessed. Rico was a total-resister – the boy's blood was deadly poison to the 'wolves, that was why Stacy and Takapa had both treasured it so in their researches.

Swagger the man may have known that – but Swagger the 'wolf had seen just another piece of meat. All sense blinded by bloodlust, he'd been the final victim of his own violence.

But Kate's eyes filled with tears as she covered the final distance. Who had he taken with him?

# CHAPTER NINETEEN

Jasmine reached Rico a second before Kate did. She scooped him up from where he lay slumped against Tom's prone body. Rico's eyes were rolling back in his head, his arm was a mauled mess. That treasured blood was everywhere.

'Stacy!' Kate yelled, panting for breath. 'We need you! Quick!' Her voice echoed and re-echoed around the vast arena.

An eerie calm was settling over the battlefield now. The surviving 'wolves had either slunk away through the exits to freedom or else changed back to human form, huddling together in small groups among the corpses dotted around the arena. Stacy left one of the groups and began to move towards them. But she was on the far side of the arena ... how much time did they have?

'Shit, Rico,' Jasmine muttered through her tears. 'Don't you dare leave me alone. Don't do this. You hear me?'

Rico coughed, his eyelids fluttering like he was falling asleep. '¿Esta sangrando mucho?'

'Only a little, Ric,' she whispered soothingly. 'It's only bleeding a little.'

Rico closed his eyes. 'Sure ... Thanks, Jas.'

While Jasmine clutched hold of Rico, Kate turned to Tom. She heard his back twist and crack as his body straightened, his ribcage snap and flutter as it shrank in on itself; watched his regular human features return. She found a heavy shawl discarded close by, and draped it around him like a blanket.

'Sorry,' he croaked, dabbing at the sticky gash on his neck. 'I couldn't reach you. I was useless.'

Kate squeezed his hand. 'No, you weren't,' she said, remembering the savagery that had possessed him on the bridge. 'You were *you*.'

Tom scrambled up, tying the shawl around his waist like a makeshift sarong, and went to help Jasmine. 'Rico?' He looked down at the boy, white-faced and scared. 'You saved my life.'

'We quits now, yeah?' Rico's eyes were unfocused. 'Swagger dead?'

Tom glanced over and nodded grimly. 'Very.'

''S'good,' muttered Rico. He was starting to shake. 'Jas? D'you think Ramone'd be proud of me? Like, real proud?'

She nodded, tears falling down her face. 'Real proud, Ric.'

Rico smiled and seemed a little more at peace. 'Gonna be good to see my bro again.'

'You're not seeing him yet,' Stacy snapped, out of breath from her rush across the arena. 'Look at my fingers instead. How many do you see?'

'Wanna go sleep,' Rico mumbled.

'Look! How many do you see?' Stacy insisted.

'I dunno.' Rico raised his good arm feebly and gave her the finger. 'How many *d'you* see?'

Stacy grinned. 'That's it, stay with me, Rico. Give

235

up now and Ramone's going to kick your ass.'

'Screw you. Wanna sleep now.'

'I mean it. Stay with me!' Stacy lay Rico down on the grimy floor and studied his grisly arm, hard-faced and professional. 'We have to find the brachial artery and close it off,' she said. 'Keep him from losing anymore blood. We need a tourniquet.'

'Look out!' Tom yelled, looking over her shoulder.

A 'wolf was dragging itself along the concrete towards them. Kate backed away, looking around for a weapon. But the monster looked sick and weak, panting with the effort of its slow movement. In its jaws it held something boxy and grey.

A self-printing camera.

'The camera strap,' Stacy ordered. 'Get it.'

Kate cautiously pulled the camera free of the creature's jaws. It growled in protest, and watched her closely. She removed the strap and gave it to Stacy, who busied herself tying it around Rico's arm. The creature quietened down when she placed the camera back in front of it.

A minute later it was Polar lying there on the freezing ground, curled up in a ball, his body covered in bruises. He was sobbing quietly, clutching the camera to his face.

'Must've found the locker key after all,' murmured Kate to herself.

Jasmine looked down at him coldly. 'Kinda late to help us out now,' she breathed. 'Him and that damned camera.'

'Guess we all need to cling on to something,' Tom said quietly. 'Hope. Friends. Memories.'

Kate nodded. 'The stuff that makes us human.' She

shivered, feeling a presence behind her. She turned to find Jicaque hovering a few metres away.

'Where'd' you go?' Tom asked accusingly.

'An ambulance will be arriving shortly in the street outside,' said Jicaque, ignoring him. 'The way to the locker rooms is clear. Paramedics are on their way there. Get Rico out quickly and he will be taken to hospital. He'll receive the medical attention he needs.' He looked at Stacy intently. 'Tell the paramedics Rico was attacked by a wild dog. Say nothing of what has happened here tonight.' He glanced around and sighed. 'The truth of what happened here must remain our secret. Think of the panic it could cause.'

'But what about all these people?' Kate gestured to the groups of men and women huddled in the bleachers. 'They're hurt.'

Jicaque shook his head. 'Only I can help them. In time they shall recover their true humanity. If they allow me to administer to them my treatment, each day for a lunar month—'

'What about Polar?' Jasmine interrupted, sneering at the curled-up figure at her feet. 'You gonna help him too?'

'Yes. But for now, this boy needs real doctors, and must go with Rico. His injuries are severe, but he also shall recover.' The old man looked at her meaningfully. 'With the aid of his friends.'

'Polar ain't got no friends,' said Jasmine, turning away. 'Not anymore.' She bent to help Stacy lift Rico, then together they carried him carefully across the slippery concrete towards the locker rooms.

'We'll see you later,' Stacy called.

Tom raised a hand in farewell. Kate found she was shivering, and hugged herself for warmth. 'So. What happens now?'

'Takapa's notes,' Tom said. 'The results of all his researches. We should destroy them.'

'It is already done,' Jicaque replied. 'I have not been entirely idle since leaving you.' He smiled wanly. 'Yes, it is fair to say we have set back Takapa's plans this night. But I fear he will not give up. And I fear there is some greater purpose that consumes him. We must discover what that is.'

'We?' Kate raised an eyebrow. 'Jicaque, we've come a long way to find you because Tom needs to be cured. He wants his life back. This isn't his fight.' She looked at Tom. His face was pale and troubled. 'Go on, tell him,' she urged. 'Tell him what we've been through to find him!'

But Tom said nothing.

Jicaque smiled at Kate a little sadly. 'I can only cure those who truly wish to be cured,' he said softly.

'So?' Kate responded. What was going on here?

'Tom still has tasks he must accomplish. He does not wish to be cured.' The ghost of a smile played around Jicaque's lips. 'Not truly. Not yet.'

Kate stared at Tom. 'He's wrong. Tell him he's wrong.'

'I ...' Tom took his hands away from Jicaque's and placed his palms on Kate's shoulders. 'I can't.' He looked into her eyes. 'This thing isn't over yet. We'll never be free until it is.'

'But this could be your only chance,' she insisted. 'You want to throw that away? You want to throw your whole *life* away?'

He shook his head. 'There's more than just my life at stake, though, isn't there?' She said nothing. 'You *know* there is.'

'This isn't about me, don't bring me into this!' Kate yelled, gesturing at the livid welt down his neck, at the bruise on his chin. The photo of Ramone's blood-ied body flashed back into her mind. 'I won't be responsible for your death too! Look at you! You were nearly killed tonight. And so many people have died ...'

'I wish I could just walk away.' Tom shook his head. 'I can't.'

'Wait.' She stared at him. 'You enjoy it now, don't you? Lupine power. You've got used to it. You *like* it.'

'It's not that!' Tom stormed. 'How can you even *think* that?'

Kate turned away. 'You don't know what I think, Tom.'

'While I'm 'wolf, I can protect us, till we're both out of this mess for good. Together!'

She wanted to shout at him: *If you weren't 'wolf, maybe we could* really *be together. Maybe we could stand a chance.*

But how could she, now?

Without looking back she set off for the locker rooms. She'd forgotten she only had one sneaker. It was hard to keep your dignity when you were walking lopsided.

'I should go after her,' she heard Tom say.

'Perhaps she needs a little space right now, huh?' the old man said gruffly.

*I don't,* Kate thought desperately. *I want you here*

*with me, Tom. Come after me. Stop me acting like a freaked-out little kid.*

But her own uneven footsteps were the only ones echoing around the freezing arena.

# CHAPTER TWENTY

That night, Tom's thoughts were heavy with what Kate had said. He knew she was just upset, knew that she'd been through a hell of a lot. But he knew too that what Jicaque had said in that little coffee shop was dead right. Takapa had to be stopped, whatever the risks – or none of them could ever rest easy again. If Tom could make more of a difference as a 'wolf, then he'd have to stay that way until this thing was over. Once and for all.

He caught up with Kate the next morning at Park East Hospital, feeling nervous as hell. She was lying on her side on the couch in Stacy's office, cleaned up from her ordeal in the meat net and dressed in grey hospital pyjamas like an in-patient. She looked like she'd been up all night, crying.

His heart sank like a stone. 'Rico?'

'He's doing OK,' she said, not meeting his gaze. 'He lost a lot of blood, but he'll pull through.'

'Thank God.'

'Polar's stable too.'

Tom nodded, standing awkwardly beside the door, uncertain what to say. 'Have you been here all night?'

She nodded. 'The ambulance was still there when I

got outside. Stacy vouched for me, and they gave me a ride here.'

'Would've been a long walk otherwise. Especially with one sneaker.'

She didn't smile, but at least she looked directly at him. 'How about you? Where've you been?'

'The arena. Jicaque was fixing people up.'

'With deranged tailors?'

Tom glanced down at his ill-fitting jeans and shirt. 'There were a whole load of old clothes down there. I guess for re-clothing the troops once they ...' He broke off. 'Anyway. I just wanted to watch him perform the first rituals of the cure.'

It had been fascinating, watching the old man chant over the prone bodies, pressing his old, gnarled fingers against pressure points of their bodies, warming the freezing air with the colourful words of his incantations.

She must have seen the faraway look on his face. 'I'm sure it was something. Maybe he should charge admission.'

Tom ignored her. It was what she did; coped with the world by holding it at arm's length and waving sarcasm in its face.

'I tried calling you ...'

'I was asleep. Dead to the world.' She half-smiled. 'Lucky for you, you didn't wake me. I feel a lot friendlier after a good long sleep.'

Tom nodded. 'I'm dying for a soft bed,' he said with feeling.

'Well, if you will stay up all night ...' The light in Kate's eyes showed him she was in better humour now. 'What about all the other walking wounded?'

'At another hospital, I think. Jicaque took care of it ... he's started work on the cure with them all.'

She nodded. 'Happy ending, then. Right?'

'I hope so.'

They looked at each other for long, silent seconds.

Then Kate took a deep breath. 'I was wrong to say what I did last night ...'

'You were upset. Jeez, we were all upset.' He cleared his throat. 'I'm sorry I didn't go after you. I felt bad all night.'

'Really?' she murmured. Her voice sounded hard, tired. 'Well, I guess it's your shit. You've got to get through it your own way. Right?'

'Uh-huh.' He paused. 'You heard Jicaque, his cure takes a month. And I don't think we *have* a month before Takapa or your mom and dad try to catch us again.'

'So what *are* you going to do? You going to see your parents?'

'Not until we've seen yours,' he said firmly. 'Not until we've cleared our names.'

Kate pulled a face at him. 'And just how do we do that?'

'I don't know. But until then we can't turn to anyone for help.' He swallowed hard. 'When I see my mom and dad again, I want them to see *me*, Tom Anderson, as I used to be.'

'You think things can ever be the same after all we've been through?'

'Maybe not the same,' Tom said. 'But maybe better. *Because* of what we've been through.'

'We have to make it count for something, right?' She rolled her eyes, but Tom saw she was trying not to smile. 'Give me a break, Tom Anderson. Stop being so damned good, saying the right things all the time.'

'OK.' He smiled wryly. There was so much he wished he could say to her. 'You look a total mess.'

'Don't push it, Anderson!' He ducked as she threw a pillow at him. But when he looked at her again, he saw the worry in her eyes. 'I wonder where they've gone now ... *my* parents.'

Tom sighed. 'What we need is a psychic.'

'Uh-huh.' Kate suddenly seemed to brighten. 'And I know where we can find a couple.' She crossed to Stacy's PC and moved the mouse to wake up the screen. 'See if we can get online. I haven't touched base with the geeky Net community in days. Maybe someone's heard something about the lupines we should know about.'

Tom smiled wryly. 'Right. That extreme possibilities chatroom you hang out in?'

'I'm beginning to think *no* possibility's too extreme these days,' she murmured.

Soon she was connected and signed in – as 'Troll Lover', her online alter-ego in these chat rooms.

'No way!' she cried suddenly, making Tom jump.

He crouched to look at the screen over her shoulder. 'What is it?'

'A message from Adam Blood,' she said, her hands flying to her mouth in excitement. 'Sent this morning.'

'Genuine?' asked Tom nervously.

'Only two people in the world know I call myself Troll Lover. You and him.'

'Well, what does he say?'

Quickly she typed in a password and hit the

ENTER button. Tom blinked as the short message appeared on screen:

Dear Trolly,
Hope you are as sexily aloof as ever
— and hope Tom isn't ripping his way
through a new wardrobe every week (down,
boy!). Heard a whisper — something big,
secret, scary and wolfy is going down in
Chicago sometime soon. All the pureblood
clans have been summoned by Takapa ... So
in case you happen to be in Chicago
right now — GET YOUR STUPID ARSES OUT OF
THERE! And if not, AVOID LIKE THE BLOODY
PLAGUE IF YOU HAVE ANY SENSE!
    AB

'It sounds like him,' said Tom dryly.

'Well?' Kate looked up at him nonchalantly. 'Am I as sexily aloof as ever?'

'He's such a great kidder, isn't he?' Tom turned so she wouldn't see his blushes. 'But I guess now we have a fair idea where Takapa's holed up. *And* your mom and dad.'

'Better than a psychic.' Kate nodded thoughtfully. 'You meant what you said, didn't you? About needing to finish this ...'

Tom nodded. 'And Takapa said his HQ was in Chicago ...' He took a deep breath and turned to face her. 'I hear the Windy City's lovely this time of year.'

'Then I guess,' Kate replied, with the tiniest of smiles, 'maybe we should check it out.' She turned back to the computer and typed a brief reply:

Dearest AB. Too aloof for sense and plague, too broke to keep running. We're going to Chicago. See you there? X

'You never put kisses on notes!' Tom protested.

She sent the message and smiled innocently. 'Don't I?'

'Well,' he grumbled, 'even with a kiss, I can't see Blood coming.'

Kate stretched and yawned. 'He'd better,' she drawled, bunching her fists. 'Otherwise – sexily aloof or not – I'll hunt him down myself and smash his face in.'

Kate slept for most of the afternoon. Rest came easier now she'd cleared things up with Tom. She knew he was right; she'd known last night he was right about what they had to do, and about being in it together. He was facing up to the future, and she knew she had to as well. Whatever it held.

A fresh change of clothes had been left out for her on the floor along with her rucksack: her black corduroys and a bottle-green sweater, and her battered Timberlands. She dressed quickly, and went out to find Tom.

He was sitting in Rico's room, dressed more normally now in blue jeans that fitted him and a grey ribbed T-shirt. She watched him, waiting in gloomy silence while the boy lay asleep in crisp white sheets. It must be tough for Tom, she knew, with his parents just down the hall.

'Hey,' he said softly, his face brightening as she walked over.

'Where'd you get the clothes?' she asked.

'Jasmine got them from the hangout, along with our gear.' Tom tapped his own rucksack and sighed. 'I think they were Ramone's. She didn't want them slung out in the trash.'

Kate nodded, and turned to look at Rico. 'He seems so peaceful.'

'Just how peaceful this place will be when he wakes up remains to be seen,' Tom said dryly.

Kate smiled. 'Where's Jasmine, anyway? I thought she'd be here.'

'She's been busy.'

Kate turned to see Stacy walking into the room with a welcoming smile.

'But she's going to be busier,' Stacy added.

'She is?' Kate queried.

'Uh-huh. She's out front right now, waiting for you guys.' Stacy held out her hand to Kate. 'Goodbye.'

Kate looked at Tom. 'We're leaving already? How're we getting to Chicago?'

'I think it's going to work out,' said Stacy, helping Tom struggle into his rucksack. 'But I'm trying to steer clear of the details. I'm already an accessory to God knows how much ...'

Tom shook Stacy's hand. 'Goodbye. Thanks for everything. Especially for looking after my parents.'

'I'm going to have to spin them one hell of a line to explain why they've spent the last thirty-six hours fit and well in isolation,' she said dryly, 'but I'll make sure they know your last sighting was somewhere on the way to Hawaii.'

He grinned. 'You've done so much for us already.'

Stacy shook her head. 'Before you two came here, I

was doing more harm than good to the people I was supposed to be helping.' She smiled. 'Now maybe I can turn that around. With some help from my friends.'

Stacy crossed the room to check on Rico, who was still sleeping peacefully.

Kate fumbled in her purse for the picture Polar snapped when she and Tom had first arrived at the tenement. Ramone stood between them, scowling in the middle of the picture; his old, habitual look. She placed the picture on Rico's bedside table. 'Someone to watch over you,' she whispered.

Then she and Tom left the room.

Jasmine was out in the parking lot, leaning against a glossy black Daimler that seemed to shine in the wintry sunlight. 'Thought you might need some wheels,' she said. 'Friend of Ramone's fixed up the plates. Should get you where you need to go without the cops on your tail.'

Kate hoped Tom's dazed grin was down to the car and not the sight of Jasmine in her leather pants and fitted top.

'I don't know what to say,' Tom said finally.

Jasmine snorted. 'Then get out of here already.'

'What are you going to do now?' Kate asked her.

'Ain't gonna be stealing no more cars, for one thing,' she said dryly. 'Stacy's rule.'

'Stacy?'

'She finally got her way. Fixed me up with a job, helping out with one of her hard luck programs.' Jasmine shrugged. 'Guess I ain't got much to go back to now. So I'm thinking I can help out them howler kids now the fighting's over ... Help them work stuff out.'

'Kids like Polar?' Tom asked gently.

Jasmine glared at him. Then her face softened. 'Maybe. I guess. Stacy says we gotta give them for real what they thought they were getting from Takapa. Kind of self-respect. You know?'

Tom nodded. 'We know.'

'Don't pay much. But Stacy knows some hostel where me and Ric can stay.' She shrugged. 'It's something.'

'It's *really* something,' Tom said. 'And you are, too.'

He went to kiss her cheek, but Jasmine pulled away. 'Just take care of yourself, Tommy-boy.'

Tom opened the door of the Daimler, his cheeks burning, threw his rucksack into the back and climbed in the driver's seat.

Kate waited till he'd shut the door, then crossed to Jasmine. 'I never thanked you for that stunt with the cigarettes,' she said. 'You saved my life.'

'So I did.' Jasmine eyed Kate coolly. 'He's in love with you, the poor bastard. You knew that, right?'

Kate took a step back involuntarily. 'What did you say?'

'Guess it's just the way life works out.' Jasmine shook her head wryly. 'Take care of him, 'K?'

Kate nodded and she crossed to the car's passenger side just as coolly as she could, doing her best not to show she was trembling.

Tom turned the ignition, and drove the car out of the lot.

Kate saw Jasmine in the rear-view, watching them go, hands on hips. Her figure dwindled then vanished as Tom swung the car out into the busy New York traffic. 'Penny for your thoughts,' Kate murmured.

'I'm saving my pennies. We'll need them if we're going to eat tonight.' He frowned. 'Know any good diners on the way to Chicago?'

Kate smiled, fastened her seat belt, settling in for the long drive. 'We'll find one,' she said.

# THE WERELING
## TRILOGY

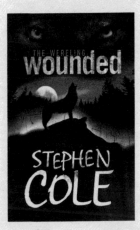

# ALSO BY
# STEPHEN COLE
## THE THIEVES TRILOGY

## BLOOMSBURY

www.bloomsbury.com